DOONGAJI
House

Also by Cyrus Mistry

The Prospect of Miracles: A Novel
Passion Flower: Seven Stories of Derangement
Chronicle of a Corpse Bearer
The Radiance of Ashes

DOONGAJI
House

SELECTED PLAYS

CYRUS MISTRY

ALEPH

ALEPH

ALEPH BOOK COMPANY
An independent publishing firm
promoted by *Rupa Publications India*

First published in India in 2023
by Aleph Book Company
7/16 Ansari Road, Daryaganj
New Delhi 110 002

Copyright © Cyrus Mistry 2023

All rights reserved.

This is a work of fiction. Names, characters,
places, and incidents are either the product of the
author's imagination or are used fictitiously and any
resemblance to any actual persons, living or dead,
events or locales is entirely coincidental.

No part of this publication may be reproduced,
transmitted, or stored in a retrieval system, in any form
or by any means, without permission in writing from
Aleph Book Company.

ISBN: 978-93-93852-73-1

1 3 5 7 9 10 8 6 4 2

Printed in India.

This book is sold subject to the condition that it shall not, by way of trade or otherwise, be lent, resold, hired out, or otherwise circulated without the publisher's prior consent in any form of binding or cover other than that in which it is published.

CONTENTS

Doongaji House / 1

The Legacy of Rage / 73

A Flowering of Disorder / 167

Notes / 244

DOONGAJI HOUSE

A Play in Five Acts

I was twenty-one when I wrote *Doongaji House*. It won the Sultan Padamsee Award for Playwriting in 1978. This competition was sponsored by Mumbai's Theatre Group, the city's most affluent and high-profile English theatre outfit at the time. The contest itself was considered a prestigious one, soliciting entries from NRI as well as desi playwrights.

I had only published one short story before writing *Doongaji House,* and was understandably elated. Not merely because my writing ambitions, so early in my career, had gained some credence nor even for the cash prize of ₹5000 (a lot of money for a college student in '78), as much as for the assurance, given in print by the Theatre Group, that the prize-winning plays would be performed. With no practical experience in the theatre, I needed to find out if my play could breathe and come alive on stage. I felt, unreasonably perhaps, that until I had had a chance to hear my own lines, learn from my mistakes, I couldn't attempt another play.

But the worthies of Theatre Group procrastinated, asked for script abridgements, made copies of the revised script, drew up production schedules and tentative cast lists, but in the end never got beyond making indefinite postponements. Until one day the truth was stated more bluntly at a committee meeting to which I had been summoned: 'We find this play commercially unviable,' I was told. 'We can produce it only if you (as playwright) undertake to raise a lakh of rupees in advertising revenue to support the production.' This, from committee members who owned and ran some of the city's largest advertising agencies. And it had taken them four years—after the fanfare of the awards ceremony, the speeches about promoting indigenous English theatre—to arrive at this conclusion about my play.

How erroneous that judgement was, was proved beyond doubt by audience responses when Toni Patel of Stage Two put on the play in Mumbai on a shoestring budget. But that was in 1990, twelve years after it had been written. Subsequently, the play travelled to other cities and towns, had a fresh production in Bangalore with Mahesh Dattani's Playpen, and a long run in its excellent Marathi version, translated and directed by Chetan Dataar for *Aawishkaar*. In retrospect I cannot but regretfully conclude that Theatre Group, lulled by its own proclivity for recycling staple Broadway and West End hits, completely missed an opportunity thrown up by a competition it had itself instituted. Sadly, since 1978, this competition hasn't been held again. As for myself, I didn't write another play until 1992.

THE CHARACTERS

HORMUSJI	Nearly seventy, slight of build
PIROJA	His wife, portly, slightly younger
AVAN	Their daughter
FALI	Their son
CAWAS	A distant relative
DARABSHAA	A retired schoolteacher
PERIN	A neighbour
DHANJISHAA	A ghost
BAPASOLA	
YOUNG HORMUZ	
PURVEYOR	
COOLIES AND WORKMEN	

The play is set in Bombay in the late 1960s. The action takes place in the living room of the Pochkhanawalla family.

ACT ONE

SCENE ONE

The living room of the Pochkhanawallas is poorly- lit. A faint, yellowish hue of mouldiness and dust seems to hang in the air. The furniture is drab and mostly antique. A little off centre-stage is a round, marble-topped table with two chairs and a stool around it. On the table is a kerosene lamp with a long, exquisitely-shaped chimney. Downstage left, an easy chair with extendable leg-rests. A dreary old cupboard with a large inset mirror, perhaps a chest of drawers, or a sideboard, and other curious articles of furniture in various stages of disuse and decay may be judiciously included to create the effect of a few decades of cluttered accumulation and, above all, of impoverishment.

The three-storeyed building, of which this is the second floor, itself shows alarming signs of age and degeneration. The walls, hung with portraits of family ancestors, are cracked and peeling. In one corner of the room, a beam of timber has been erected to support some sagging portion of the ceiling above. Upstage right is an elevated platform with two steps leading up to it, beyond which, angularly placed, is the front door to the apartment. When the front door is open, we can see a part of the landing and a section of the stairway leading to the floor above. Upstage left is a window overlooking the street. The point of intersection of two beams of a scaffolding built along the exterior facade of the building, is framed by the window. At stage right and stage left are two exits leading supposedly to the kitchen and bedroom of the flat respectively.

When it is evening, the kerosene lamp on the round table is lit. If the window is open, light from a street lamp streams into the room. However, most of the time, until we reach Act Four, the window remains shut.

It is not necessary to match the very naturalistic description given above. It may even be desirable to try and achieve the same overall effect by using somewhat more abstract means.

Perin, *a plain-looking girl in a long, dumpy frock, is seated at the round, marble-topped table. A few moments later,* Piroja *enters from the kitchen with two plates of french beans and two knives, and joins* Perin *at the table.*

PIROJA: Take care to peel the threads off both ends. This house is full of fusspots.
(*They work silently; then* Piroja *puts down her knife and fans herself with a piece of cardboard.*) Ohoho… What heat. Unbearable heat.

PERIN: Terrible heat… Will the rains be here by next week? I wonder…

PIROJA: No sign of rain.

PERIN: Landlord said anything about your new wire fittings?

PIROJA: Two years since our wiring rotted. I've grown so used to this lamp, I think it will hurt my eyes if we ever get back our lights. But I miss the fan.

PERIN: If you were to keep the windows open, at least—

PIROJA: The house would be coated with dust in five minutes. These buses pass right under our noses now; people can look straight in. Ever since they cut the footpath to widen the road.

(*As if in confirmation of her grievances, a loud bleating of horns mixed with general traffic noises.*)

PERIN: Next week, my Mummy will be sixty-three.

PIROJA: Depdin Roj?

PERIN: Sherevar… Just think, Piroja aunty…

PIROJA: What?

PERIN: First, your Rusi went away to Canada. Then, Fali went away to Chikkalwadi. The Bogdawallas and their children moved out lock, stock, and barrel. Who's left in the building now? Only old people.

PIROJA: Looks like the landlord's just waiting for our wickets to fall, one by one…

PERIN: All oldies. Except Avan and myself, who else in the building is below sixty?

PIROJA: That's if we are not all buried together, one of these days… (*Looks up at the ceiling, apprehensively.*)

PERIN: Remember? How we used to play on your landing… racing up and down the stairs till late in the evening, till you would shout at us to go home…? (*Tunefully*) L-O-N-D-O-N, *London!*

PIROJA: Hmm…every step I take on the staircase now makes my heart quake. The boards feel like they'll give way any day.

PERIN: After dinner, we'd bundle ourselves into your large, soft bed and play rummy. Everyone. Mummy, sometimes Hormusji also, if he was not too busy with his books and papers… (*giggles.*) All the children would fight to sit next to him. He'd pretend to be very absorbed in his cards, but slyly he was tickling whoever sat beside him. The way he could wag his big toe!

PIROJA: I think the vegetable-man has really cheated me today. Just keep the bad ones aside, Perin. I'll throw them in his face when he comes tomorrow.

PERIN (*after a pause*): How boring everything has become… Everyone's left… Shall I say something, Piroja aunty?

PIROJA (*slightly irritable*): What is it?

PERIN: Sometimes I think it's for the best that Fali changed his mind about marrying me. Even if it was at the last minute. (Piroja *throws her a contemptuous glance and continues working.*)

You don't know the kind of talk that's flying around Chikkalwadi. Comes home late every night, reeking, and really gives it to her. First, he makes her squeal, then he makes her whimper. Keeps up the neighbours till one in the morning, with his swearing and shouting. I heard the tenants have put out a petition to the Panchayat to have him evicted.

PIROJA: Stop jabbering! You know the tiffin-man will be here at eleven. If I make him wait one minute, he starts shouting and runs away.

(Perin *bends her head obediently and concentrates on trimming the beans. But* Piroja *is uneasy. When she speaks again, her voice is charged with an emotional urgency.*)

…I know. He broke off with you a week before the wedding. He went and married Jal Talati's ayah instead. He drinks. He smokes. He gave up a good job and became a matka-bookie instead. I know everything!… (*Bitterly sarcastic*) Everyone used to say 'Pirojamai, you are really blessed with such beautiful, bright children.' Actually, they couldn't bear to see it. They were burning with jealousy… How well he played the piano…. His father talked of sending him to Germany, Vienna…. Suddenly he picked up a stick and smashed everything around him…. See his state now… (*Turns on* Perin, *in a flash of anger.*) Why do you moon about the house all day like a parrot that's losing its feathers? Why don't you go out and find someone else while your flesh is still unwrinkled? (*At this moment, we hear* Hormusji's *voice humming* La Marseillaise *off-stage. His singing and his approaching footsteps grow louder, then stop abruptly. He has become aware of the two women in the living room. He tries to sneak into the bedroom unnoticed by Piroja. He raises a finger to his lips, cautioning Perin, who has seen him, not to give him away. He is halfway across the stage, when—)*

PIROJA (*aggressively*): Ah, back already? So early. Where have you been roaming?

HORMUSJI (*sighs*): Yes…this heat is really something outside. No sign of the rains at all…

PIROJA: Is that so? (*to* Perin) Saw his foxiness? What question I ask and what answer he gives. (*Shouts*) Say at once! Where were you?

HORMUSJI: What is the need to roar like that? Just went down to Mayrose for a cup of tea.

PERIN (*incredulous*): Uncle! You *never* like tea!

HORMUSJI: Be quiet! Whole day you sit here and butter her up.

PIROJA: She'll say whatever she wants. (*Rising from the stool*) Let's see since when you have become a tea-lover? Open your mouth!

HORMUSJI (*backing away*): Am I a child or what?

(*A slight scuffle ensues, in which* Hormusji *tries to turn his face away, but* Piroja *manages to catch a whiff of liquor on his breath.*)

PIROJA (*striking her forehead*): See? From this hour in the morning he begins scorching his throat. This is poison for you, poison! Dr Lalkaka has warned you thousands of times. When you are flat on your back, your liver all chewed up and rotted, then don't expect me to bring the bedpan to your cot.

HORMUSJI: Okay, so it's poison. I'll die. Few days I have left; let me live those in peace at least?

PIROJA (*mimics*): Okay, so I'll die. Spoken like a brainless ass!

PERIN: Uncle, why don't you be reasonable? Piroja aunty worries so much about you.

HORMUSJI: *Chaal,* shut up! I'll drive you out of the house this minute!

PIROJA: Shall I remind you what happened to your friend Dinshah Kanga? When you went to his bedside in those last days, you came away dripping with sweat. (*Mimics*) 'Piroja, Piroja, now I have seen too much, now I will never touch a bottle again.' Before his *uthamna* was done, you had started again. (*Pauses for breath*) As for that great friend of yours downstairs, I wouldn't say any better fate awaits him: Darabshaa: *Saalo* loafer!

HORMUSJI: Just now you were talking about me; now you've gone on to him?

PIROJA: Whatever is the truth I will say it. Of course he is giving you encouragement. He is two steps ahead of you. Hmph. Wanted to be a schoolmaster, it seems. Are you listening, Perin? Flask in his coat pocket, and he would suckle at it every half hour. One-two pegs before every class, like a newborn babe! (*Turns to* Hormusji) But he is a bachelor, Hormusji. Even if he locks himself in the bathroom and gargles with carbolic acid there is no one to ask any questions. If something happens to you, who is going to pay the hospital bills?

HORMUSJI: Say. Say more. Say whatever comes to your mouth.

PIROJA: Who would believe this man is approaching seventy? Have you given your wits a scrubbing and put them out to dry or what?

HORMUSJI: Bas? Finished? Say some more. Cast your

spells. (*Darkly*) I hope every word comes true.... In those days who would have believed that this would be my state today?... (*In a tone of mock puzzlement*) 'Hormusji?' they would have asked, 'Which Hormusji?' (*Utter disbelief*) 'Hormusji Pochkhanawalla!... Na, na, not possible, heh, heh, not possible...'

PIROJA: Come, baby. Better light the primus. Once Hormusji starts his theatrics, there will be no interval for hours. (Perin *is too engrossed.*)

HORMUSJI (*theatrically*): One crate would be delivered here every week... Tell me if it is not true! Tell me if I lie! Scotch, cognac, vodka! Whatever you want—ask, and you shall have it. Today, to get two pegs of rotgut from that mad Irani in the bar, I have to fight tooth and nail. How many gallons of my liquor has he downed? Forgotten? Lost count?... Because I have lost my wealth, I have to listen to these words today— from you, from my friends, from everyone.... But I did not lose it. Ah! Correction! I was cheated out of it. Swindled. By one who had my own mother's blood in him.

PIROJA (*tensely*): For whose sake these long-winded recitations? We have heard the story many times before.

HORMUSJI (*raises his voice*): You shut up! I am talking to myself. I am mad!

PIROJA: Okay, talk. I am busy with my kitchen. (*To Perin*) Are you coming or no?

(Perin *reluctantly follows her into the kitchen.* Hormusji, *calmer now, ruminates over the past, a certain bitterness in his voice as he talks, now addressing the audience, now only to himself.*)

HORMUSJI: ...What made me do it, I wonder...? To this day, I still think about it. What made me offer him that job? For that matter, why did I ever let him set foot in my house, knowing his nature...? And why did I trust him in the end, when sickness preyed upon my senses... Blood is thicker than water, they say. Sometimes it curdles, and then it is so thick you could slice it with a knife. That's what he did to me. He ripped me up. Hacked me, and then fled. My own stepbrother. Sohrab. I had this strange illness, which nobody could diagnose. Rest, rest, take rest, they all said to me. So I went to a sanatorium and rested for three months.... When I came back, I found the ice cream factory closed. Heavy debts. Our cycle shop, which used to hire out bicycles to the children of Dhobhi Talao—devastated! Cycles lying in heaps, mangled... But worst of all...my bookshop...the bookshop which belonged to my father, and to his father before him.... He had sold the bookshop! Rare volumes, priceless manuscripts, disposed off for a song by a callous boor who could not even have guessed at their value. It was too great a blow for me...too much...

PIROJA (*emerging from the kitchen*): Don't add too much chilli powder.

HORMUSJI (*snaps*): What's that?

PIROJA: I am talking to Perin. What are you getting excited about?

(*She has come out only to take something from the table, and goes back into the kitchen.*)

HORMUSJI: ...Sohrab never returned from Bangalore with all the money he had accumulated at my expense, he built a house there, for himself and some bazaar slut he had taken for wife.... But there is, after all, a justice that governs our universe. And swiftly it took its course. One month after Sohrab moved into his new house, he suffered a paralytic stroke. Three weeks later, he was dead.... His son, Cawas,

has grown up now. Must be twenty-eight…twenty-nine…
(Piroja *comes out again, issuing some final instructions to* Perin *about the cooking, and settles into the easy chair.* Hormusji's *last sentence evokes a sudden interest.*)

PIROJA: You told me he was doing very well for himself?

HORMUSJI (*stiffly*): So I heard. And do you think he will be able to eat his ill-gotten wealth? He will choke on it.

PIROJA (*reasonably*): But Hormusji, he seems quite a nice boy, really…

HORMUSJI: Who?

PIROJA: Why, Cawas. Remember, he sent us such a lovely card last Papeti.

HORMUSJI (*mutters*): Tricks. All tricks. I should have sued that family long ago.

PIROJA: We are the only family he has left, poor boy. Maybe he wants to make up in some way for what his father… Maybe, if he comes to Bombay.

HORMUSJI: I will spit in his face, if he dares to show it.
(*But* HORMUSJI *is suddenly transported by the memory of a verse from Shakespeare, and he declaims, gravely, introspectively*):
'Ingratitude…thou marble-hearted fiend…
More hideous than the sea-monster, when thou show'st thee in a child…'
(*A subtle change of mood takes place in* Hormusji. *He chuckles.*)
…Major Bamji…heh, heh…Major Minocher Bamji. How he taught us Shakespeare. How he instilled in us a love for the great Bard of Stratford…(*to* Piroja) Well? I may have put my wits out to dry, but at seventy the memory is still giving good service, eh?
(*Sings*) '*Then sing heigh-ho the holly, this life is most jolly, most friendship is feigning, most loving mere folly…*' (*Playfully*) Say

something? Some words of praise for an old wretch?

PIROJA: Very good, we'll announce it in *Jame* tomorrow.

(Perin *comes out of the kitchen.*)

PERIN: I've turned the flame down. The beans are nearly done.

PIROJA: Just pass me my specs, dear, and newspaper... (PERIN *gives them to her.*) Haven't had a moment since morning, even to glance at the Deaths column...

HORMUSJI (*sarcastically*): Going? So soon? Sit a little longer (Perin *puts her tongue out at* Hormusji, *on her way to the door. He raises his foot comically, as if aiming a kick at her. When she is gone and the old couple are alone,* Hormusji *suddenly looks very tired, drained. He takes off his jacket and hangs it on the back of the easy chair; then asks, gravely*): Anyone we know?

(Piroja *shakes her head mutely. He takes off his shirt as well and hangs it. Then sits on a stool and begins unlacing his shoes.*) I have a memory that never fails me. I am not boasting, Piroja. It is my special curse... When I think of old times, I feel so brittle...worn...I feel I could just pluck the fingers off my hand and toss them away. Then my toes, my nose, my ears, my tongue...till at last nothing remains, but a thought... that rankles. How things have changed in the last few years.

PIROJA: Not few, Hormusji. Things changed nearly thirty years ago.

HORMUSJI (*bitterly*): I don't care. Whatever followed has only been an endless desert for me.... Do you remember those days, Piroja...when Rusi was only five or six, and Fali was still learning to walk...?

(Piroja *turns a page of the newspaper and continues reading.*)

Things were so cheap then, we had plenty of money. Every evening, coming home from work, I'd pick up something...

those eclairs from Monginis? Pineapple cake! Liqueur chocolates!

(Piroja *puts down her newspaper, drawn into the web of nostalgia herself. Now she and* Hormusji *speak associatively, without really talking to each other.*)

PIROJA: Everything was cheap. Eggs five annas a dozen. Only later, after Avan was born, they went up to fourteen annas. Everything started going up then. And never stopped.

HORMUSJI: Yes, Avan.... How much she has changed, too. What a cheerful, sprightly little devil she used to be.

PIROJA: You gave us all the comforts. You called me your Queen Sheba of Princess Street. But you never had time for me. Only your drinking-mates...your precious books.

HORMUSJI: A most talented child, Avan. At school she won essay competitions. Two of her poems were published in *Kaiser-e-Hind*.

PIROJA: I had to look to others for companionship.

HORMUSJI: Now she does not write any more. She has become so serious, so sullen...as if she is carrying some secret inside her...something she will not share.

PIROJA: Sohrab left so suddenly for Bangalore. Not a word from him. Then the news of his death...then everything fell apart.

(*A long pause.*)

HORMUSJI: Is there no letter from Rusi this month also?

PIROJA: No letter.

HORMUSJI: How can it be? I have a feeling that postman is behind this. Spiting us for not giving him his Diwali bakshish. Let him come next time—

PIROJA: You think he has no better work than to steal your son's letters?

HORMUSJI: You don't understand these people, Piroja. They've got completely out of hand. They think it is their Raj now. There was a time when they would bow and scrape to us. If a Parso got on to a bus, they would rush to offer him a seat. Today, walking down the street, they make fun of you. 'Bawaji aya. Parsi bawaji ko dekho.' Sometimes I just feel like taking a horsewhip and flaying them! But those days are gone. The Parsis of old are all gone. This is a generation of schoolgirls. See in our own family. We have a good example.

PIROJA: Okay. Enough now. Less said the better.

HORMUSJI: How can I keep quiet? How low he has stooped.... These people who don't even wash their arses after shitting—he's married one of them!

PIROJA (*shouts*): Didn't I say enough?

(*Another long pause ensues. Street noises fade in, fade out.*)

HORMUSJI: If only we could get away from here... If only Rusi would just sponsor us.

PIROJA: What plans you make, Hormusji.

HORMUSJI: Why, don't you want to go?

PIROJA: To Canada? At one time I did. Now my bones feel too old to carry me such a long way... Go now? To die there?

HORMUSJI: Yes. Yes, even that I would not mind... To meet Rusi...to see the big cities...the snow... You know Piroja, I've never sat in a plane.

PIROJA: Read his letters. I always say: 'if you want to be blind, all you have to do is shut your eyes.'

HORMUSJI (*reluctantly*): It is strange... Always the same letter... Is this a letter? 'Hi folks, how's everything out there? I'm fine. It's freezing out here, but everything is centrally heated so it's quite pleasant. Bye for now, your loving son Rusi.' Is that a letter? God knows...God knows what he is doing there. But I'll tell you one thing, Piroja. See this... (Hormusji *extends his right palm.*) Travel to a foreign land is very definitely in my fortune line. Besides—no, never mind.

PIROJA: What?

HORMUSJI: No. Nothing. You'll laugh at me again.

PIROJA: Say? Say?

HORMUSJI (*in a hushed, reverential tone*): Some months ago. I saw Dhanjishaa Bapasola. He told me...

PIROJA: Dhanjishaa Bapasola! (*Starts laughing*) At this rate you'll go totally crack!

HORMUSJI: See. You're laughing. Don't laugh! I don't like it. Besides, I am not the only one who has seen the spirit of Dhanjishaa Bapasola. Darabshaa has seen it. Also old Burjorji.

PIROJA: One is a drunk who will agree with anything you say. The other is half-crazed with age.

HORMUSJI (*sadly*): After all these years, Piroja, you still do not understand me... Poor Dhanjishaa...no one understood him either...

PIROJA: Go in and lie down. You've talked enough for one day.

HORMUSJI: No one in the whole building...hardly anyone ever spoke to him. Sometimes for weeks on end he would not be seen at all...but once in a while, a housewife caught a glimpse of him on the landing, saying his prayers, or down by the well doing his kashti. And she would run, panting with excitement to the other housewives in their kitchens and announce: Dhanjishaa Bapasola is still alive....

PIROJA: And where was Burjorji?

PIORMUSJI: I am talking about more than sixty years ago.

Burjorji and his wife moved in much later. At that time, there was only Dhanjishaa upstairs. With his six dogs.

PIROJA: Six dogs!

HORMUSJI: Mongrels he had picked up in the streets, grown ferocious from being chained all day.

PIROJA: No wonder the neighbours hated him.

(As Hormusji *begins his story, lights dim and narrow in on him.*)

HORMUSJI: One day...I was on my way home from school...when I saw a tall, willowy man standing at the top of the stairs...

(*The ghostly figure of* Bapasola, *gnarled with age, wrapped in a voluminous white sudrah and flowing white pyjamass, appears on the elevated part of the stage, glowing dimly in the darkness. The figure on stage never speaks. His lines, spoken backstage, are amplified and booming with echo. The rest of the stage is dark.*)

BAPASOLA: ... Hormuz!...Hormuz...!

(*Sound of footsteps. A small boy of eight or nine in school uniform, carrying a satchel, approaches from the darkness the aura of light surrounding* Bapasola. *Hesitantly, he climbs the steps leading to the platform.*)

HORMUSJI (*in darkness*): I wondered where he could have learnt my name, and faltered...up the stairs.

(Bapasola *bends down and whispers something in the boy's ear. He puts his arm around his shoulder and leads him out of the light into darkness.*)

That day I found out, that under his gruff exterior which everyone feared, lived a very kind and loving man.... He took me into his home and told me not to be afraid. (*The boy and* Bapasola *appear in another part of the stage which lights up. The boy puts down his school-bag.*) The furniture was old and dusty, and it made me sneeze. (*The boy sneezes: 'Aachoo!'*)

The six dogs were lying in a row, quiet and drowsy, as if they had been drugged... He told me their names and made me pat them on the head...Bruno, Caesar, Cerberus... (*The boy bends and cautiously caresses each of the dogs.*) Then...

BAPASOLA: Hormuz...

HORMUSJI: ...he said to me...

BAPASOLA: Do you know why everyone in this house hates me? Do you know? (*The boy shakes his head slowly, from side to side.*) Because I hate them! Men and women I hate them both!... But I love dogs...and little boys... These have not yet been corrupted by Ahriman's forces... (Bapasola *bends down and begins unbuttoning the boy's shirt and helps him out of it. The boy takes out a white hanky from his pocket and places it on his head. Then he begins untying his kashti*).

HORMUSJI (*still in darkness*): Then he made me say my kashti prayers, because he wanted to check if I was really a good boy.

(*The boy is now holding his kashti outstretched between thumb and fingers.* Bapasola *kneels, embraces the boy tenderly and kisses his forehead. Then, in an amplified whisper*):

BAPASOLA: Tomorrow night, when everyone is asleep... come quietly to my door and knock thrice...I will let you in and show you such wonders that even when you are old and ready to die, you will not forget the great Bapasola...

(*The light on* Bapasola and *the boy fades out, and now* Hormusji *is in the spotlight.*)

HORMUSJI: The next night, trembling with excitement, I got up when everyone was asleep, and made for the front door. But as my luck would have it, I stumbled over the servant sleeping in the passage. He screamed in fright and woke the whole family. After that, a strict check was kept on my whereabouts, constantly. Only, it wasn't necessary for long. Poor Dhanjishaa... Only a week later, something happened which shook everyone in the building out of their wits. At sunset, one evening, the old man was seen doing his kashti at the well. Then suddenly, without warning, everyone heard a loud—SPLASH! (*Silence*) That was the last they saw of him. His body was never recovered. The well was boarded up forever. That night, the dogs in his house howled and howled, till all the dogs in the street joined in, and all of Dhobhi Talao knew that Dhanjishaa Bapasola was dead.

(*Stage lights fade in to show* Piroja *again, stretched out in the easychair. She has been a silent spectator to* Hormusji's *story. Though she appears not to be listening.*)

But was that really the last we saw of him? He was a very holy man. On certain nights, when the moon is only a slit in the sky, the Good Spirit of Dhanjishaa Bapasola appears at the well. He is seen in a long white sudrah that touches his knees and spotless white pyjamas. He can be heard doing his kashti late into the night, cracking it like a whip that can put the fear of God in the meanest and lowliest of devils...

(*The high drama of* Hormusji's *tale is rendered anti-climactic by a suppressed giggle from* Piroja, *which abruptly grows into unrestrained laughter.*)

HORMUSJI (*contemptuously*): Don't jeer at things you can't understand! It is a boorish trait.

PIROJA (*provokingly*): I never said I don't believe in spirits. But the spirits that linger behind are unhappy, or evil. Good souls travel smoothly.

HORMUSJI (*snaps*): Watch what you say! There may be higher reasons.

PIROJA: Such as?

HORMUSJI: To aid those mortals it has known in its earthly life.

PIROJA: Meaning you?

HORMUSJI: Yes. Perhaps even me. (Piroja *laughs again.*) You have no imagination, Piroja, no will to live. You think our condition will never change for the better. But how do we know what life holds in store for us? Avan is still young…

PIROJA: Avan?

HORMUSJI: Yes, Avan.

PIROJA (*mysteriously*): Yes… How do we know? How do we know anything…?

HORMUSJI (*puzzled*): Why? What do you mean?

PIROJA: Nothing. Nothing…

HORMUSJI: Cheer up. Cheer up, Piroja. Never be a pessimist in life.

(*He collects his shoes and socks, his coat and shirt.*)

I think I'll go lie down for a while.

(*He starts humming the* Marseillaise; *then suddenly stops short, as he remembers something.*)

Guess who I met today? Kelso! My old school buddy. The first thing he asked me was, 'Remember the *Marseillaise*'! (*Laughs.*)

PIROJA: Now! What is it again?

HORMUSJI: Our French teacher, Father Gaston. He had this long, thick beard he was very proud of. You could tell by the way he stroked it. 'Fr. Gaston has bugs in his beard!' By God, he was wild. He spent two hours trying to make us confess who had written these words on the blackboard. In the end he gave up and said, 'For this grave insult, each of you shall write out the French national anthem 500 times.' Guess who had written that line on the blackboard.

PIROJA: How do I know? Must be you.

HORMUSJI (*terribly amused*): Me and my friend Kelso.

PIROJA: No shame to boast about it at this age?

HORMUSJI: Kelso can never remember the words beyond the first verse. As for me, I would be able to rattle it off even on my deathbed.

(*He begins singing lustily, shoes and all still in his hands.*)

> *Allons enfants de la Patrie,*
> *Le jour de gloire est arrive.*
> *Centre nous de la tyrannie,*
> *L'etendard sanglant eleve...*

(*At the culmination of the first verse, a rude knocking on the front door tapped out to the beat of the song's martial rhythm. The old couple start. There is a shocked silence, before* Hormusji *drops his clothes and shoes and goes to the door. It is* Fali, *who enters, swaggering.*)

FALI: Kem? Some song and dance party in progress, Dad?

HORMUSJI: You!

FALI: Who do I look like?

PIROJA: For six weeks you didn't show your face. We didn't know if you were dead or alive.

FALI: Mummy I'm so busy, you have no idea. Whole day, no time even for a gulp of water.

PIROJA: How come?

FALI: I am expanding my business. Too much work...

HORMUSJI: Business? We know what kind of business. Sitting here we get all the news.

PIROJA: Is it true they are going to evict you?

HORMUSJI: Of course, it's true. They will throw him and his ayah out on the footpath. Why shouldn't they? It's a Parsi colony. Not for dheras like—

PIROJA: Bas! Go in and rest now, will you? You've talked enough for one day.

FALI: No fighting, no fighting, please. Actually I'm in a bit of a hurry. I just stopped by to give Daddy a tip.

HORMUSJI: What?

FALI: A number. A sure bet for tomorrow. Put a little something on it, make a few hundred bucks…

HORMUSJI (*furious*): A number! Besharam! Not enough that you have degraded yourself, you now come to your own father with a tip?

FALI: Now, now. (*To* Piroja) See how he behaves. (*Tauntingly*) As if Hormusji Pochkhanawalla has never betted on a matka number before.

HORMUSJI (*very emotional*): I? Matka number? You monster! Because I am old you think you can talk to me any way you like? I've eaten the ghee of earlier days. I'll remove your whole set of teeth—I'll—!

(*He rushes up aggressively, but* Piroja *intervenes, speaking firmly but kindly, as if to a child.*)

PIROJA: Sit down. Sit down. Sit down at once.

HORMUSJI (*appeals*): This boy has cut off our noses. I can't show my face to half of Dhobhi Talao—(*starts coughing and clutches his chest. Backs down and sits, muttering*). His happiness will come only when he sees me dead. That is his one mission in life…

(Hormusji *holds his head in his hands. A pause, during which the metallic grating sound of someone roller-skating on the floor above begins to be heard. First faintly, then louder and faster.* Fali *and* Piroja *seem not to hear at first, but it is making* Hormusji *visibly tense.*)

PIROJA: And how is—Lucy?

FALI: She's okay.

PIROJA: What stories I hear about you...

FALI: Stories?... Mumma, in from one ear, out the other. Malicious people will talk. Why bother? (*The noises have grown louder.* Hormusji *can't take it any more. He rushes to the window and yells*)

HORMUSJI: How are we to live here? Burjorji! Burjorji Bonesetter! Stop it at once!

FALI: What! That *buddha* is still alive?

PIROJA: He's eighty-four now, and still a proper nuisance. If he breaks a bone at this age, he'll never leave his bed alive. Stop it, Burjorji!

(*Gradually the noise comes to a halt.*)

Every time he starts roller-skating, we have to shout some sense into his head. Sometimes he won't even listen, he'll go on.

FALI: Poor fellow. *Jara*... ? (*Makes circular gestures in the region of his temple, to say: screw-loose.*)

PIROJA (*nods*): Ever since that night...

FALI; I remember. But that was ages ago.

HORMUSJI: What difference does it make? The pain remains.

PIROJA: *Dhandar* and *kolmi no patio*. The little one's birthday, they were feasting. But the prawns must have been very old or not properly cleaned. All three of them were poisoned. And poor Burjorji—the only survivor of his daughter's birthday dinner. Since then, everyone in the building has stopped eating prawns.

FALI: If you're going to die, you can die of a pomfret as well. (*For some reason, this statement angers* Hormusji *again.*)

HORMUSJI: Spare us your philosophy! If you think you're so

smart, go! Look at yourself in the mirror. See what you've made of yourself... If I had had all the opportunities I gave you as a father, where would I have been today. At sixteen I was LTCL in violin. Old Arthur Furtado used to call me Homi Heifitz! But fate was against me, my family responsibilities too many... And look at you. I gave you everything—leisure, comfort, the best teachers, the best piano in Bombay. And all you could make of yourself is a contemptible *matka* bookie!

FALI: And suppose I wanted to be that? Did you ever ask me if I was even interested in music?... Come to think of it, we haven't heard you play in a long time. Where's the old Stradi? Come on, Dad, give us a performance.

HORMUSJI: If two strings were not broken—(*livid*). He's trying to make fun of me... He's trying to taunt his old father... Tell him to get out, Piroja! I can't stand the sight of him! (Hormusji *hurriedly wears his shirt and jacket again.*)

PIROJA: Now, now. What do you think you're doing?

HORMUSJI: Better still. I'll go myself.

PIROJA: You're not going anywhere.

(Hormusji *ignores her and wears his socks determinedly. There is another loud knocking on the door.* Fali *answers. It is* Darabshaa. *He is about the same age as* Hormusji, *slightly taller, plump and effeminate.*)

DARABSHAA (*gasping*): Hormusji! Hormusji! Hormusji!

HORMUSJI: What has happened, Darabshaa?

DARABSHAA: It's the heat. It's gone to everyone's head. The city is in ferment. Rioting may break out any minute, who knows? Bloodshed!

PIROJA: He's drunk, if you ask me.

DARABSHAA: I swear. I swear I'm sober. I heard it just now

on my transistor. You can use my ice-box. Fill it up with foodstuffs. Tomorrow, who knows, nothing may be available in the market.

FALI: Rubbish! Old wives' gossip!

(Darabshaa *is stunned by this verbal assault. But a moment later, he starts grinning foolishly, obsequiously.*)

DARABSHAA: Pardon me son, pardon me. You must know better, of course. Heh, heh, anyone can see I'm an old buffoon, heh, heh, what do we know, Hormusji? We must watch this younger generation. Watch how they will sweep us off our feet and into the gutters of —

HORMUSJI: Talk sense, Darabshaa. Get a hold on yourself. What's all this about?

PALI: I'll tell you. It's nothing serious. Last night two Maharashtrian boys were stabbed in a fight. Some political thing. They were members of that group Yuvak Sangh or something. So their gang retaliated. Some shops in Null Bazaar were looted. A few windshields smashed. Some Muslim fellows were beaten up at random. That's all. No one's going to bother you.

DARABSHAA: There. Bravo. How well put. What did I tell you, Hormusji? This generation understands things much better than we ever could. We old dodderers will mumble and fumble, but they will come straight to the point. Of course, I'm only speaking for myself ...

HORMUSJI: Shut up.

DARABSHAA: Sorry, sorry...

HORMUSJI: This is serious. No laughing matter. In 1921, when the Prince of Wales came to Bombay, the same thing happened. Parsis vs. Hindus. A few shops looted, a few of our women molested...before we knew it, it had spread through the whole city and we were fighting to save our lives. What a licking we gave them! Remember, Darabshaa?

DARABSHAA (*also animated by these memories*): I was only eight years old, Hormusji. But I remember, my father and uncles were up on the terrace, singling out the Hindus one by one... (*Pretends to take aim with a rifle.*)

HORMUSJI: We even poured pots of boiling water on their backs. In three days they were on their knees, begging for mercy... But those days are gone, Darabshaa. This is a generation of sissies. The blood has been polluted... (Hormusji *slips into his shoes.*) I'm going out with Darabshaa now. Don't say anything, Piroja. I'm really angry today... Oh, but before I go...

(*He goes into the bedroom and comes out a moment later, carrying a large airgun.*)

Take this. Keep it with you.

(Piroja, *taken aback, only reluctantly accepts the gun from* Hormusji's *outstretched hand.*)

My grandfather's. Only an airgun, but it can kill a man.

PIROJA: Giving me a gun and going loafing yourself?

HORMUSJI: No arguments please, no arguments...

FALI: I'm going, too. If you want to put something on that number you know where to find me.

PIROJA (*anxiously*): Don't go, Hormusji. Darabshaa can sit here with you. You never know. It may be dangerous outside.

HORMUSJI (*already at the door*): Don't worry, Piroja, don't worry! Never fear for Hormusji! Ha!

(*recites*) 'Danger knows full well that Hormusji
    Is more dangerous than he!
    We were two lions littered in one day,
    And I, the elder and more terrible...'

(*The three men troop out laughing loudly. Suddenly everything is quiet.* Piroja *is alone now. She walks slowly towards centre-stage, looking worn-out, still carrying the airgun limply in her hand. Softly, at first, the noise of roller-skating begins again. It grows louder.* Piroja's *voice is full of anger and despair, as she rushes to the window and screams*):

PIROJA: Burjorji!

BLACKOUT

ACT ONE

SCENE TWO

This scene follows without a break. In the darkness on stage, a pendulum clock strikes seven times. While the last of its chimes is still ringing, Piroja *lights the lamp on the round table. The set comes alive with shadows. She lights another smaller lamp and carries it into the kitchen. Street sounds fade in as the front door opens and* Avan *enters. She is about 26, dressed quite conventionally in a sari. Tall, thin, with a slight slouch. A pretty face, marred by a thick-framed pair of spectacles.*

PIROJA (*off-stage*): Avan? (Avan *deposits her handbag and a plastic folder on the table.*) Avan? (*Still no reply.* Piroja *emerges from the kitchen, a knife in her hand.*) Can't answer? (*Then, excitedly*)... Did he come?

AVAN. Yes. I was with him just now. He dropped me home.

PIROJA (*dismayed*): Dropped you home? Came all the way here and didn't come up to see me...?

AVAN (*sits at the table, looking tired*): And how were we to know my father would not be home this evening?

PIROJA: Yes...yes... That's why I gave him your office address. If he had come here directly, Hormusji might have... But you don't think he may be offended? Why has he not come to see me yet?

AVAN: He's been busy. I've told you already. He does not believe in the old family feud. He's not exactly dying to meet Hormusji and be insulted. But he's very keen to meet you. He'll come.

PIROJA: You look tired, I just made some tea. I'll bring you a cup.

Piroja *goes in and comes out with a cup of tea. Sits at the table.*) What's that? (*Pointing to the folder.*)

AVAN: Some of the stuff I used to write. Cawas wanted to see it.

PIROJA: Years ago I stopped thinking of these things... Struck them out of my memory. The father was dead. I never expected to see his son... Is he fair, Avan?

(*She nods.*)

And tall?

AVAN: Not very.

PIROJA: And he has big eyes? Wait. I'll show you something. (*Opens a drawer in the cupboard and fishes out an old photograph.*) Does he look like this?

AVAN: Who is this?

PIROJA: Does he?

AVAN: ...Yes... There is a likeness. This is his father, then?

PIROJA: Yes, Avan. This is Sohrab.

(*pause*)

If Hormusji finds out Cawas is here and you've been meeting him on the quiet ...

AVAN: I don't care what he thinks.

PIROJA: Don't talk like that. Your father dotes on you, Avan. Don't hurt him.

AVAN: Hormusji gets hurt much too easily.

PIROJA: He's an old man now, remember. Things haven't gone so well for him.

AVAN: And if they haven't, whose fault is it? Whose fault but his own?

I've drudged too long... I can't stand it any more. That

stinky hole of an office. I feel like throwing up listening to their sick jokes, their loud, shameless farting—

PIROJA (*alarmed*): Whose?

AVAN: Those petty clerks and accountants whose company I keep… Yes. It may be a shock for Papa. But one can't live for others all the time. Sometimes it's a good thing to be selfish. One has to *learn* how to be selfish.

PIROJA: Do you understand yourself what you are saying? Where have you learnt all this madness?

(*The lights dim slowly to a blackout.*)

ACT TWO

SCENE ONE

Hormusji *is stretched out on the easy chair.* Darabshaa is *sitting in one of the chairs. Between them, on the floor, a bottle and two glasses. They talk softly.*

HORMUSJI: No end to this heat...

DARABSHAA: The hottest summer in fifty years, today's paper says.

HORMUSJI: They've been saying the rains will be here in forty-eight hours.

DARABSHAA: For the last ten days! If they say it often enough, their luck is bound to change. It's like bluffing in flush.

HORMUSJI (*laughs*): Haven't had a good game of flush in years... (*burps*) ...Excuse Excuse me. Had a little too much to eat at lunch. Piroja's *dhandar-sauce*.

DARABSHAA: Mine was that sickly *khichri-kuhri* from Patuck's. Everyday the food they send gets more and more inedible.

HORMUSJI: Such are the travails of bachelorhood, Darabshaa. Put an ad in *Jame*—Wanted good-natured, middle-aged Parsi lady from good family...for handsome, elderly, retired schoolmaster...

(Darabshaa *breaks into a loud giggle.* Hormusji *hushes him quickly.*)

Shhh. If Piroja wakes up, we've had it.

DARABSHAA: Shall I go...?

HORMUSJI: No, no. Sit. We'll keep our voices low. Be comfortable.

(Darabshaa *slips off his shoes and shares the easy chair's leg- rest with* Hormusji).

DARABSHAA: Last night, three more people were killed. One had acid thrown in his face.

HORMUSJI: I read about it. For two days, everything was quiet. Now they've started again.

DARABSHAA: Who knows where all this may spread?

HORMUSJI: A bunch of illiterates! That's what they are. Choking with jealousy...

DARABSHAA: It's not easy to understand all this hatred... When there's not enough to go around, I've seen even brother turn on brother. It has happened in my own family. In yours too.

HORMUSJI (*disagrees*): The old acquisitive instinct, Darabshaa... Snatch, snatch! Maharashtra for Maharashtrians! Indeed! After we Parsis have built the whole city!... Now if the British were here, they would have just flogged one or two of them in a public place...

DARABSHAA: Shhh. Don't get excited. Piroja.

HORMUSJI (*softer*): Yes. You're right. I get excited too easily ... (*sadly*) Do you know, Darabshaa? In this very house, there's something going on, which I don't know of.

DARABSHAA: What do you mean?

HORMUSJI: I don't know. There's some conspiracy afoot. For one week, Avan has been coming home late from work. If I ask her why, I get no reply. Sometimes both *maidikri* sit together and whisper. If I come into the room, they stop: abruptly. Do they think I'm a fool?... To tell you the truth, Darabshaa, in this house I am made to feel no more important than a pile of old newspapers waiting to be sold for small change.

DARABSHAA: Every morning before I leave my bed, I give my blessings to old Aimai aunty. Without the cheque she sends every month, where would I have been?

HORMUSJI: It all boils down to money, doesn't it? Because I'm not earning, they treat me like dirt ... What about Fali? He makes a packet at his bookie business. Rusi doesn't send a pice. And he won't even write regularly.

DARABSHAA: Tomorrow I will go and see Aimai about this month's cheque.

HORMUSJI: Harkness Road! Why don't you ask her to post it?

DARABSHAA: No, no. She'll never do that. Every time I see her, it's the same story. She'll be waiting for me in the huge mirror room, with her silver tea-set and her Flemish porcelain. We will drink the pallid, lukewarm tea which she insists on pouring herself, even though her hands shake so much, half of it she spills. Then she will mumble to me ... (*Hoarsely*) 'Darab' and put her head in my lap so that I may caress it. I don't mind, Hormusji! I will caress her if I want to. Why should I not? For thirty years I have lived off her. Aimai will be 90 soon.

HORMUSJI: I have made some mistakes too, in my time. But none but the One-Above has any right to judge us harshly.

DARABSHAA: He will understand, Hormusji. He understands better than any of us. They will call us scoundrels and wastrels because we drink. But no. We drink *because* we are scoundrels and wastrels and worthless pigs and because we *know* it. Forgive me if what I say is wrong. But I drink so that I may feel twice as bad and twice as sad for still being alive. Without a bottle I would feel dead ... (*Suddenly starts and looks around as though he had heard a voice.*) Who said that? I've heard that somewhere before... But it's so true. So true.

HORMUSJI: What you say is true, Darabshaa. No one understands me so well as you do. You're my best friend. (*They are both slightly sentimental, as friends drinking together can be.*)

DARABSHAA: I was an idealist, Hormusji. I wanted to teach ...heh, heh, yes... But I did not have the temperament of a teacher. I could never keep discipline in my class. The boys would hoot and whistle at me. When I walked into class, I would find the blackboard scribbled with obscenities. Then they even started shooting paper pellets... I tried to bully them, thrash them. But they saw through my threats. They could see clearly I was nothing but a pompous fool. Every evening when I went home, I would find the back of my shirt and the seat of my trousers fully covered with ink-stains... One day I thought it might help to go to class with a half-peg inside me... (*Pours himself another drink*) ... I tried another job only once. As a clerk. By then I was drinking too heavily. I was sacked even there... (Hormusji *nods sympathetically, sighs*). Yes, I drink. And I will keep on drinking, and I'm glad that I drink. I drink so that I may never forget what a wretch I am. The day I can't have my pint I'm a dead man. (*pause*)

HORMUSJI: Darabshaa...

DARABSHAA: Yes?

HORMUSJI: I can't bear it any longer...

DARABSHAA: What?

HORMUSJI: Being treated like the black sheep of my family.

A second-class citizen in my own home. I will tell you a secret too, Darabshaa. I want my family to live again in peace and happiness. God has provided me the answer! (*He beckons to* Darabshaa *to come closer and, in a hushed, reverential voice*): Last night I saw by the well…old Dhanjishaa Bapasola!

DARABSHAA: What!

HORMUSJI: Yes. It's true. There he was cracking his kashti fearfully. Anyone else would have fled for his life. But I stood there and watched. Then he looked straight at me and spoke two words…words that sent a shiver up my spine. 'Sixty-seven,' he said. 'Back sixty-seven, tomorrow.' And then he was gone.

DARABSHAA: Sixty-seven?

HORMUSJI: Do you know what that means? I am being given a chance to recover my family's fortunes. We will be rich again. And I'm not forgetting you, Darabshaa. You must put something on this number, too. At last, Dhanjishaa Bapasola has taken pity on us.

DARABSHAA: But are you sure? Where will you find the money to back this number?

HORMUSJI: Yesterday Avan received her salary. Eight hundred rupees. Tonight, I will take six hundred from the cupboard where Piroja has put it and give it all to Fali. And tomorrow we will be rich again. In one night, I will have made a clean fifty thousand! Dhobhi Talao will bow before us again.

DARABSHAA: Do you know what you are doing, Hormusji? You are stealing her salary! God forbid, but if the number doesn't come?

HORMUSJI (*in hushed excitement*) It will come. It will. Don't say another word.

BLACKOUT

ACT TWO

SCENE TWO

The opening bars of a lilting Viennese waltz, full of charm and nostalgia, effect the scene transition. When the lights come on again, Piroja *and* Cawas *are seated at the round table.* Cawas, *pleasant-looking, young, with straight hair, a warm, reassuring voice; yet something oily, too smooth about his manner, which is faintly disquieting. He drains a cup of tea and puts it down on the table.* Piroja *is dressed neatly, in her best sari.*

PIROJA: So you have come back at last to your father's city.
CAWAS: Yes. He really loved this city, didn't he? This is my first time here. Yet somehow, it feels as though I've seen it all before. As if I'm returning home after a long absence.
PIROJA. But it is, this *is* your home. Your father should never have left it.

  (*Warily*) But you must have come to Bombay before?
CAWAS: Yes, several times, in fact. On work.
PIROJA: And what made you look us up *this* time?
CAWAS: Some months ago, Pirojamai, I was going through some old trunks in our storeroom at home. I found Sohrabji's diaries.
PIROJA: Diaries?
CAWAS. A dozen notebooks, filled cover to cover, in his minute scrawl…. Such wonderful descriptions. Of this city, this house…the happier days you saw together…
PIROJA: I knew he used to write things down. He never

showed me anything.

CAWAS: He should have been a writer, my father. Such loving observation, such detail... Those good old days of gaslights and victorias. British soldiers on furlough, during the War. Nights at the Opera House...

PIROJA: Yes. We have seen some good times, too.

CAWAS: He writes about the first time he met you, at a wedding.

PIROJA: I remember.

CAWAS: And Hormusji caused a panic by getting a fish-bone stuck in his throat, at dinner.

PIROJA: Yes.

CAWAS: And my father pulled it out for him with a pair of tweezers...

(*They are both amused by this detail.*) ...I sat down and read through all the diaries. That's when I decided I wanted to meet you. And Hormusji. And your children.

PIROJA (*doubtful*): Hormusji...

CAWAS: I know. I know everything about the old quarrel. Avan told me that he's never stopped hating my father. But I say, let us end all this. Let us forget the past.

PIROJA (*with a trace of bitterness*): And what good are his diaries to us now? Why in God's name did he not write me a single line, after he went away?

CAWAS: But that is what he wanted, what he suffered for. A few days after reaching Bangalore, he had his first stroke. Till the day he lost his speech completely, the only name on his lips was always 'Piroja'. My mother told me about it years later, as she lay sick, dying herself, choking with remorse... He would beg of her to write you a note for him. And she would punish him. She would not clean him. 'Where is your

Piroja now?' she would ask. 'Will she come to clean your shit?' And he would lie in the dung and wetness for hours, and moan...

(Piroja *is visibly moved and horrified.*)

...She was never able to forgive him for having loved another woman more than he could ever love her.

PIROJA: And he was never able to forgive me for not breaking off my engagement with Hormusji. One year after my marriage...what a revenge he took! I would not have found it difficult to forgive him anything. If only he had just written a line... Two days after our last meeting, Hormusji was taken ill. Couldn't breathe. He had to be given oxygen. Then we went away to Deolali for three months, so he could rest. And all the while, I was thinking, there will be some news, a letter waiting for us when we return home. But no. Nothing. He just vanished... I felt so cheated. So ashamed...

CAWAS: Did Hormusji never find out about your feelings for each other?

PIROJA (*shakes her head*): He was too self-obsessed, too busy. He had no time for me.

CAWAS: I say again, let us forget the past and all this bitterness. There's nothing to be gained by dwelling on it.

PIROJA: I'd forgotten...almost... But it has all come back... God forgive, I don't wish to speak against the dead. Yet what could be more horrible than what he did to us?

CAWAS: I believe my father was an honest man. But let us leave that. It is not my intention to revive painful memories. Let the dead bury their secrets with them; their shame... or their honour. I want to make up for the past in whatever way I can. Avan has such talent. She's wasting it as a steno.

In fact, we were talking about a plan. A possible job for her. One way in which I *can* help.

PIROJA: What plan? Hormusji will never agree to anything. (*Just then,* Avan *enters, carrying a tea-tray. She is bubbly, effervescent, quite unlike the gloomy and angry* Avan *we saw before.*)

AVAN (*She calls, cheerfully*): Tea! Tea! Tea for everyone. (*Puts the tray down on the table.*)

PIROJA: What is this, Avan, what have you been plotting behind my back?

AVAN. It's true, Mama, it's true. (*Grabs her mother by the arms, in a kind of hug, excited.*) I'm going away.

(Piroja *recoils, in shock. Freeze.*)

BLACKOUT

ACT TWO

SCENE THREE

The pendulum clock chimes eight. Piroja *and* Avan *are laying the table for dinner.* Hormusji *emerges from the bedroom, whistling, knotting the string on his striped pyjamas, and joins them at table.*

HORMUSJI (*dismayed*): Cabbage…?

PIROJA: Eat it if you can. Otherwise, don't. There's nothing else.

HORMUSJI: I *like* it, I like it…

(Piroja *and* Avan *are tense, in no mood to talk.* Hormusji *is quite the opposite—cheerful, loquacious. He hums a tune while serving himself. Then talks, between morsels.*)

When Bombay first got electricity—1928, I think—ours was one of the first buildings to install a meter. You know, Avan? It was the tallest building around for miles … At night it would glow brightly, like a lighthouse in a sea of dimly-lit fishing boats. At one time it was a matter of pride to be able to say 'I live at Doongaji House'.

PIROJA: Eat your food.

HORMUSJI: …What a state it's come to now! That rascal of a landlord… Anway, we'll have to spend some money. First thing we'll get done is the wiring. Then maybe a coat of paint. Some repair work…

PIROJA (*sharply*); What nonsense are you talking!

(Hormusji *is silenced, momentarily*).

HORMUSJI (*with a solemn dignity*): Remind me to clean the

lamp tomorrow. The chimney's all black.

PIROJA (*offers*): Some more...

HORMUSJI: Luck hasn't been with the Pochkhanawalla family for many years now. But things may change soon... Yes, I have a feeling things will change. The wheel of fortune turns... restores to the righteous what is theirs.... The main thing is family. The family must stick together. The family must not get scattered...

PIROJA: What's with you tonight?

AVAN (*to* Piroja.): Why is the salt always less in our food?

PIROJA (*crossly*): If you find it less, go and get some from the kitchen.

AVAN: Doesn't matter. I've nearly finished.

HORMUSJI: In my father's day, there was never any shortage. Food was always cooked for fifteen people. Guests would come and go as they liked, always welcome. Every month, pounds and pounds of grain would arrive from the grocer's and be stored in those massive enamel jars.

PIROJA: Don't swallow your food.

HORMUSJI: They were really huge! Like this... (*indicates height and roundness*). After a point, it was no longer possible to reach the grain from outside. Then my mother washed my feet and lowered me into the jar...and I would scoop up the remaining grain and pass it out to her...that feeling...so dark and cool and roomy inside...my feet would sink into the grain. I'd never want to come out. I'd have to be dragged out, screaming and kicking.

PIROJA: Chew. Or you'll get gas and groan through the night.

HORMUSJI: Piroja, my dentures are hurting me, I can't! Where did they go? I can't seem to remember what became of those jars...(*They munch quietly for a while.*)

PIROJA (*to* Avan): Take some more.

AVAN: I've finished.

HORMUSJI: I have an idea. Why don't we all play a game of cards tonight. Rummy, what say? Like before...

PIROJA: What has happened to you tonight? How strangely you are talking.

AVAN: Been tippling again, I expect. With Darabshaa Dalal. (*Her words are laced with the casual contempt of youth. They sting.*)

PIROJA (*harshly*): Go in and wash your hands, if you've finished.

(Avan *takes her empty plate to the kitchen.*)

HORMUSJI (*bitterly*): I may not have been an ideal father. But I never thought I'd live to see the day when my children would talk to me like that...I know you have to work, I know how you hate your job. Don't think I'm not aware of it. It torments me... Let me tell you that. And let me tell you one more thing, Hormusji Pochkhanawalla may be down, but he is not out. I can tell you that. I will change things completely! Overnight! Then you can even leave your job if you want to—

AVAN (*she has just re-entered*): That's exactly what I plan. Things are going to change tomorrow. Definitely. At least for me. Daddy please don't go out anywhere tomorrow morning.

HORMUSJI: Why?

AVAN: We are expecting a visitor.

PIROJA (*in a tense, low voice*): Let them go, Hormusji...let them all go...

HORMUSJI: Who? What are you talking about?

PIROJA: The family will scatter...the family will chip and splinter...

HORMUSJI (*shouts*): Answer me!

AVAN: Everything can be answered tomorrow. I'm too tired and sleepy. Good night.

(Hormusji *pushes his plate away.*)

PIROJA: Finish it, Hormusji. Don't waste food.

(Hormusji *is sunk in a deep silence,* Avan *is walking towards the bedroom, when there is a sudden knocking on the door.* Perin *steps in and announces, stiffly, like a messenger.*)

PERIN: There have been more stabbings, soda-water-bottle fights. A chawl was set on fire in Parel. The police have ordered a curfew in many areas: Girgaum, Pydhonie, Khetwadi, Dhobhi Talao: that includes us.

BLACKOUT

ACT THREE

SCENE ONE

Cawas *is seated at the round table, looking slightly disinterested. Near him stands* Avan, *tense, clenching her fists.* Hormusji *has sought refuge in the bedroom and locked the door,* Piroja *is outside the door, knocking, entreating. She wears a sari-petticoat, a blouse and looks as if this morning has erupted on her before she could quite ready herself for it. Her long hair, usually tied in a bun, hangs loose giving her a wild look.*

PIROJA (*knocking on the bedroom door*): Come on out!
(*There is no reply.*)
Open up! Are you opening, or no?
HORMUSJI (*shouts offstage*): No!
PIROJA (*exasperated, turns to the others*): Now what shall we do?
AVAN: This is the way he always behaves.
PIROJA (*gentler*): But come out at least. We can talk it over.
HORMUSJI: Never! I'll never come out.
AVAN (*to* Cawas): He should have been on stage, my father.
PIROJA: Hormusji, please! We just want to discuss something. Is this any way to behave?
HORMUSJI: I don't want to hear anything. I don't want to see his face. (*A moment's pause. The front door is ajar, and* Perin *enters, in some state of excitement herself.*)
PERIN: Listen! They are breaking down Burjorji's door. Not a squeak from his roller-skates since yesterday. His tiffin-box has been lying untouched outside since last night. The ants have got at it.

PIROJA (*shouts*): What do you want?

PERIN: I just came to tell you. All the neighbours are going up to force his door in. Adesar Uncle thinks he might have slipped while skating and broken his hip or something.

(Hormusji *has quietly opened the door an inch to listen to* Perin. *He creeps out.*)

HORMUSJI: I am going up to see what the trouble is…

AVAN and PIROJA: No, you're not! Sit down now.

(Piroja *tries to take him by the hand and help him to a chair, but he recoils from her touch and yells*):

HORMUSJI: Don't touch me! Don't you dare! Oh! Oh!

(*Clutches his chest and hobbles to a chair, moaning.*)

PIROJA (*to* Perin.): Go away. We have enough problems of our own already.

(Perin *leaves.* Hormusji *continues to moan and wheeze in a most disturbing manner.*)

HORMUSJI: I can't breathe… My pill…

(Piroja *finds his pills,* Avan *fetches a glass of water.*) HORMUSJI (*breathing more easily now, looks only at* Piroja *and* Avan, *never at* Cawas): …You want to kill me…? Is that it? Is that the sole intention? I knew there was something going on. Some plot. But with him?

PIROJA: Hormusji…

HORMUSJI: Go! You can all go! What are you waiting for? You don't have to attend my funeral also…

PIROJA: Be calm now! Behave yourself. Enough is enough.

HORMUSJI: Seditious witch! Why did you wait thirty years to do this to me?

PIROJA (*striking her forehead in exasperation, close to tears*): What has happened to him? How he's talking…

HORMUSJI: Why don't you go to Bangalore as well? What

auspicious day are you waiting for? Hasn't he invited you?

PIROJA: Don't be so selfish. This is for Avan, don't you see? She is getting a much better job. Twice as much salary!

HORMUSJI: ...Ah...so that's it... Money!... Paisa!... O fickle breed, that can be bought and sold for money, I don't need you...I don't need any of you. I will stay here all alone...like Dhanjishaa...

CAWAS (*warm, slightly patronizing*): If I may say something. Uncle, you must not become so bitter. Whatever's past is past. Why let a quarrel thirty years old stain her future? Avan is very talented. She'll be invaluable to my agency. It's so difficult to find good writers...

(Hormusji *turns to him and stares, drinking him in.*)

HORMUSJI: ...So you are Cawas...Yes, I had heard of you. They tell me you have done well for yourself. What agency?

CAWAS: Advertising.

HORMUSJI. Ah, advertising.

CAWAS: It's still quite small, but—

HORMUSJI (*interrupts*): You're a cleverer opponent than I thought.... You think you have age on your side.... You think you are dealing with a man who has one foot in his grave...

CAWAS: Nothing of the sort.

HORMUSJI: Do you remember your father's death? No, of course not. You were too young. But you may have heard... He suffered... He had to pay for everything in the end. He suffered terribly...And in death, his body gave off such a foul stink, the khandhias refused to carry it, until their fees were doubled.

PIROJA: What has all that to do with us now?

HORMUSJI: The Universe is a strange place, far more

mysterious than young people tend to think. When you are young, you think you can get away with anything… It's not true. There are Laws operating, though we cannot perceive them… There is Fire…Atash… The Atash in our temples is a blend of fires ignited in sixteen different combinations. The sixteenth and most terrible is the fire obtained from lightning that strikes the earth. We have prayers to produce even that! Do you think in such a world a man can get away with anything?

AVAN: Oh really, Mummy. This is worse than I thought it would be.

PIROJA: First, he didn't want to talk at all. Now he's giving us lectures on religion! But what are you trying to say? I can't understand anything.

HORMUSJI (*Suddenly his attention has wandered. He looks dazed, dream struck*): Nothing…nothing…really…I just remembered…last night… (*The anger and arrogance in his voice have evaporated. A gentle vulnerability takes their place.*) It was here… At this very table…I was sitting here and weeping. Every time I passed my hand through my hair, large tufts of it would fall out, painlessly. I was simply pulling out all my hair, just by caressing it. And weeping, because I knew that soon there would be none left. The strange thing is, every time I removed some hair and laid it on the table, it would go up in flames immediately. I enjoyed this immensely. Soon a small bonfire was dancing merrily before me. I laughed. Then I realized the whole building was burning. Doongaji House was up in flames. I ran to save my life. When I reached the street, there was no fire any more. But the building was not there either. Only a vacant plot of land. And a wizened, half-naked beggar standing there. In his hand, he held a small jam bottle which was filled with ashes. He gave it to me and said, 'Doongaji House…'. I remember marvelling at how a whole building could be reduced to ashes that filled only one jam bottle…

PIROJA: Okay, now let's not waste everyone's time.

HORMUSJI (*raises his voice*): Do you think you can get away with this?

PIROJA: Here we go again…

HORMUSJI: You fools! Why did you entertain him in this house even for a minute? He has come here to complete his father's work. Suddenly he's been inspired by sublime motives. Who is Avan to him? It is all a plan… One morning he walks into our life; when he walks out of it, in the evening, our family is in pieces, ruined!

AVAN: There is a limit even to nonsense. If he can't learn to be civil, we'll both walk out this instant. He's not come here to be insulted.

PIROJA: Watch your own tongue, you puppy-bitch! Suddenly you think you have grown up too much!

AVAN: As much as the two of you have dawdled back into infancy.

PIROJA (*reaching for her sapaat*): Don't back-answer! I'll throw this in your face! (*They exchange baleful glares.*)

HORMUSJI: You want money. Is that it? Are you going to Bangalore for money? From today onwards I will support you. Leave your job! I will keep you like a princess. From today—

AVAN: If time is money, we'd certainly like to catch up on some of that.

PIROJA (*threateningly reaches for her sapaat*): Again? Again? Suddenly she has started twittering like a European madam.

(*sarcastically*) Because she is going to *Bangalore*! (*A brief pause.*)
HORMUSJI: Do you remember, Avan? When Fali left us, that night you came to my bedside and comforted me. You said, 'Don't worry, Daddy, I'll stay with you forever. I'll take care of you…'
AVAN: One can't live on sentimentality. Old times, old times. In this house there's nothing else. Do you remember this? Do you remember that? I'm still young, don't you see?
HORMUSJI: And one day, you, too, will be old. And lonely. Desperately lonely. Then, perhaps, you will remember your old father, who will no longer be alive. Don't think I am putting a curse on your head. A father can never do that to his own child. I'm just telling you the way it is. It's a law of nature. Today I would not have been half so unhappy if I did not know that the man you are running away with is the son of my worst enemy. The man who reduced me to what I am today.
AVAN: I am afraid that is just not true!
CAWAS (*cautioning*): Avan…
AVAN: But the truth has to be stated, Cawas. The sooner, the better. (*To* Hormusji): Sohrab never cheated you. Your precious bookshop was already in financial trouble even *before* you fell ill.
HORMUSJI: Says who?
AVAN: His father's diaries. Cawas found them. He read all about it.
HORMUSJI: Ha! Diaries! Who cannot fabricate a diary, to explain away his villainy…
AVAN: And, besides, he found a letter.
PIROJA: Letter?
HORMUSJI: What letter?

AVAN: A letter signed by you...dismissing Sohrab from his job. It is dated three weeks before your illness began. At the time your business collapsed, Sohrab was no longer even working for you.

CAWAS: He went to Bangalore not with embezzled money. He went there to take possession of a house left to him by Uncle Cooverji, who had just died.

(*All through these disclosures,* Hormusji *is completely stunned. He is looking at his palms, moving his lips silently.*)

PIROJA: Oh God...am I going mad?

CAWAS: I didn't want to bring up all this...

HORMUSJI (*rising from his chair, slowly*): Lies! Lies! Lies! ...He has come here with a bunch of lies to poison your minds... I'll kill him! (*leaps at* Cawas. Piroja *jumps up and wrestles with him, as* Cawas *backs away, startled.*)

PIROJA (*struggling*): Cool down! Your blood pressure!

HORMUSJI (*gasping for breath, softer*): I told you. He has come here to destroy me.... He is evil.... Come to complete his father's work.... Letter. Where is the letter? Come on. Let's see that piece of forgery. Well?

CAWAS: It's in Bangalore.

HORMUSJI (*triumphant*): See? See? Bangalore!

CAWAS: It was never my intention to bring up this matter at all. There was no reason for me to bring this letter along.

HORMUSJI: Don't go with him, Avan, don't go.... You don't know where he's taking you...Bangalore!? Stop her, Piroja!

PIROJA (*holds her head*): Now something is going to happen to me...something will happen to me.... My head is spinning!

AVAN: I'm afraid there's nothing more to discuss. I have said what I had to say. It's a pity we could not discuss it decently, like adults. Now I've got some shopping to do. And a six o'clock flight to catch this evening.

PIROJA: Six o'clock flight! Today! You never told me you were going today! Avan! Avan! (*She is almost wailing with anxiety and confusion.*)

CAWAS: Please, aunty. Office work. I simply have to get back. And both of us felt there was no point in her coming later, on her own…isn't that right? (*Smiles at* Avan.)

HORMUSJI: Saw that? Now do you understand? We don't even know where she is going, what fate awaits her…

AVAN (*at last showing some signs of emotional stress herself*): Daddy, *please* Daddy! Don't worry so much about me, I'll be alright. I'll write to you as soon as I get there. Everything will be okay.

(*Enter* Perin)

PERIN: Don't worry. Everything okay. Burjorji Bonesetter was only having a good snooze. When we broke down his door, he sat up in bed and gave a big yawn. I find it really funny (*Giggles, but her mirth fizzles out as she registers the expressions on their faces*). Wha—Wha—What's happening here? Is anything the matter?

(*Enter* Fali, *trundling in quite casually, announcing in his slightly effeminate, undulating voice*):

FALI: Where is he? Lost, Everything gone…

HORMUSJI: Fali! (*Rushes up and grabs his arm.*) What happened?

FALI: What did I tell you, Dad? Never put everything on one number.

HORMUSJI: O Dhanjishaa Bapasola! What have you done?

PIROJA: What has happened, Fali? What is this now?

HORMUSJI (*shaking his head*): I'm going. I'm going now. Now there's no point in living. Don't try to stop me…

FALI: Come now, be a sport, Daddy. Money comes, money goes…

(*To* Piroja, *while hanging on to* Hormusji's *arm*):

I warned him. But he insisted on putting everything on one number. Six hundred rupees washed away in one night.

PIROJA: Six hundred rupees!

AVAN: Six hundred rupees! (*She goes to the cupboard and confirms her hunch.*) My salary! Oh, so that's how he was going to make me a princess!

HORMUSJI: Let me go, Fali! Don't try to stop me…

(*Enter* Darabshaa)

DARABSHAA: Er…excuse me…

HORMUSJI: Darabshaa! My friend! I am undone! My family's broken. This devil has come to take away my Avan. I have lost everything. I am nothing but a petty thief.

DARABSHAA: Ah! Ah! Who—? (*Points to* Cawas).

HORMUSJI: He is evil! He is Iago himself!

DARABSHAA: It's the younger generation, Hormusji! They've caught up with us. The younger generation is waiting to wash us into the gutters of history!

HORMUSJI: Let me go! Now the only place for me is at the bottom of a well…

(*He makes a sudden dash for the door. Fali is undecided as to whether he should give chase, Piroja, clutching her long hair, is making most alarming and extraordinary panting sounds*).

AVAN: Let him go. He'll be back in half an hour.

HORMUSJI (*screams, backstage*): If you ever have children by him, remember! They'll be shrivel-headed dwarves! It's a law of nature!

DARABSHAA (*panting*): Wait…wait for me…Hormusji!

PIROJA: Ah…hoh…ho…ha…

(*A moment's pause. Then* Fali *notices* Perin).
FALI: Arre? Hello, Perin. Sorry unh, I didn't see you.
PERIN (*very sweetly*): Hello, Fali…
FALI (*leering at* CAWAS): And who's this?
(*Just then, the grinding sound of* Burjorji's *roller-skates, rapidly growing louder*).
PIROJA (*screams*): Stop him! I am going to faint! (*She swoons, everyone rushes up*).

BLACKOUT

ACT THREE

SCENE TWO

(That evening. It is very dark. The set is deserted. HORMUSJI waits in the doorway for a moment, listening. He walks stealthily, first to the kitchen, then to the bedroom, peeps in to see if anyone is at home. He is not sure of his step and totters a little. Occasionally, he grunts to himself.

He lights the lamp, and the room swells with shadows. He seems lost in thought. He picks up the stool and carries it to the cupboard on which his violin case is perched. He climbs on to the stool and retrieves the faded case. When he takes out the violin, he wipes it lovingly with his handkerchief; then picks up the bow and, staggering towards centre-stage, scratches out a tune. The tone he produces is harsh, he gets many notes wrong, which he goes back to and corrects … Half-way through the song, he stops playing and puts the violin back in its case.

Then he notices a note left for him on the table. Reads it aloud, in a husky voice):

HORMUSJI: If you feel hungry, take three potatoes, one piece of meat and half of yesterday's vegetable. Don't eat the food without heating it… I have gone to see Avan off at the airport…

(He crumples the note and throws it on the floor. He is mumbling, making indecipherable, grunting sounds. Suddenly, he recites, in a low mournful voice):

'O Gertrude, Gertrude…

When sorrows come, they come not as single spies,
But in battalions.
(*He goes to the door and before slamming it shut, announces*):
Tonight I will be very drunk...

BLACKOUT

ACT FOUR

(*The table lamp has been turned down. Its dim, eerie glow reveals* Piroja *stretched out on the easy chair, snoring gently.* Perin *seems to be asleep too, her head resting on the table. She sits up, looks at her wristwatch. Rouses* Piroja).

PIROJA (*mumbles in her sleep*): ...Ummm...What?...Who?
PERIN: Wake up, Piroja aunty! Wake up!
PIROJA: What time is it?
PERIN: Ten to one.
PIROJA: I fell asleep... Ten to one! (*Sits up with a start.*) They're not back yet! O Perin, what must have happened.
PERIN: I checked: there's a lock on Darabshaa's door, also. They must be doing the rounds of the bars, as usual.
PIROJA: But so late? Shapoor closes at midnight...and all this trouble in the streets. Isn't there something we can do?
PERIN: What?
PIROJA: I don't want to just sit here cracking my knuckles. Let's go and drag them out.
PERIN: From where? They could be in any one of those Goan joints in Agiari Lane. They'll be back any minute, singing their *Marseillaise* soulfully, waking all the neighbours. You go back to sleep.
PIROJA: No, I won't be able to. You go down if you want. I'm alright.
PERIN: I'm wide awake now.
PIROJA: ...How many things happened today...Hormusji was very angry. I've never seen him so angry before.

PERIN: Naturally. After all the nasty things Cawas accused him of. And on top of everything, he's run off with your daughter.

PIROJA: Don't talk any nonsense. She's gone there to work. She's got a new job.

PERIN: Where will she stay in Bangalore?

PIROJA: We don't know, Perin. She said she would write as soon as she reached. She's just packed one small suitcase and left. Hormusji was right. We should have found out more about this. What was the great hurry?

PERIN: Hormusji can never be angry for long. He's such a gentle, understanding person.

(*Pause. Piroja is restless.*)

PIROJA: ...Just look out the window. See if you can see anyone.

(Perin *strolls up to the* window. *Stares outside for a while in both directions.*)

PERIN: Not a soul. Not even a stray dog in sight.

(*She comes back and sits.*)

PIROJA: I had a dream just now when I dozed off.

PERIN: I love listening to dreams.

PIROJA: I was going back to my father's estate outside Lahore. I was happy to be going back home. But when I reached, I saw that everything was ruined. The garden was overrun with brambles and wild grass. The bungalow had decayed and crumbled... Then I saw Avan. She was standing in the middle of the ruin, carrying an infant in her arms. It was a monster...swollen head...two holes for a nose...eight fingers on each hand...'Who is its father?' I screamed at her. She just pointed some distance away, in the tall grass, was a body...covered with a white sheet. I went up to it and pulled back the sheet... It was my father. Kaikushroo. I touched his cheek. It was icy cold. Then he opened his eyes and smiled at me...I was not scared. I felt happy...

PERIN: If I was to think of all the weird dreams I have, I'd go bonkers in no time.

PIROJA: You're a good companion, Perin. I'm glad you're here with me tonight.

PERIN: Everyone thinks I'm stupid. Mummy says I haven't the brains of a sparrow. But I can be quite intelligent sometimes.

PIROJA: Now, now. Don't let it go to your head... (*They smile.*) ...Even if my son didn't marry you, at least I found a friend.

PERIN: What do you mean? You mean if I had married him...

PIROJA: We would probably have hated each other. Don't you know? A saasu and wahu can never get along.

PERIN (*laughs*): How funny you are! As if it's a hard and fast rule... Do you have someone in Lahore still?

PIROJA: We lost touch...I don't know... My mother left him. She took me with her and came to Bombay. I was only seven.

PERIN: What did he do to her?

PIROJA: A hard-livered man...arrogant... He was a rich landlord. His one great passion was hunting. Animals and women. One day, he had a child by one of the women who picked fruit on his orchards. My two elder brothers stayed on with him. We came to Bombay, After Partition, we never heard of them again. (*pause*)

Now I will have to start sending out dabbas again. Like I used to, before Avan found her job,

PERIN: You mean she won't be sending you any money now?
PIROJA: Oh yes. She said she would. But I've still got two hands, two legs. I'm not bedridden yet. I don't want to keep waiting every month for money-orders to arrive.... Most of last month's salary went down the drain, I'd almost forgotten about that. At the airport, Cawas gave me two hundred rupees. I didn't want to take it. But he said I should consider it an advance on Avan's first salary. And anyhow—

(*She does not complete her sentence.* Perin *has risen from her chair, excited about something, taking deep breaths.*)

PERIN: You know what?
PIROJA: What is it? Can you hear them on the stairs?

(Perin *shakes her head mysteriously. Goes to the window and leans out.*)

PERIN: Can't you smell it? It's unmistakable. There is a smell of rain in the air.
PIROJA: Rain?
PERIN: Yes. It's going to rain at last.
PIROJA: I can't smell a thing. My nose is blocked. But it has suddenly become very cool. Come and sit here, Perin I want to ask you something.
PERIN (*sits*): What?
PIROJA: Think carefully before answering. Do you think what Cawas said about Hormusji…and his brother…was not true?
PERIN: I've been thinking about that question, too, ever since you told me what he said.
PIROJA: Yes…?
PERIN: …And, I thought, perhaps it doesn't really matter any more…
PIROJA (*angry*): Doesn't matter? Doesn't matter that he made his brother out to be a thief when he was innocent? How

many years I suffered because of that...I tore him out of my heart, learnt to despise him.

PERIN: But Sohrabji has been dead thirty years... If Hormusji has believed for the last thirty years that he was cheated out of his shop, who is Cawas to come now and say he wasn't. Has he got any proof?

PIROJA: He has... But he didn't bring it with him.

PERIN: There you are... To tell you the truth, I didn't like him one bit. Smart-looking fellow. But I wouldn't trust him an inch.

PIROJA: We just have his word for it... Why should he lie? He didn't even want to talk about it.

PERIN: Anyone can make any claims. Where's the proof?

PIROJA: And yet, if what he said was true, it explains many things... If Sohrab was dismissed, it explains why he went away quietly, and never tried to contact me again... If Hormusji dismissed Sohrab...it can mean only one thing...

PERIN: What?

PIROJA: That he knew...he knew all along... All these years... If Hormusji dismissed Sohrab, all of a sudden, it means he must have suspected something... Perhaps it was the pain of that that made him ill... Afterwards, he heaped curses and slander on his brother's head and blamed him for our bankruptcy...for his own mistakes... What shame. What shame on my head... What a curse I brought on the family... How much I made him hate his own brother... and how much he must have hated me... But silently... inside himself... All these years, he never said a word in reproach...I never even suspected for a moment that he might know...

PERIN: Know *what?*

PIROJA (*shakes her head*): Never mind.... This is not for you, my child...

PERIN: Were you and Sohrab lovers...?

(Piroja *hides her face in her hands. Her large body heaves, overwhelmed by emotion. Just then, very softly at first, we hear the slow patter of rain.* Perin *stands up slowly, fascinated.*)

PERIN ...It's come at last... What did I tell you?

(*Suddenly, the sound of the rain increases, becomes a deep, drumming sound. A strong breeze dashes the window against the sill, twice.*)

PIROJA: Shut the window! Quick! Those are the last panes in the house that haven't cracked.

(Perin *shuts the window. The sound of the rain is reduced to a muffled hum.*)

PERIN: ...At last the rains have come...

(*After a brief silence, we begin to hear the irregular shuffle of two pairs of footsteps slowly making their way up the wooden staircase. The sound grows steadily louder.* Piroja *stands up too; both women are waiting for the knock on the door. It comes: a loud, persistent knocking.* Perin *opens the door. She screams.*)

PIROJA: What has happened?!!

(*From the darkness of the landing, a battered* Hormusji *limps into the dim light of the room. He has his arm around* Darabshaa's *shoulder, and is half in a faint. There is blood on his forehead, and his left arm seems injured, if the manner in which he is holding it is any indication. Both men are drenched. The rain has washed some of the blood from* Hormusji's *face onto his shirt, which has acquired a pink hue. His spectacles are missing.*)

PIROJA: O God save us...

DARABSHAA (*talking through effusive gasps and sobs*): Piroja, Piroja... There was nothing I could do. I could only stand and watch... (*Lowers* Hormusji *into a chair.*)

PIROJA (*screams*): But what happened?

DARABSHAA: We were coming back home… A bunch of five or six boys were passing. They would never have done anything to us. But Hormusji started shouting all kinds of dirty names. Ai-chi tai-chi, he started abusing their mothers and sisters. He said their kind were illiterate pigs, who should be shot. I begged him to stop, but he was very drunk, very angry…Piroja, when they crossed the road and collared us, I froze completely…I am a coward…I should have fought them. One ugly dark fellow slapped me so hard, I fell in the gutter. (*All through* Darabshaa's *speech,* Hormusji *has been sitting frozen, in a limp position, gazing fixedly at a point, muttering abuses.* Darabshaa *extracts a broken pair of spectacles from his pocket and extends it towards* Piroja). They broke his specs.

(*But* Piroja *doesn't take the spectacles from his hand. He is left holding them, as the old woman turns to* Perin *and shouts*):

PIROJA: Run! Wake up Dr Lalkaka! …O God, what new mischiefs will you invent for us every day…?

BLACKOUT

ACT FIVE

Rain and thunder. A storm rages. The first few bars of the Marseillaise *blend with this symphony of the natural elements, as the lights come on for the final scene. The set has been altered in a violent and disturbing manner. The round, marble-topped table is no longer at centre-stage. It has been pushed nearer the door, and its marble top wrapped in old newspapers and tied with a string. The two chairs are placed one on top of the other, seat to seat, and a rolled-up mattress rests on them. The lamp which used to be on the table is on the floor, next to a large bundle of household odds and ends wrapped together in a sheet. The corners of some family portraits and the handle of a badminton racket stick out from the bundle. The front door is wide open.*

The window, too, is open—flung open violently, it would seem, for one of its sides has come off its hinges and rests on the floor, the other still hangs by one hinge. The timber scaffolding, of which we have glimpsed a section in earlier scenes, is also slightly altered—a log sticks through the window at a diagonal slant.

Hormusji *is resting on the easy chair, which has been pushed into a corner. He has a sticking plaster on his cheek, and his head and left wrist are swathed in bandages.*

It is afternoon. The rain clouds have cleared and a mild afternoon light suffuses the room. From a distance, we hear the monotonous droning of two male voices reciting Avestan prayers.

Piroja *enters from the kitchen, carrying another bundle—cooking utensils wrapped together in a sheet. She places it on the floor, next to a trunk. She is dressed in a rather ragged-looking sari. She goes back in, and comes out once again with another piece of luggage.*

Then the sounds of several pairs of footsteps coming down the stairs …the prayers get louder.

HORMUSJI (*to* Piroja): Ask them to wait! I want to pay my last respects to Burjorji Bonesetter.

PIROJA: Come… (*She gently helps him up, and he hobbles to the door with her. As the stretcher-bearers cross their landing, they bend their heads and fold their hands in a silent prayer. The chanting and the footfalls fade away,* Piroja *and* Hormusji *walk back. When they speak, there is a bleakness in their voices, such as people have at funerals.*)

HORMUSJI: The vultures will have a meagre meal today…

PIROJA: He waited twenty-five years for this day. He had become just skin and bones… When the roof caved in, a beam fell straight on his chest and flattened it. He was asleep in bed… (*pause*)

…All this while I was packing, it still felt like a dream…. An ugly nightmare caused by the *masoor* we ate last night. In the morning, the breadman will come and wake us. Then the milkman. I will fill water in our tubs, before it becomes a trickle and disappears from the taps. Then I will fry you an egg…. And we will laugh at our silliness and put everything back in its place; get down to the cooking. Are you hungry, Hormusji? You haven't eaten anything all day… (Hormusji *shakes his head.*) …Even the pain…it's like the pain in a dream. I have never seen this Jeejeebhoy sanatorium. What is it like?

HORMUSJI: A smelly hovel.

PIROJA: I hope there are no rats. I'm terrified of rats.

HORMUSJI: A slum, a footpath, a sewer! Does it matter?

PIROJA: We have a few years left still. We'll have to fill our term somehow…

HORMUSJI: Was anyone else hurt?

PIROJA: Poor Adesar. Both his legs were smashed. His wife and his old mother had a miraculous escape. And Goolmai's thigh is fractured. That whole side of the building is open to the street.

(Piroja *feels* Hormusji's *throat, with the back of her hand.*)
Hormusji, you have a fever still. If you say so, I'll ask them to send an ambulance.

HORMUSJI (*angrily*): If you will send me in an ambulance, you may as well ask them to take it straight to Doongerwadi!

PIROJA: Shut your mouth!

(*Enter the* Purveyor. *A comical, nasty sort of fellow. Thin, short, with a Chaplinesque moustache and gait, gold-rimmed spectacles balanced on the tip of his nose. He wears a white shirt and trousers, bow, and sola topee. He carries a chart in his hand and a pencil stub. He speaks in a rather high-pitched, sing-song cackle.*)

PURVEYOR (*snapping his fingers*): Come 'long. Come 'long Everything ready I hope? Your turn next. Truck will be here in ten minutes. Can't keep a truck waiting, eh? Trucks cost money. And whose money? Not *your* money... Hmm, now let's see, what do we have here...?

(*He refers to his chart and walks around the room, examining the baggage that has already been packed and the remaining furniture. Both* Piroja *and* Hormusji *just gape at him all the while he is there, dumbstruck by his officious manner.*)

...What a lot of furniture you've been collecting! Why, look at this—this—and that! A proper godown. Well, you'll have to sell it off to the *jaripuranawalla,* sometime later I'm afraid. Now see. You can take one cupboard. That one. Take the mattress if you want. But not the bed. Certainly not the bed, eh? You're not shifting to the Maharaja of Udaipur's palace, mind you. You'll have to share a room ...And don't bring along any termite-infested furniture, see? Don't want a pest-control problem on my hands at the sanatorium. You people are famous for that.... Hmm. What a lot of trouble you've caused.... What's this now?

(*He has noticed* Hormusji's *old violin case, among the luggage. He opens it.*) Oh-ho-ho! A guitar! Does it work? (*He strums a ridiculous discord*). It works! He-he-he-he...

HORMUSJI (*shouts*): Don't touch that violin!

PURVEYOR (*saunters up*): What's the matter with your head, old man? Been taking a few knocks, eh? From the missus, eh? He-he-he-he. (*He starts walking towards the door.*). What a house this is! By God! I didn't know such places existed. It's a museum piece. A zoo! Such samples I've met today...one better than the other. This house should have been certified unfit for habitation long ago!

(*A long pause, as* Hormusji *and* Piroja *recover.*)

HORMUSJI: Who was that man?

PIROJA: He's from the Panchayat. He's taking care of the transport arrangements. Calls himself Purveyor.

HORMUSJI: Swine... (*pause*)

PIROJA: Hormusji, dress up now... They'll be here any minute to take things away... (Hormusji *looks away.*) Are you feeling alright? Shall I help you to dress?

HORMUSJI (*almost in a whisper*): I am not coming, Piroja...

PIROJA: Hormusji...

HORMUSJI: You go, Piroja...I'm not coming... (*Raising his voice a little.*) Why can't I stay on? What's wrong with these walls? I don't see anything wrong with them.

PIROJA: It's not safe any more. That's why they are evacuating us in such a hurry, don't you see? The next heavy shower and the whole structure may collapse. We're lucky to be getting another place, however small or filthy...

HORMUSJI: Then *you* go, Piroja! Leave me here alone. Let these walls collapse on me. I'd rather be buried alive under Doongaji House, than found dead in some rat-ridden gutter, picked at by crows... No...not the Panchayat nor any chicken-livered purveyor will be able to drag me out of this house... (*In a whisper.*) I will stay alone...shutter the doors and windows, drive nails through them...I will not see the light of day again.

(*Suddenly hysterical, he jumps up and starts banging on the walls with his fists.*)

Perish, walls! What are you waiting for? Prostrate yourselves! Release me, as you released Burjorji.

(Piroja *puts her arm round him and comforts him, while he has a coughing fit.*)

PIROJA: *You* talking this way, Hormusji? And I used to think you were a man of unlimited optimism... You have a fever raging in you, Hormusji. Come quietly. You were talking in your sleep last night, do you know? Mumbling all kinds of strange words...

HORMUSJI: Yes...I had a very fitful sleep... Racked by horrid, meaningless nightmares...I was travelling in a train, at dead of night.

PIROJA (*interrupts, bitterness in her voice*): Tell them to me sometime later! My head feels like it's going to burst. My legs are breaking. All this I've done since morning, do you hear? And I haven't had anything to eat either (*They are both silent for a long time. Then* Piroja *says, gently*): tell me about your dreams, if it helps...

HORMUSJI: I was asleep on the topmost bunk of a

compartment, in a moving train. It was a cold night, and I was shivering in the dark... The train was crowded. There weren't enough bunks for everyone. A whole mass of people jostled on the floor, quarreling, huddled in their blankets. Then one young man saw me sleeping. He started shouting, pointing me out to all the others. 'Why should he be allowed to sleep up there, all by himself? Why should he?' Suddenly, everyone was angry and, on their feet, shouting, threatening me, while I pretended to be asleep. 'Come on down, or we'll pull you down!' one of them shouted. And they all surged forward and grabbed my blankets and bedding and pulled! Then I was falling... falling endlessly, through space...

PIROJA: And now the house has fallen on our heads...

HORMUSJI: Wait. That's not all... Suddenly I was back in school. I was an old man, alone in the examination hall. There was some kind of exam I had to appear for. I didn't even know what.... Then my examiner walked in and sat down at his desk. He took off his spectacles and put them down. And I saw—it was—Dhanjishaa Bapasola! He said, 'So, Hormuz? I hope you are well prepared?' I nodded my head dumbly. Then he asked his first question. He asked me to recite the *Marseillaise* for him... I couldn't remember it, Piroja... I couldn't for the life of me remember a single line! Then I was alone on a deserted street at night... Out of nowhere, a beautiful white stallion came galloping at me. I moved aside in the nick of time, grabbed its bridle and swung myself on to its back. The horse just collapsed under me. Then I saw that it was dead...bloated...a yellow fluid was pouring out of its mouth and nostrils. My leg was pinned under the horse...Oh... (*He stops.*) That's all.

PIROJA: You were crying bitterly in your sleep, Hormusji... I had to caress you and whisper 'It's alright...it's alright...' Then you slept peacefully for a few hours. Then the morning awoke with a terrific crash.

HORMUSJI: You're a good woman, Piroja. I'm glad I have you.

PIROJA (*smiles*): If you are, then come quietly. Come. You can start dressing slowly.

(Hormusji *nods, and* Piroja *picks up his shirt and helps him into it.*)

I forgot to mention. There was a telegram this morning from Avan.

HORMUSJI: What did it say?

PIROJA: Arrived safely. All is well. Love, Avan.

(Hormusji *is silent.* Piroja *helps him into his trousers, which he wears over his striped pyjamas. Then she fishes out his shoes from somewhere and slips them on his feet.*

HORMUSJI: Piroja.

PIROJA: Yes?

HORMUSJI: Piroja, I have to ask you one question. Swear to me that you will speak the truth.

PIROJA: What is the question?

HORMUSJI: Did you believe what Cawas said...about me, about my business?

PIROJA: No, Hormusji, I didn't. The moment he said that, I knew he was a liar.

(*Just then, the coolies enter. There are four of them: swarthy, muscular men, perspiring profusely. The sweat glistens on their oily skins. They are all barefooted and dressed in shorts. One of them, the leader, has a red scarf thrown around his neck. They work silently, completely ignoring the old couple whose furniture they are taking away. First, they walk around the room, in a circle, silently menacing. The man with the scarf suddenly snaps his fingers, and points to the cupboard. They lift it quite easily and take it out. Then we hear its noisy descent down the stairs.* Piroja *and* Hormusji *watch all this with a subdued horror.*)

HORMUSJI: They are taking it away, Piroja…

PIROJA: So, they are…

HORMUSJI: Then it must be time to leave…

(Piroja *nods.*)

There's trouble in the streets. It's not safe—

PIROJA: There's no trouble any more. We have to go, Hormusji…

(*Two of the coolies return. This time, they stride in and take away the round, marble-topped table.* Piroja *collects a few last things and carries them out on the landing.* Hormusji *walks around, slowly, gazing incredulously at the walls, the scaffolding, the furniture.*)

HORMUSJI: So… We are leaving you now… But remember. It is not of our own choice that we part. In this past week, I have learned many things. I learned there is a weakness in human flesh that makes it untrustworthy…

I learned that spirits too do not always speak the truth… But today, you have taught me something new. You have taught me that even stone walls can betray…O Faredoon Doongaji, old scoundrel, wherever you are, could you not have employed a sturdier stone, a faster cement, when you decided to raise this house? Something that could have held together just a few years longer; so today, two old people would not have been forced out of their home to some strange new hole where their miseries will increase a hundredfold…surrounded by strange faces, strange voices, unfamiliar smells.… Who am I talking to? Faredoon Doongaji died years ago. Now Doongaji House too, is dead. (*More coolies enter and take away the last of their luggage.*) ...Come, Piroja. (*She has just finished everything she needs to do. She passes a hand over her hair, straightens her sari, and collects a large padlock from the window sill.*)

Remind me to write to Rusi as soon as we get there. We'll tell him what has happened. We'll tell him we have nowhere to go. Maybe—(*He shakes his, head, slowly, and does not complete his sentence.*)

Slowly, Piroja... I'm not so young as I used to be...You'll have to help...

(*Piroja retreats a few steps and puts her arm around Hormusji. Both of them hobble out of the door. Piroja shuts it from outside. We hear the sounds of it being bolted and locked. Then slowly, the lights begin to fade on an empty stage.*)

THE END

THE LEGACY OF RAGE

In the heart of overcrowded Mumbai, an elegant, one-storeyed bungalow, suggestively Portuguese in style: wooden gables, latticed balconies, thick creepers along its walls. Ensconced in a quiet churchyard at Bandra, it wasn't exactly the country house I had imagined in my set notes, but nevertheless made a highly evocative backdrop for the play which was enacted on its porch, as it were, with characters, entering, exiting, or passing through the interior of the ground floor apartment.

There were other striking parallels: a builder had evinced interest in redeveloping the property, and putting up a high-rise where the old bungalow was. This had led to contentious differences of opinion between family members. Despite the fraught situation, one of them agreed to let my director have the use of some rooms of his apartment, and the space outside it, to enact the play. But before agreeing, one reluctant request was made. The family had lost a dear one in tragic circumstances not too long ago; as it happened, the name of my play's main character was identical to the deceased person's name. To avoid raking up painful memories for the entire family, it was suggested we change this character's name during performances.

Although I could not be present in Mumbai during most of the play's rehearsals, it was a learning experience for me to observe how much the script had evolved, acquired depth and verisimilitude; how, serendipitously, elements of an elaborate, decidedly difficult production had fallen into place once a certain momentum picked up. *The Legacy of Rage* remained in manuscript form for fifteen years before it was first staged. The beleaguered conditions in which serious English theatre continues to operate in Mumbai may have something to do with this unseemly hiatus. On the other hand, I had never completely been convinced myself about the high emotionality of certain moments in the script, that they could be pulled off without sounding maudlin. So, in a sense, I had hesitated, myself, to seek out production opportunities wholeheartedly.

Perhaps a playwright never quite knows if something he has written will work on stage or not, until he sees it in performance. It took an exceptional director, who believed in the play and convinced me to let him produce it, and a fine team of actors, to breathe life into a script which would otherwise have remained an only partially successful literary effort. This director's approach was to let actors play their parts in a forthright, unembarrassed fashion, relying on the power of the drama, and their lines, to carry it forward. The tumultuous applause and appreciation of parishioners after every night's performance, in the otherwise quiet churchyard in Bandra, showed that somewhere, somehow, he had got it right.

THE CHARACTERS

ROBERT : An ageing landlord, fifty-eight

REGINA : His sister, slightly younger

JOEBOY : Robert's son

BLENDINA : Joeboy's wife

ROSCOE : Blendina and Joeboy's son, nine

GEORGIE : Regina's son

FATHER RUFUS : The parish priest

FRANCIS LOUELLA : An old farmhand and family retainer

VILLAGE WOMEN, PROFESSIONAL MOURNERS

The characters of the play belong to a Christian community which, though not specified in the text, may easily be identified as that of the East Indian Christians of North Konkan. These original settlers of Bombay are believed to have been converted to Christianity in the third century AD by St. Bartholomew. They belong to three traditional sub-castes of landed agriculturalists, fisherfolk, and toddy-tappers. In 1857, to coincide with the coronation of Queen Victoria, the community officially adopted the name of 'East Indians' to indicate their loyalty to the British East India Company and seek preferential treatment in the matter of jobs. The name is something of an anomaly, since they in fact belong to the west coast of India. Apart from their mother tongue, Marathi, the East Indians also speak a quaint pidgin English. Though the language of the play does not consistently attempt to find a literary equivalent for this dialect, occasionally certain idiosyncracies of speech have been retained for their flavour.

The above information is not crucial to an understanding of the characters or to the enjoyment of the play. It merely provides an approximate idea of the social context in which the play is set.

THE SET

The action of the play takes place in the large living room of a country house at Vasai, on the outskirts of Mumbai. The place is rather rundown. Bare floor. A roughly hewn oblong wooden table with four wooden chairs and two stools around it, upstage left. Downstage right, positioned at an angle, is a tacky old sofa. Facing the audience, is the family altar—a shelf covered with a richly embroidered cloth, with two candles in stands at either end. At the centre of the altar is a framed picture of *Madonna and Child* and, in front of the picture, possibly encased in glass, is an electrically illumined Sacred Heart that glows hypnotically in the dark room. Some distance away, on the same wall, hangs a panther skin or perhaps a mounted tiger's head. Below it, a shotgun rests diagonally on clamps fixed in the wall. In one corner of the room, resting on its stand at a jaunty angle, is a child's bicycle.

There are three exits leading offstage. Upstage extreme left is one exit, leading supposedly to the kitchen. The kitchen area can be made partially visible. Downstage left is another exit leading supposedly to the bedrooms. Upstage right is the front door, which opens onto the porch of the house.

The porch area may be elevated to demarcate it from the

living room. A hint of foliage, or the section of a tree trunk can be touched on, to suggest the vast open spaces and greenery outside which we do not see but are expected to imagine.

The set designer may judiciously include other artifacts, which give the room an untidy, lived-in look. On the other hand, he could also take recourse to a certain amount of abstraction. Whatever the approach, the overall effect should be one of bareness and gloom. In several of the scenes, appropriate lighting can heighten the brooding, primitive quality of the setting.

ACT ONE

SCENE ONE

The room is in total darkness, except for the red glow of the Sacred Heart. Very gradually, light seems to seep in from the outside. The room grows brighter, suggesting the approach of dawn. A dark figure walks across the stage and goes through the motions of opening the front door. Early morning light streams in, along with faint sounds of nature, the chattering of birds. The figure—it is Regina—stands at the door for a few moments, gazing out; then she turns and goes into the kitchen. Presently, she re-enters, carrying a pot of tea which she places on the table and covers with a tea cosy. She busies herself setting cups and saucers, laying the table for breakfast. Regina is thin, tall, and tensely strung. She wears a housecoat that reaches below her knees, and her greying, straggly hair is tied loosely in a bun. Francis, who presently appears on the porch, is an old man with a rather shrill sing-song voice. Short, hunched, he has a peculiar splay-footed walk—a sort of jerky scurrying, with knees perpetually bent. He wears baggy khaki shorts and a stained singlet. He is carrying a small wicker basket.

FRANCIS (*offstage, tentatively*): Auntie… Auntie! (*Appears on the porch*) Auntie… Good morning.
REGINA: Good morning.
   (*In deference to the early hour, their first few exchanges have a muted quality about them.*)
FRANCIS: Fresh brinjals. Just plucked.
   (*She gestures to him to leave the basket in the kitchen. He doesn't move. Picks up a brinjal and regards it lovingly.*)

See my blushing black brides! So tender...

(*He kisses the vegetable with a loud smack. Regina ignores him. Chuckling, he enters the kitchen area and deposits the basket. Outside again, he dallies.*)

REGINA (*after a pause*): Going to market, Francis?

FRANCIS: Today? But Robert Uncle said be ready by nine. What to do? If you say—

REGINA: I forgot. Today's the big day.

FRANCIS: Big day?

REGINA: No, you better stay with Robert.

FRANCIS (*giggles*): I look after Uncle. He looks after me.

(*At the door, he raises a finger in the air, a stern reminder.*) Nine o' clock!

(*But he doesn't want to leave yet. Turns to go, then comes back in.*) Lots of prawns in the bazaar, auntie. Fresh. Fresh' n' cheap... Prawns, brinjal.... Brinjal and prawns. Makes what love curry...

REGINA (*severely*): You hungry or what?

FRANCIS (*shakes his head*): No, no, Not hungry...just thirsty... One? Just one? (*indicates peg measure with hand between index finger and thumb*).

REGINA (*displeased*): Hmmm...

(*Francis goes into the kitchen and comes out with a jerry-can and a glass. She pours him a slug of country liquor. Francis knocks it back greedily. He looks disappointedly at his empty glass. Pauses a moment, then remembers something. He reaches into his pants pocket and brings out a grubby white envelope.*)

FRANCIS: Ah...ahem...this... (*holds it out to Regina*)

REGINA: What?

FRANCIS (*in a hushed tone*): Uncle told me to post... Remained in my pocket.

(*Regina snatches it from his hand, reflexively glancing over her shoulder in the direction of the bedroom. She reads the address, then crumples the letter, stuffing it into her own pocket.*)

REGINA: No money in the house. And he goes wasting it on foreign postage.

(*Francis waits, contemplating his empty glass sheepishly.*)

Now what?

FRANCIS (*extremely apologetic*): One last…?

(*Regina glares at him. Then accedes to the price of his treachery. Francis knocks it back cheerfully.*)

God bless you, Auntie…

REGINA: Now don't forget. Nine o'clock.

FRANCIS: I'll be here. (*yells, offstage*) Nice juicy prawns. Big-big prawns I'll bring you…

(*Pause. A dragging of footsteps precedes Robert's entry. Robert is a thickset, heavily-built man, affected by a slight disability. His left arm hangs stiffy and he drags his left foot a little while walking. But he is still strong. Even in his pyjamas suit he is an imposing rather than pathetic figure. He ignores Regina's presence entirely and walks past her to the porch, where he stands surveying his fields. She pours out a cup of tea and, after a moment, calls*):

REGINA: Your tea will get cold.

(*Robert turns, walks slowly to the table, and lowers himself into a chair.*)

Up early?… (*No reply. Challengingly.*) Going out somewhere?

ROBERT: Umm…to court.

REGINA: Dear Lord…this court business will never end.

ROBERT: Where's it begun yet?… That Mad Dog Alex's worms are tickling his anus again.

REGINA: What?

ROBERT: He's slapped another suit on us. Now he wants a

share of the creek property also.

REGINA: Creek property! Man's got a tapeworm on his brain.

ROBERT: And the worm's name is BA, LLB.

REGINA: Degrees painted larger than the name on his front door. Never got a chance to practice. So now the old crow diverts himself with litigation.

ROBERT: I'm not worried about Alex. By the time his cases come up for hearing, he'll be in one himself: his coffin.

REGINA: Domasso lived to ninety-three, remember? And Alex himself boasts he hasn't lost a single tooth yet.

ROBERT: All the better to bite with, eh? I'm told he had a tough time finding a new lawyer.

REGINA: What did they fight about? The last one…?

ROBERT: Got him arrested.

REGINA: That I know.

ROBERT (*shrugs*): Maybe he told Alex his cases don't hold any water.

REGINA: So what, he just flew into a rage and bit…

ROBERT: Dug his teeth into the lawyer's shoulder. Bit off a chunk of flesh! Bloody cannibal… Now he wants to eat up our land. Wakes up after twenty years to make his claims!

REGINA: What nuisance. Can't sell a square inch till all these—matters are settled.

(*Robert reacts with a menacing though subdued aggression.*)

ROBERT: Who wants to sell?

(*She remains meekly silent.*)

It's this case against the government. That's the bigger nuisance.

REGINA: And that's to come up today?

ROBERT: Supposed to. For the last eight months.

REGINA: To court and back, court and back. What headache.

Not sick of it yet? (*He doesn't reply.*) Watch your health, Robert. That's more important than dry earth. (*pause*) He can't go without you?

ROBERT: Who?

REGINA: Your lawyer.

ROBERT: One thousand rupees for each appearance. Five thousand if the case is heard.

REGINA: Five years ago you sold the jeep. Bit by bit all the jewellery's gone.... And the liquor? You insist on selling it at cost. Or loss, I should say. Counting all the guzzlers who drop by to pay their respects to Robert Uncle.

ROBERT: They are our people. We are not bhandaris to make a profit on brewing liquor.

REGINA: Vegetables. Once a week Francis takes something to market. A few dozen coconuts...

ROBERT: Then what's your worry? You don't have enough to run the kitchen?

REGINA (*sarcastic*): Worry? What worry? (*stridently*) ...Acres and acres of land all tied up in lawsuits! Go, run to the courts, run!

(*Robert doesn't answer her. After a pause, softer.*)

ROBERT: ...When Grandfather built this house, what was there? Nothing. Jungle. A few Kolis had their huts by the beach. Panthers came down from the hills and carried away their livestock; sometimes their children.... Papa cleared the land, planted the fields. He built pucca houses for his workers in the village. He hunted down the wildcats...what was it worth then? A paisa per square yard? Nobody wanted to buy jungle land...

When the builders started calling, I sent them off. Don't need your bloody money. This is my grandfather's land. My children will inherit it when I'm gone… Suddenly the city's grown bigger. Suddenly it's knocking at our doorstep…

(*with rising anger*) And now this bloody government, these bloody socialist whitecaps have rek-ek-ek-ek (*stammers*) *requisitioned* my property! To build an S.T. depot, it seems! Three acres gone? And compensation? Ten years ago the builders were offering me more.

REGINA (*quietly*): But you didn't sell to them… Let someone else handle these court matters, Robert.

ROBERT: Who?

REGINA: Georgie could do it.

ROBERT (*disdainfully*) Georgie. Hmph. Let him see to the harvesting. I'm happy if he can manage that.

REGINA: Georgie's smarter than you think, Robert. He's got contacts. He's young. He can run around—do what it takes.

ROBERT: What does it take? Answer me! What does it take? Have I become such a bungling fool in your eyes that your son must tell me how to conduct my affairs?

REGINA (*quietly, after a pause*): I'll get your porridge.

(*She goes into the kitchen. Robert sits there brooding hunched over his tea. Then he starts to exercise his left arm, bending and stretching it at the elbow. Regina returns with porridge and places the bowl before him.*)

REGINA: No need to lose your temper, man…you know I've always admired you so much. But we worry…

ROBERT: No need.

REGINA: Your doctors are all fools, then?

ROBERT: Look. What has my doctor been able to do about this?

(*He lifts his left hand with his right and lets it fall on the table with a thump.*)

See? (*He repeats the action.*) Deadwood. Go on, jab me with that fork... One half of me has gone to sleep.

REGINA: You haven't been doing your exercises, Robert. It had got better.

ROBERT: Only one thing helps, sister.... Somewhere here... (*indicates left half of this body*) ...buried in this part of me, is my conscience... For years I gagged it, stamped on it. So now it's taken its revenge...only when I take a glass or two, it rouses...I can remember things. I can feel... It hurts. But at least this unfeeling flab begins to twitch again... (*pause*)

REGINA: God knows I've done my best. Spent my life looking after your children. And now your grandson, too... When Mother Margaret refused to let me join the order, I didn't understand... She suggested I do a course in nursing...

ROBERT: Ha! (*laughs spitefully*) Your very first patient was your own husband, and you nursed him nicely to his grave.

REGINA: Don't talk nonsense. I did my best for him. Hillary was always a weakling... Not destined to see his own child's first birthday... You've suffered enough, Robert. You have paid for your mistakes. We have both suffered... But do you know what your biggest mistake was, Robert?

(*Robert doesn't speak, but looks up at her, coldly.*)

To marry that woman who wouldn't stand by you.

For better or for worse. She broke the marital oath. She deserted you...

ROBERT (*freezing*): We'll not talk about her, Regina.

REGINA: We'll not talk about her. Very well. What shall we talk about, then? Your porridge has grown cold. Your fields are lying fallow, all but one. And what does that one give us? A few baskets of brinjals and chillies and cauliflower?

ROBERT: But that's what keeps us going, isn't it?

REGINA: That? We are to be happy with just that? If it was all the Good Lord gave us, yes, we would accept gratefully. But when he has given us of his bounty—all lying out there, overgrown with weeds and thickets like our own lives, our children's—then I ask you, what drives you to haunt these courtrooms? Why bang your head on brick walls? Let Georgie do it.

ROBERT (*puzzled*): Georgie?

REGINA: Just takes a piece of paper, man. Give him the power to negotiate. Come to some settlement.

ROBERT: You stay out of my affairs, Regina. You and that smart-arse son of yours.

REGINA: Of course, of course. In the end, that's all the thanks we get. I'll go rub my nose in kitchen soot. But Georgie? He's not done enough for you?

ROBERT: What he's done, what he hasn't, I know. And where would the two of you have been if I hadn't taken you in, paid for his schooling?

REGINA: So now I must thank you for letting me live in my own father's house?

ROBERT: You got married and left. A fat dowry went with you.

REGINA: All that got eaten up by Hillary's illness.

ROBERT (*aggressively*): So? I'm responsible?... (*after a pause*) I don't want you or Georgie to ever forget: my son is still alive. There'll be no talk of settlement for now. Let him come back and decide what's to be settled and what sold. All this is his.

REGINA: Your son...

ROBERT: I've written to him. Explained our problems. He'll come.

REGINA: Feed. Feed on dreams... A delicious diet, but never filled anybody's stomach.

ROBERT (*stands up, menacingly*): Look, don't smart talk me.

REGINA: It's the truth. Joeboy has gone, Robert. He'll never come back. He's like her. He's deserted.

ROBERT (*shouts, raising his good hand to strike her*): Shut up! Shut up I say!

(*Roscoe charges into the room at that moment, and Robert slowly lowers his hand. The boy is carrying an airgun slung over his shoulder. He senses the tension immediately and stops short. A moment's silence before Robert speaks*)

Aha! so the little hunter is awake.

ROSCOE: Good-good morning, Grampa.

ROBERT: A very good-good morning to you, my son.

REGINA: Shikar can wait till after breakfast. Put that gun down. What do you want to eat?

ROSCOE (*shakes his head*): Not hungry, Auntie.

REGINA (*threateningly, grabbing hold of his wrist*) Again? Want to eat two slaps for breakfast, then?

ROSCOE (*pleading*): I won't be able to eat any thing. I swear I'll vomit.

REGINA: Everyday, everyday. Your friends are waiting by the jackfruit tree?

ROBERT: Give him milk.

(*Regina releases the boy and goes in to get the milk. Robert takes Roscoe by the shoulders and pulls him closer, affectionately.*)

Have to eat, son. How you'll grow? And what'll you do if you meet a panther on the road? Who's not had his breakfast like you?

ROSCOE: I'll shoot him down! *Dishaon!*

ROBERT (*laughs*): That's if he doesn't eat you first... (*Fondles his hair.*) Gun slung over shoulder, tearing off into the morning. Just like you—Ditto copy...know who I'm talking about?

(*Roscoe shakes his head.*)

Your daddy.

ROSCOE (*playfully*) You're my daddy.

ROBERT: Oh no, I'm your grandpa.

ROSCOE: Okay, you're my grampa. And Georgie-porgie's my daddy.

ROBERT: No, no! that's not true. Who told you that?

ROSCOE: Mummy. She said Georgie-porgie's like your daddy.

ROBERT: Like your daddy. In some ways, yes. Best of friends they were. Thick as thieves. But your real daddy...he sent you that gun. That cycle. Don't you know? He'll be back. You see.

(*Regina comes out with a glass of milk. Roscoe drinks half and puts the glass down on the table.*)

REGINA: Finish it.

ROSCOE. Enough. (*Runs to his cycle and begins wheeling it out.*)

REGINA (*to Robert*): See? The tramp! Hasn't looked at his schoolbooks once since his holidays began.

ROBERT: Don't go near the highway!

REGINA: Make sure you're back in time for lunch!

(*Exit Roscoe*)

That boy's growing wild. What he needs is a good belting... Where's that cane you whittled from the drumstick tree? How your sons grew up in terror of it. If that was not handy, you'd have your belt out in a jiffy. And think nothing of using the buckle end, too... You've grown soft, soft, Robert.

ROBERT: Is it good then to be hard?

REGINA: How will children learn if they are not punished?
ROBERT: And the boy's mother? Where is she?
REGINA: In bed, I suppose. Growing fat on pastries and chocolates. Certain luxuries she's used to, what to do?
ROBERT: Her father frittered away a fortune and left her penniless.
REGINA: What can I say if she wants to indulge her sweet tooth? It's her money.
ROBERT: My son's money.
REGINA: But your son sends it to her. And without what she gives us for expenses, I wouldn't be able to run this place… I try to save, Robert. (*emotionally*) I slave and drudge for all of you. I'm not complaining. I want nothing for myself. I just want to see you happy. To see our family happy…
ROBERT: Wake her up. She can help you 'round the house?
REGINA: Ah, let her be. I can manage. (*pause*)
ROBERT: Well, I have to get dressed.

(*Robert exits. Enter Blendina. Tall, lovely long hair. In loose, modest nightgown.*)

BLENDINA: He's gone out?
REGINA: Dressing up for court. Case is on today, it seems.
BLENDINA: I meant Roscoe.
REGINA: Oh, he's out somewhere, with his gun… Gave me an earful, too.
BLENDINA: Who? Robert?
REGINA: Who else? Stay in the kitchen and mind your business, he tells me.
BLENDINA: You all are pushing him too much. I keep saying, Papa needs more time.
REGINA: Hasn't it been dragging on long enough? Who knows, tomorrow if he has another stroke or something…

BLENDINA: Oh, don't say such things, Auntie.

REGINA: Georgie's been meeting some builders. One of them knows a politician. Something can be worked out fast... Have to plan for the future, my dear. For all our sakes...

(*She reaches out to caress Blendina's hair. Blendina looks a bit disconcerted by the gesture. A pause. Then Robert emerges, fully dressed, carrying a briefcase.*)

ROBERT: Where's that idiot? I told him nine o'clock.

(*Sees Blendina.*) ...Aha. Morning sun has risen early today?

BLENDINA (*embarrassed, amused*): Don't tease, Papa. I overslept.

ROBERT: Three meals and plenty of sleep shorten the day, but expand the waistline. (*To Regina*) Give her something to do, man. Grind masala. Knead the dough. Take the dogs for a run. When Joeboy's back he'll wonder, who is this fat auntie in my bed?

REGINA: Now, Robert. Leave her alone. (*To Blendina, who is reaching for the teapot.*) Wait, I'll heat it for you. (*She takes the pot in.*)

ROBERT (*conspiratorially*): Any news, Blendina? Letter?

BLENDINA: Nothing, Papa. No news.

ROBERT: Well. He was never one for writing letters. You let me know soon as you hear from him. Okay? Now what's there to grin in that? Like a fat pussycat you've become!

BLENDINA: I'm not grinning. Of course, I'll tell you if there's any news.

ROBERT (*looks at his watch*): Where's that idiot? I told him nine sharp!

FRANCIS (*offstage*): Here I am. (*appears on the porch*) At your service, uncle. Punctual as an alarm clock.

ROBERT: Alarm clock indeed. You've been winding up your spring, have you?

FRANCIS: If your blessings are with me, I can keep ticking forever, Uncle.

ROBERT: You're old enough to be my uncle, you rogue.

FRANCIS: That may be. But you're a great man, Uncle, and I, a poor beggar. So you will always be my uncle, my father, my everything.

ROBERT: Buttering me up won't get you another drink. Come on, let's go. Hold this.

(*In the action of handing him the briefcase, he stops short, suddenly noticing Francis' clothes.*)

What! You're coming to court like this? In half pants? Where's the ones I gave you? Sold them?

FRANCIS: So hot, Uncle, feels too hot to wear those. If you say, I'll go change...

ROBERT: Come on. But don't blame me if the judge puts you in.

(*Francis tugs at the lobes of his ears in a gesture of mock contrition, as Robert laughs and they march out. In the meanwhile Regina has come out with the teapot. Holding it in her hand, she watches them leave.*)

REGINA: There go the court jesters. Which is the king and which the fool, God alone knows.

BLENDINA: They keep each other company at least.

REGINA: Pucca boozards both.

BLENDINA (*after a pause*): Papa believes Joeboy will come back. What do you think?

REGINA: Even as a child, I could never have my way with him. Tried to be strict, but never could bend his will... He hates Robert. He'll never come... I think he hates all of us.

BLENDINA: Even Roscoe?

REGINA: No. Maybe not you either. You're recent, both of you. But he hates this place and everything it reminds him of… Though, he used to love it once… The coconut grove sloping down to the beach… He would spend hours there, wandering alone…or by the old well up on the hill, hunting frogs…

BLENDINA: It's months since he scribbled a few lines. That too, just thanks for the pictures of Roscoe I'd sent.

REGINA: Ah. Poor Roscoe. It's him I feel for.

BLENDINA: I showed him some pictures of his dad the other day.

REGINA: How could they mean anything to him? Nine years have passed.

BLENDINA: I can't remember much myself. Only the face of the boy just out of school who promised me happiness. And pots of money. He said he'd make his fortune in the Gulf and come back and marry me.

REGINA: So he did.

BLENDINA: Yes. But the man who came back was different from the boy. He didn't love me any more. And he left again, when our child was born. Why did he marry me? Just to keep his promise?

REGINA: Robert's big dream: the happy family he could never make real for himself… Happy children, a loving father and mother…a doting grandpa… Not just Robert, why, the whole village felt he should marry you. The poor orphaned girl who had been his childhood sweetheart.

BLENDINA: I should have joined the orphanage then, when Fr. Rufus suggested it. God knows, I might have been happier doing some useful work…

REGINA: ...At least Roscoe has you...poor Joeboy and Willy, they never knew the love of a mother.

BLENDINA: But surely she loved them? She must have. How can you say such a thing?

REGINA: They were still growing up when already she was too far gone. Crouched in a corner of her room, muttering a hundred Hail Marys every day. Once in a fit of anger against our Lord she snapped the string of her rosary. The beads danced away to every corner of the room like pieces of her broken heart, and she scrambled after them... Sometimes she would lose control and weep before strangers, tell her woes to common villagers. She loved to show her wounds. Her martyrdom.

BLENDINA: And he?

REGINA: He had no time for any of them. Neither her, nor the children. Except when he used his belt on them. Or his fists.

BLENDINA: Can't believe it.

REGINA: He's grown soft now. But I'm still scared sometimes. Even this morning, for a moment I thought he would strike me.

BLENDINA: To me he's always so kind.

REGINA: But naturally. You're his daughter-in-law, mother of his grandson, the hub of his happy family. Besides, you're fair and pretty.

BLENDINA: But so was his wife, wasn't she? I remember seeing Daisy when I was a child, singing in the church loft with the rest of the choir. She looked to me beautiful as an angel...and you say he never loved her?

REGINA: Never got a chance to. Daisy kept her legs so tightly crossed, no man could have tolerated it. So my brother took another woman. And *she* could not bear it.

BLENDINA (*after a pause*): No woman can bear that, don't you think?

REGINA: Everyone in the village knew. Only poor Daisy was in the dark. Though she suspected it. He would come home late, reeking of perfume. But bottles and bottles of Old Spice couldn't disguise the reek of fish. She never failed to smell it on him, when he came back after seeing her.

BLENDINA: That woman? Louella?

REGINA (*nods*): The Koli. They call her Ella. She stopped her fish business long ago.

BLENDINA: When he left from here the second time, Joeboy said he would wind up his affairs and then return. Later, he wrote to say it would not be so easy, it would take a while... Nine years have passed...

REGINA: By now he must have amassed a fortune. For all you know he may have another wife and children out there.

BLENDINA: Somehow, I don't think that's so.

REGINA: ...The children had seen him knock her down, bang her head against the wall. (*Blendina listens silently.*) They'd scream in terror and hang on to his arms and legs. And get knocked about themselves... Then Robert would go on a binge and not return for days, while Daisy tortured herself. Not eating. Stubbing his cigarette butts on her body. To earn his pity, if not his love...Joeboy hates him... But the foolish man is convinced that his prodigal son will return. And the fatted calf will be slaughtered. And there will be much feasting and merriment. And the son who was lost, but is now found, will preside over his dream of a happy family... Only, he doesn't realize that the fatted calf may well be himself.

(*After a pause, Francis strolls in casually.*)

REGINA: Francis?

FRANCIS: Father is coming. Father is coming. Met him just now, crossing the graveyard.

REGINA: Where's Robert?

FRANCIS (*despondently*): No prawns in the market. Yesterday, it was chockful. And today, not a single prawn. I was shocked…

REGINA (*sharply*): Where's Robert?

FRANCIS: Georgie-boy had come. Robert said they might be late, and sent me off. So I went to bazaar. And not a prawn in sight. Here—

(*He holds out a soggy packet of fish wrapped in newspaper.*)

I bought you some mooshi.

BLENDINA (*to Regina, coming out*): That means the case came up for hearing, if Georgie was there…

FRANCIS: That all I don't know. They just packed me off. Here.

(*Extends the packet of fish once more*).

Mooshi.

BLENDINA: Give it here. (*She takes it into the kitchen.*)

FRANCIS: But Father is coming now. He told me.

REGINA: Did you tell him Robert is not at home?

FRANCIS: Oh. He didn't ask. (*softly*) Auntie…

(*She doesn't hear him.*)

Auntie… (*Indicates peg measure.*) Very hot day outside…

REGINA (*shouts*): Go on, get going!

FRANCIS (*beats a hasty retreat*): Yes, yes. I'm gone.

(*Mutters to himself, petulantly.*)

Tempers also hot. What to do? Can't eat prawn then eat mooshi…

(*Francis goes out and squats in a corner of the porch. Suddenly, there is a terrific barking of dogs. Francis leaps up and begins scolding the dogs, his shrill voice rising some decibels above the ruckus they are making. He curses them in Marathi.)*

Stop it! Stop it I say! Can't see who it is? No shame to bark at a man of *God?* (*Utters a string of curses in Marathi.*)

(*Regina has got up from her chair and is moving towards the door as Fr. Rufus enters, a podgy, short, slightly hunched priest in a white cassock.*)

REGINA: Father Rufus!

RUFUS (*out of breath*): My Lord! Those big dogs of yours. What a scare they gave me. I thought they would snap their chains, the way they lunged!

REGINA: They're quite harmless, Father. Like kittens, once they get to know you.

RUFUS: Oho, they don't look harmless to me. I thought they'd eat me alive. What a fright I got.

REGINA: I'm really so sorry, Father.

RUFUS: Well, never mind. Dogs will be dogs.

REGINA: Really sorry. Come sit, Father. A drink to steady your nerves?

RUFUS: No, no, thank you. Where's Robert?

REGINA: At court, Father. Nowadays you are more likely to find him there than here.

RUFUS: Oh, never mind then, I'll come again some other time.

(*Blendina emerges from the kitchen.*)

BLENDINA: Sit, Father. I'll prepare some tea.

RUFUS: No, no, I must go. We have started our annual collection drive for the orphanage. I stopped here first.

REGINA: Father, pray that our land disputes be settled. That Robert should come to his senses. He wants to go on fighting the government. And here we have not enough for our daily needs.

RUFUS: The Good Lord will provide, have faith. (*quoting*) 'Take no thought for the morrow: for the morrow shall take thought for the things of itself. Sufficient unto the day is the evil thereof... Consider the lilies of the field...'

REGINA: What lilies, Father? Our fields are bare as a hag's bottom.

RUFUS: The Heavenly Father knows our needs. And then there are those of our brethren even less fortunate...I must be on my way. Oh please, just see me past those dogs.

(*Blendina moves towards the door to escort him. Francis jumps up on the porch.*)

FRANCIS: Father, I'm here. Come. Not to worry. I'll see how those bloody dogs bark at you.

(*Exit Francis, muttering curses, and Rufus; Blendina stands on the porch.*)

RUFUS (*offstage*): Now, now Francis. Language.

(*There is a terrific barking of dogs again, with Francis' voice screeching over it.*)

FRANCIS (*offstage*): Shut up! Shut up I say! Mad fellows. No sense?

(*The barking subsides. Blendina is looking out into the distance. A few moments pass before she says*):

BLENDINA: Georgie!

REGINA (*going to the door*): Has he come?

BLENDINA: There he is.

REGINA (*out on the porch*): I can't see...oh yes, there he is. But he's alone. Where's Robert? That's his briefcase he's carrying.

(*A few moments later Blendina and Georgie enter the living room together, followed by Regina. There is evidently a physical ease and familiarity between the two of them. She relieves him of the briefcase.*)

Georgie is a smart young man, rather dapper, and, judging by the sophistication of his clothes, which seem incongruous in a country setting, also well-heeled. He wipes his feet at the door.)

GEORGIE: Before the rains come, we must get the road to this house paved. Or we'll all have to swim through muck.

REGINA: What happened at court? Where's Robert?

GEORGIE *(chortling with amusement)* Your brother's BP really hit the courtroom ceiling.

REGINA *(anxiously)*: Is he unwell?

GEORGIE *(shakes his head)*: Lucky I was there. Or he'd have had to spend the night in the cooler.

REGINA: What! Speak clearly. What happened about the case? Where is he?

GEORGIE: The case? Ha. After all these months, bit of an anti-climax. Magistrate disposed of it in fifteen minutes flat.

REGINA: You mean, Robert—

GEORGIE: Has lost. Case dismissed. He's given Robert a month's time to appeal to the High Court if he wants to.

BLENDINA: Poor Robert...

GEORGIE *(chuckles)*: Couldn't believe his ears. Charged up all red in the face and hammered at the magistrate's desk. *(imitates)* Government is right? And I'm wrong? Magistrate was a thin Muslim fellow with a long goatee. I could see Robert eyeing it vengefully... Believe it or not, when the magistrate ordered him to be silent, Robert accused him of taking bribes. In a full courtroom. That was the last straw. Magistrate was so angry, he could hardly pronounce the sentence. He ordered Robert to be locked up for contempt of court.

REGINA: Locked up!

BLENDINA: My God!

GEORGIE: One week in jail. That was his sentence.

REGINA: Holy Mother of God! He's in jail!

GEORGIE (*impatiently*): No, no, just listen. Mama. He would have been. But then his lawyer pleaded for him. He's a sick man. When his blood pressure shoots up he becomes temporarily insane. He'll never survive imprisonment. Finally, the magistrate calmed down and reduced the sentence to a fine of two thousand rupees. Lucky I was there, and had the money on me.

REGINA: I can't believe this man. That's the way to behave in the court? My ears are burning with shame just to hear of it.

BLENDINA: How awful for Robert...

REGINA: Two thousand rupees! Would have been cheaper to let him cool off behind bars.

GEORGIE: No, no, Mama. What're you saying?

BLENDINA: He must be feeling so humiliated as it is.

GEORGIE: It's better this way, don't you see? He has been humbled. And for once in his life he was grateful I was there at his side. To pay the fine.

REGINA: You're right. Maybe now he will come to his senses. God knows. God alone knows how his brain works. Do you think he'll want to take the fight to High Court?

GEORGIE: I think not. It'll cost too much.

BLENDINA: Anyway, where's he now?

GEORGIE: Stopped by at Henry's place for a drink.

REGINA: To boast of his exploits at the magistrate's court, no doubt.

GEORGIE: Well, to drown his sorrows at any rate.

BLENDINA: His disgrace.... Blot it out with drink...

GEORGIE (*raises her fist, with thumb extended*): To us, I have a feeling things will begin to move soon.

REGINA (*returns the gesture*): Cheers, son. I think you may be right.

(*Blendina wears a half-smile as she looks from one to the other, but she is evidently bewildered by the general sense of satisfaction at Robert's misfortune.*)

BLACKOUT

ACT ONE

SCENE TWO

Late evening. The stage is in semi-darkness. Regina enters and switches on a light, which does little to dispel the shadows. But it reveals Georgie slumped on the sofa, lost in thought. He stands up, and Regina starts.

REGINA: You gave me a start
GEORGIE: Just came in. Where's Blendina?
REGINA: Inside. Putting Roscoe to bed.
GEORGIE: And Robert?
REGINA: You should have seen his state. Two of Henry's farmhands carried him home. Eat something?
GEORGIE: No. Sit, Mama. We have to talk.
REGINA (*sits*): What is it?
  (*Silently, he hands her a page of a tabloid newspaper.*)
REGINA: Good God. What does it mean?
GEORGIE: Have to wait and see. Good thing Robert doesn't take the papers.
REGINA: Once in a while he sends Francis out to buy one.
GEORGIE: That's what Francis must be told. No newspapers in the house. Not for the next few days, at least. (*He folds the newspaper and puts it away.*)
REGINA: I can tell him. But if Robert wants one?
GEORGIE: Any excuse. Forgot. Sold out. Newspaper strike is on. Anything.
REGINA (*nods*): He'll do as I say.

GEORGIE: Don't want her to hear about it either. She'll worry.

REGINA: Have you taken her for a check-up?

GEORGIE: Everything's okay.

REGINA: Then we just have to *wait*… (*Pauses, smiles faintly as though contemplating a distant pleasure.*)

GEORGIE (*tiredly*): Go to sleep, Mama.

REGINA: There's some curry and bread loaves in the meat-safe, if you get hungry.

GEORGIE: Good night.

REGINA: Good night.

(*Exit Regina. A moment later, Blendina walks in and settles beside him.*)

BLENDINA: Somehow I sensed you were here. Sure enough, I come out and see you two whispering.

(*Georgie laughs nervously.*)

BLENDINA: What were you talking about?

GEORGIE: Robert came home in a sorry state, I hear.

(*Blendina doesn't respond, he continues*:) Roscoe's asleep? Mama said you were putting him to bed, so we kept our voices down.

BLENDINA: Why are you keeping things from me?

GEORGIE: What?

BLENDINA: …Something dreadful is going to happen. I feel it. And you know it, too. Don't lie to me, Georgie.

GEORGIE: You're imagining things, Blendina. It's not unusual for a woman in your condition.

REGINA: I want to hear it from you…

GEORGIE: What're you talking about?

BLENDINA: …Just now, while telling Roscoe his bedtime story, I remembered a dream I had last night. It's all beginning to make sense now… Joeboy had come back. A pauper. He was dressed in rags, filthy, with sores on his body, the smell of pus about him. It was a pitch-black night. He was standing outside. I saw his face through the window, and he saw me. The dogs must have been barking just then. In my dream, they came charging at him, they flew at his throat. Joeboy's dogs. They didn't recognize him. Instead of opening the door to let him in, I stood and watched them attack him. I fastened all the bolts. As though he were a thief trying to break in … What'll we do, Georgie?

GEORGIE: About what?

(*She doesn't answer.*)

What makes you feel he'll ever come back? Just a dream inspired by guilt feelings?

BLENDINA: Oh, stop it. Why can't you be honest for once?

(*Pulls out a soiled page of a newspaper neatly folded in a square and hands it to him.*)

Don't tell me you didn't know about this.

GEORGIE (*unfolding it*): Where did you get this?

BLENDINA: Francis brought home some fish wrapped in it. I'd thrown it out. Then something caught my eye.

GEORGIE: I read about this. (*shrugs*) Don't think it's much cause for alarm.

BLENDINA: How can you say that? You're just trying to make a fool of me.

GEORGIE: Look. A few hundred soldiers have marched into a small country. Doesn't mean that all the thousands of Indians living there are just going to up and leave. All that property, wealth, are they going to just abandon it and flee?

BLENDINA: But it means war, Georgie. People flee from war.

GEORGIE: Kuwait's not going to put up a fight. It has no

army of its own. It's been annexed. Taken over. That's all. There's no reason to panic.

BLENDINA (*getting worked up, a slight edge of hysteria in her voice*): No reason to panic? No reason for you. And if he does come back, who'll have to do the talking? You'll run with you tail between your legs. I know you.

(*She breaks into a muted sob, but pulls herself together. He puts his arm around her.*)

GEORGIE: Blendina...

BLENDINA: How will I explain? What can I say to him. And about the money as well? There's nothing left in the account.

GEORGIE: I don't think he would grudge you the money. There's lots more where that came from. And once this plot is sold...

BLENDINA: And me like this? With a swollen belly...

GEORGIE: He's had a long leave of absence. He should expect to find some changes here. (*quietly*) Even if there is a war, Blendina, a war can mean many things. People sometimes disappear in wartime. They're reported missing. They become casualties of war.

BLENDINA: What are you saying? You're cruel. I saw that today when you were talking about Robert's defeat in court. You and your mother. You're cruel people. All of you... So now you are hoping Joeboy will die in the war?

GEORGIE: I'm realistic person, Blendina. I don't wish anything to happen... But in life, sometimes there are neat solutions...and sometimes messy ones...I just want that we should be happy. You, me, our child... Once all this is settled, we'll have plenty of money. We can send Roscoe to a good boarding school. We can even sell this whole dump if we want to and move someplace else. Don't you see?

(*Blendina is silent for a few moments.*)

BLENDINA: And Robert? How long can we keep it from him? I'm already so big.

GEORGIE: Ha! That man can't see beyond his nose. We don't need to worry about him. Not until you're in your seventh month or so. We'll think of something then. Say you're going to spend time with your aunt in Poona. We'll go away together, maybe to the hills, Panchgani...

BLENDINA: And then I'll come home with a newborn baby?

GEORGIE: Don't worry, sweetheart. I'll think of something. Trust me... Just keep to your room. Wear loose-fitting gowns. Anyhow, you look so beautiful in them.

BLENDINA (*sighs, stimulated by his caresses*): Oh, Georgie. Are we doing the right thing?

GEORGIE: I have no doubt about it. I want this baby. I love you. I do.

BLENDINA: Take me away from here, Georgie. I can't bear it any more. Even if Joeboy does come back—Promise me you'll take me away. I long so much for our baby... A little one, to hold in my arms again...

(*She clings to him in a desperate embrace. They kiss.*)

GEORGIE: There's nothing to worry about, Blendina. Just stay calm.

(*Slow fade-out begins*)

The important thing is that Robert should not find out about this war.

Not yet.

BLACKOUT

ACT TWO

Late morning, a month after. The stage is deserted. The dogs set up a fierce barking. Robert emerges and heads for the door as Father Rufus appears on the porch.

RUFUS: May I come in?
ROBERT. Father Rufus! Please come in. (*Rufus makes the sign of the cross; then, from a shoulder bag that hangs at his side, he takes out an ornamental silver sprinkler which he uses to sprinkle holy water on the threshold of the house. As he walks to the four corners of the room and, with light jerks of his forearm, proceeds to sprinkle holy water in all directions, Roberts calls out:*)
ROBERT: Regina! Blendina! Roscoe! come! Father Rufus is here to bless the house. (*Rufus goes in and out of the other rooms of the house, with Robert striding behind him, and then the whole family stands under the altar hands folded, heads bowed in prayer.*)
RUFUS: Almighty and Everlasting God, bless this house and all who live in it, for they are Thy faithful servants who promise to honour and respect thee till the end of their days. Extend unto Thy faithful, O Lord, the right hand of Thy heavenly succour, that they may seek Thee with all their hearts, and obtain of Thy mercy whatever is necessary to their condition. Cast out evil from their hearts and from the four corners of their place of dwelling, so that they may rejoice in Thy infinite perfection, beatitude, and loveliness. (*softly now all join in*) Hail Mary, full of grace, the Lord is with thee: blessed art thou among women and blessed is

the fruit of thy womb, Jesus. Holy Mary, Mother of God, pray for us sinners now and at the hour of our death. Amen. (*They cross themselves and greet each other.*) Happy Feast.

ALL: Happy Feast, Father.

ROBERT: Come, Father, sit. We were expecting you. You'll stay for lunch, of course.

RUFUS: Well, you know, every feast day I always start on my rounds early. I like to finish off with the village houses and come here last. So I can stretch my legs a bit.

REGINA: Glad to hear that, father. Knowing we'd have your company, I've specially roasted a pigling.

RUFUS (*giggles delightedly*): Tender pigling! Ooh, how delicious. Thank you, thank you.

ROBERT: But no hurry about eating. First, let's take a little something to nip up the appetite.

RUFUS: Oh no. I won't drink.

ROBERT: Wait. Just see what I've got to offer you. (*He goes inside.*)

REGINA: Blendina, you go and rest inside. I'll get the lunch ready. Excuse us, Father.

RUFUS: Please, please. No formalities. (*He is left alone with Roscoe.*) What's the matter with your mother? She's not well?

ROSCOE (*sullenly*): She's well. She just likes to sleep.

RUFUS: Ah...so? Young man? What have you been doing with yourself in your holidays? Do you help your Mama and your Auntie? Or are you always up to some mischief or other?

ROSCOE: I help.

RUFUS: What do you do?

ROSCOE (*peevishly*): This morning I shot two frogs and brought them home for our lunch. But Auntie's refusing to cook them.

RUFUS (*laughs*): Ha, ha! Am I glad! Anyway, it was a kind thought. Though not so kind to the frogs. (*Robert comes out with a bottle.*)

ROBERT: Look, father. Genuine Scotch whisky. Roscoe! Bring out the tray. (*Roscoe fetches the tray with glasses and a bottle of water*)

RUFUS: Careful…thank you, my son. Helpful little fellow you have here, Robert. Oh, very little for me, please… (*Robert pours*)

ROSCOE: I'm just going out for a while, Grampa. (*Roscoe exits.*)

ROBERT (*shouts after him*): Ask your Mama! Little devil. Slipped out while they're busy in the kitchen. You'll never find him in the house. Always loafing.

RUFUS: Well, boys will be boys. What do you expect at his age.

(*They settle down to their drinking. A subtle change in lighting, and we become aware of Francis squatting on his haunches on the porch. His presence is by no means highlighted. He sways gently, at times. He could well be dozing. But there is something about his facial expression that suggests that this silent listener has his own opinions on the conversation: he is registering in his own native way the ironies and affectations implicit in the proceedings.*)

ROBERT (*appreciatively*): Hmmm. Years since I tasted any of this. We are used to our home brew. Now that's not any worse, would you say? But, of course, Scotch is Scotch. (*takes another sip*) Delicious, eh?

RUFUS: Ummm.

ROBERT: This nephew of mine—

RUFUS: Georgie?

ROBERT: The other day he gave me a whole crate of Vat 69. A dozen bottles! I asked, what man, you've hit the jackpot or something? He said, no uncle, I hate to see you drink this country. Some smuggler friend he has, who supplies it to him cheap... Well. A few luxuries in old age... What you say, Father?

RUFUS: Yes, yes. This is matured whisky. Good for health... But one thing is there, Robert. Everything in moderation... Twelve bottles! Your nephew must be a rich man. I must remember to ask him for a big donation for our orphanage. Where is he now?

ROBERT: He'll be here for lunch. He and his partner have taken a place in Borivili. One Gujarati fellow. Enterprising boys. Just one year ago they started this business—supplying building materials to contractors. Bricks, sand, cement. Doing very well. Lots of new houses coming up in that area. Soon, wait and see, Father, there'll be no difference between Borivili and Bombay. Or even Vasai and Bombay. All one big huddle. Or should I say muddle?

RUFUS: Huddle, muddle, in the monsoon it'll be one big puddle. (*They laugh.*) The Lord said, Go forth and multiply, a long time ago. People are still taking it literally. Especially we Indians. A time will come when they'll be fighting for every inch of space,

ROBERT: I have so much of land, Father, but it's become a millstone round my neck. How many thousands I've already spent in the courts. And got nowhere. Last month, that bloody fool of a magistrate fined me just for telling him what's what. Wanted to put me behind bars.

RUFUS: I sympathize, Robert. It can't be a joke running to court at your age. And with your health...

ROBERT: What have I got to live for now, Father? Last few years, a man should spend them quietly. Thinking...

RUFUS: Yes, introspecting...

ROBERT: Making peace with his soul.

RUFUS. After all, all this property, wealth, can't take it with us. (*quoting*) 'As he came forth from his mother's womb, naked shall he return...'

ROBERT: When my father was alive...you came to this parish in '55, Father?

RUFUS: '58.

ROBERT: By then our problems had already begun. But before that...

RUFUS: I've heard. I've heard so much.

ROBERT: We lived like kings. My father was king of Vasai. His word was law. Villagers used to come to him to settle their land disputes. And he would arbitrate.

RUFUS: Yes, yes... I know. I've heard...

ROBERT. Jeeps, trucks, a hundred farmhands working the fields... One by one, things started going wrong. Everyone's heart was black with envy. Then tax fellows started getting greedy. In those days who paid tax? Suddenly—land ceiling. Then there was the big fire that razed the stables. Then mother died... On his deathbed. Papa wept. He believed some curse had been put on his head. He compared his sufferings to the misfortunes of Job.

RUFUS: But remember, Robert, everything was restored to Job in the end. He withstood his trials with strong faith.

ROBERT: When Papa died, the government slapped such a heavy estate duty on me, I could not pay it. They took away almost half my land. Now they want some more. The curse is still hanging over our heads, Father.

RUFUS: Really, nobody has any respect left for the rights of citizens any more.

ROBERT: Money talks. The only language that's understood in this land of Babel. In the old days, at least—

RUFUS: The old days are gone, Robert. They can never come back. A new morality is born. The worship of Mammon.

ROBERT: I'm sick of fighting the government, fighting my madcap relatives. That mad dog Alex bites his lawyer! His share was settled when my father died. He's still fighting for more ... few acres I have left. Take, take everything.

RUFUS (*nodding sagely*): Peace of mind, Robert. What you need most of all, is peace of mind.

ROBERT: I'm thinking now, Father, let Georgie handle all this. Georgie knows a builder who is willing to put up some money. He's been telling me, the only way is to bribe a minister. Not your type, Father, no offence meant (*they laugh*). A cabinet minister. Get him to dereserve the land. Once the land is freed, the builder will develop it. We'll get a few lakhs in the bargain ... end our days in some comfort. And there'll still be enough left for the children when we are gone. What d'you say, Father?

RUFUS: Sounds like a good idea to me.

ROBERT: I've asked Georgie to set up a meeting with their lawyer. He wants me to sign some papers... Shall I tell you something, Father?

RUFUS: What is it, Robert? Speak freely. There should be no secrets between us.

ROBERT: You've been a good shepherd to our family, Father. I am very grateful for it.

RUFUS: After all, it was I who buried your wife. Poor Daisy, may her soul rest in peace. And then later, your eldest son. After that horrible motorcycle accident. I buried him as well.

ROBERT (*overcome by emotion*): My eldest son... That I

couldn't bear…when the villagers brought his body home, I went wild with rage. Against whom, I do not know. But I whipped out my belt and started thrashing those poor village folk—they were crying for me, not the blows I rained on them… Then I wept. I lost hope.

RUFUS: The Lord is our shepherd… We have to bear our afflictions bravely, Robert… (a *slight pause*) But, you were going to tell me…?

ROBERT: What were we talking about? Oh yes, Georgie. You know, I never liked that boy, Father. Sneak. Carrying tales, always trying to curry favour. But if I think about it, he's the only one who's stayed with the family all these years. He has his own business now, but still, always ready to help out. He'll take some commission from the builder, of course. Fair enough… My sadness is only that my own sons are not here to guide me… I had such hopes for Willy, Father.

RUFUS: Poor Willy…so young…may his soul rest in peace.

ROBERT: Now with Joeboy it was different. He was always a tramp.

RUFUS: You're telling me. I was vice-principal when he was at school. Such a devil of mischief I've never seen. Somehow or other, goading and pushing, got him to finish school, heh, heh…

ROBERT: But, before we knew it, he'd packed his bags and left… I should have stopped him… Father, I believe he has steeled his heart against me.

RUFUS: But why?

ROBERT: He was very close to his mother… He never forgave me when she died. And he's right not to. I did make her life very unhappy.

RUFUS: But he was only eight or nine at the time.

ROBERT: Quietly, the boys watched everything. They heard us shouting abuse. Like animals, ready to tear out each other's hearts. And once...I am ashamed to tell you this, Father...once, I was with her, that woman. In her hut by the beach. You know who I mean...Father?

RUFUS: I think so...

ROBERT: I heard some noise and turned. There was Joeboy and Georgie walking away. I'm sure they had been hiding behind a tree and watching... The shame of it... Anyway, the whole village was talking! When Daisy died there could have been a real fuss. Luckily, Dr Hendricks gave us a certificate. And you were kind enough to give her a decent Christian burial.

RUFUS: I was only doing what was right, Robert. Maybe she was not of completely sound mind. Her suffering had driven her to distraction. But, after all, it was nothing more than an unfortunate accident. I still think Hendricks should have been more cautious about giving her such strong medication. Her body had become so frail.

ROBERT: Hendricks claimed she must have exceeded the dose.

RUFUS: We'll never know what happened... Perhaps it's best that way. The only odd thing about it, I seem to remember... That bottle of pills was never found, was it?

ROBERT: No. It just disappeared. Everything that happened afterwards... I know it has been punishment for my sins. I could never resist that woman, Father, she was such a temptress... Even after Daisy died, I couldn't stop seeing her. I needed her more than ever before. Only when my Willy died, I learnt my lesson. I went down on my knees and said, no more, oh God, no more punishment. After that day, I refused to see that woman's face... I gave her enough money so that she should never know want for the rest of her days. But she wanted me. Not my money. She never forgave me either.

RUFUS: Even the worst of sinners can be reformed, Robert. Take her own example. How she used to drink, man! And what ruckus she would create in the market. She's stopped all that now. And she's working full-time in the orphanage kitchen.

ROBERT: The reminds me, father. I'm sorry I could not contribute very much this year...

RUFUS: Don't mention it. I haven't forgotten how much you gave us in better times. We couldn't have started the orphanage without the help we got from you. (*Enter Roscoe. He goes to the kitchen door.*)

ROSCOE: Auntie, I'm hungry.

REGINA (*offstage*): Lunch will be ready in ten minutes. Just wait.

ROBERT: Sometimes I wonder if that boy will ever see his father. Your child is only three months old, I said to him, stay a couple of months. It's difficult for Blendina to manage all alone... I don't know what I said so wrong... The hatred that welled up in his eyes then. I saw it... Can he reject me so completely, Father? His own flesh and blood? At times, I feel sure he'll come back. But then all these people tell me I'm living on dreams. And I begin to doubt... I've written so many times. He doesn't reply.

RUFUS: Now, with all this trouble in Kuwait, he probably doesn't even get your letters. (*A terrible cry from the kitchen in Regina's voice. Thwack! Thwack! The sound of beating. Roscoe shrieks in pain. He can't stop crying.*)

REGINA (*offstage*): Get out! Get out, I say! I told you we don't want to eat your nasty frogs.

ROBERT (*on his feet*): What's happening? Why're you beating the boy?

REGINA (*stepping out*): He's slipped two frogs into my khuddi curry while my back was turned. Monster! Here I'm stirring it on the fire and what do I see?

ROSCOE (*through hideous sobbing*): I want to eat them! I want to eat them! Mama, Mama… (*He heads for the bedroom, clutching his ear. Regina goes after him, trying to land another slap on the back of his head.*)

ROBERT: Stop it! Control yourself, Regina.

REGINA (*breathlessly*): My chicken khuddi… I'm sorry, father. I won't serve it.

RUFUS: I understand… Not to worry.

REGINA: But there's plenty else. (*Goes back into the kitchen. Robert returns to the sofa.*)

ROBERT: I'm sorry, Father. You were saying… Trouble in Kuwait?

RUFUS: Don't you know? Iraq has invaded Kuwait.

ROBERT (*shouts*): Regina! Regina! (*She comes out.*) What's this I hear? Do you know about it? There is trouble in Kuwait. You know, that means our Joeboy may be coming back sooner than we expect.

REGINA: If all the trouble in his own family couldn't drag him here, do you think some trouble there will do it?

RUFUS: There's nothing to get worried about, really. A lot of Indians are still there. (*Enter Georgie.*)

GEORGIE: Hi, everybody.

ROBERT: Georgie, you didn't tell me? Just now Father was saying Kuwait has been invaded.

GEORGIE: Good afternoon, Father.

RUFUS: Good afternoon, Georgie.

GEORGIE: Yes, there's been all this trouble.

ROBERT: So don't you think Joeboy—

GEORGIE: But all the world is pressuring Iraq to withdraw.

ROBERT: There is a chance that Joeboy may come back now, if he has any sense.

GEORGIE: Who knows. He has his business there. His two garages.

ROBERT: I think we'll wait, man, before signing any papers. We can consult Joeboy also.

GEORGIE: Won't be good to wait too long, Uncle.

ROBERT: Why?

GEORGIE: Your appeal will come up for hearing soon. If that goes against us, it'll be very difficult to change anything. We should settle all this quietly and quickly as possible. Before the High Court comes into the picture.

RUFUS: Anyway, Robert, what you are doing is for everybody's benefit. Why should Joeboy object?

REGINA (*coming out*): Georgie, you're late! Eveyone's starving.

ROBERT: I hope he's alright. We must try and get some news.

GEORGIE: I'm ready to eat. There's not much we can do, Uncle. Except wait for him to write to us. (*Brief pause*)

REGINA: Shall I bring out the pigling then?

ROBERT: No, no. Wait. Let's have one more round, men. Father, your glass? Georgie, grab a glass. Regina, where's yours? Where's Blendina? Call her out.

REGINA: She's not well.

ROBERT: Never mind, she's going to eat with us, no? Blendina! (Blendina *comes out.*) Blendina, join us. What's the matter with you? You look well to me.

BLENDINA: Just a slight flu.

ROBERT: Your cheeks have come out like apples.

BLENDINA: Puffiness, Papa. Don't feel so good.

ROBERT: A drop of Scotch will do the trick. Get a glass for Blendina.

BLENDINA: No, no, I'll just have a sip from yours. (*She takes a tiny sip from Robert's glass and returns it. Then she and Regina begin laying the table, while the men continue their drinking.*)

ROBERT: Sukala! Bottoms up! Lovely whisky, Georgie-boy.

RUFUS: You're spoiling your uncle, my son.

ROBERT: Francis! Where's Francis? Let's give him a taste of it.

REGINA: Now don't go spoiling Francis.

FRANCIS (*hurrying in from the porch*): Yes, Uncle?

ROBERT: Come on, take one. Good whisky.

FRANCIS: No, no, Uncle. (*joins his hands in supplication*) Whisky, please excuse. Country for me.

ROBERT: Go on then, take it from the kitchen, you country bumpkin. (*laughs*) These fellows can't appreciate the good things of life. What say, Georgie?

REGINA (*to Francis*): Take the khuddi curry with you when you go, Francis.

FRANCIS: Thank you, Auntie. (*He leaves the room with his glass. Regina goes in and carries out the main platter with a certain pomp. Fr. Rufus crosses himself and they gather round the table in hushed solemnity, for grace. Roscoe comes out a little late, sheepish and also sullen. He joins them at the table.*)

RUFUS: Bless us O Lord, and these Thy gifts we are about to receive from Thy bounty and goodness. Through Christ our Lord, Amen.

REGINA (*whipping off the cover with a triumphant flourish*): And now for the pigling!

GEORGIE: Attack!

(*Lights begin to fade over the clattering of cutlery, appreciative grunts and small talk, as the company falls to eating with serious gusto. Simultaneously, on the porch outside, Francis stands up, tottering a little, glass in hand. Now lights dim over the rest of the stage, and there is a spotlight only on Francis. As though raising a toast, he declaims, in his naturally shrill, sing-song tone: he's tipsy, but his tone has the choric detachment of an observer.*)

FRANCIS: I like frog curry. Tastes just like chicken.

But alas, it makes me belly swell with gas…

Like the clouds that darken our skies,

About to burst in storm

the foolish bubble of willful ignorance.

(*He chuckles with delight.*)

BLACKOUT

ACT THREE

SCENE ONE

Late morning, a few weeks later. Georgie paces about, fuming. Regina is seated on the sofa.

GEORGIE: But the man is completely insane. Completely!

REGINA (*sardonically*): Just found out, or what?

GEORGIE: Everything's ready. Ball is set rolling. I fix up a meeting at the lawyer's. And then the bastard says he's changed his mind. Won't sign. He needs time to think. One and a half months later, he's still thinking.... What do I tell my friend? He's already paid out some money on my assurance. The minister's started re-opening files. The builder's architect has drawn up plans for an apartment and shopping complex. I myself paid Alex thirty thousand to withdraw his plaint.

REGINA: You're always in such a hurry, son.

GEORGIE (*angrily, anguishedly*): But who would have thought, once he had agreed to everything... (*dully*) I hate wasting time.

REGINA: He gets more feverish day by day. Right after breakfast, goes out for the newspapers himself ... The walk will do me good ... Then every day I must sit and listen to him read his litany of headlines: thousands of refugees fleeing Kuwait. UN issues ultimatum to Saddam. War clouds gather... Every word in the papers spells only one thing for him: Joeboy is on his way back.

GEORGIE: How can I trust him now? Even if he does sign, how do I know he won't retract a few days later? Other parties are involved. My arse is on the line. Robert doesn't even know them.

REGINA: Can he do that?

GEORGIE: Do what?

REGINA: Change his mind even after giving you power of attorney?

GEORGIE: Power of attorney? Ha! It's a joke. I had it for less than a week. He cancelled it almost as soon as he gave it. But why did he give me his word if he was not planning to keep it?

REGINA: I don't know what to say. You know best what to do, son.

GEORGIE: He has a moral obligation to me. I'm going to make that man sign those papers even if I have to...

REGINA: Don't tell me anything. I don't want to know... You all just talk, talk, and nothing happens... Just spend some time with Blendina, son. She's getting more anxious with every day that passes

(*Slow fade-out, quick fade-in to next scene*)

ACT THREE

SCENE TWO

Night. Roscoe is asleep, on the sofa beside Blendina and Georgie. The two sit silently for a few moments, before Blendina speaks.

BLENDINA: So, war has broken out…
GEORGIE: You should come over one day and watch it on TV.
BLENDINA: What do they show?
GEORGIE: Planes taking off, bombings, aerial combat, the works. Like a war movie. More exciting, actually.
BLENDINA: Do they show Kuwait? What's happening there?
GEORGIE: Not much. They haven't got in yet. But they will. Once they bomb the shit out of Iraq… Why do you ask? (*Laughs*) You're hoping I might have seen Joeboy's mug on TV?
BLENDINA: Don't be silly.
GEORGIE: If I had, that would make you happy? Or sad? (*She doesn't reply.*) You're still worrying about your Joeboy, eh? Two souls hopelessly entwined…
BLENDINA: Oh, stop it, Georgie! Stop needling.
GEORGIE: I'm jealous. (*She doesn't respond. Pause.*)
BLENDINA: We should go away soon.
GEORGIE: Already?
BLENDINA: Can't you see? (*Stands up and displays her stomach. A slightly hysterical edge to her voice.*) Anybody can! …How many hours can I hide in my room every day?

GEORGIE: But he's accepted you aren't well. The strange fever that comes and goes... Robert even suggested that Roscoe shouldn't be sleeping in the same room.

BLENDINA: I keep feeling they all know. That skunk, Francis? Suddenly, he's so concerned. So smug. Just to let me know he's on to me. Rufus, too. I've caught him staring at me in a peculiar way... Maybe not Robert. Maybe he doesn't know as yet. But how much longer—?

GEORGIE: Don't worry about Francis. He's our man... I just have to slip him a bottle every now and then, and his lips are sealed. (*laughs*) On the bottle's mouth... Okay, listen. We'll go. We'll go away very soon, Blendina. Wherever you want. But just give me a little time. A few days, to wrap, things up here.

BLENDINA: We don't know how long that could take.

GEORGIE: No, It's just a matter of two or three days. This is a very important phase. Can't leave here just yet. Believe me. (*pauses*) Don't know why I got involved in all this... Family property. I thought I'd help. And see where it's got me. I'm wedged in the middle.... You have to believe in me, Blendina. You have to believe in our baby...

(A *long silence, during which Roscoe stirs in his sleep. Blendina pats him gently, and he settles back into deeper slumber.*)

BLENDINA: And what will you do with our baby?

GEORGIE: That's my problem. Don't even think about that. I've planned everything. Baby will be in a safe place, well looked after.

BLENDINA: I don't think I could live without my baby.

GEORGIE: It's just a matter of a few days. As soon as I have those papers in my hand, you can sue Joeboy for divorce. On grounds of desertion.

BLENDINA. How can it be called that? He's been sending money regularly.

GEORGIE: My lawyers will deal with him. Don't worry.

BLENDINA: You hate Joeboy, don't you? Why do you hate him so much, Georgie?

GEORGIE (*after a long pause*): We were always best friends. That's how everyone else saw us. Grew up together, went to the same school, studied together, played together after school… Maybe because we got to know each other so well, we couldn't stand each other after a while… He was always trying to get the better of me. So lofty, so superior. I can just imagine the way he'd look at me if he knew I was having an affair with his wife. As though I were a worm. He probably wouldn't even say anything.

BLENDINA: Affair …? Is that it, Georgie?

GEORGIE: Oh come on, Blendina. You know what I mean. Until we get married, what else can one call it?

BLENDINA: You will, Georgie? …You will marry me, won't you? (*There is fear in her voice.*)

GEORGIE: Now what kind of silly question is that? Of course, my darling, I love you.

(*They embrace. Slow fade-out*)

ACT THREE

SCENE THREE

Dusk, three days later. It is just beginning to grow dark. Francis enters, realizing there's no one about, he walks about gingerly, peeping into the kitchen, then looking in at the two exits leading to the bedrooms. He is surprised in his snooping by Regina, just as he ventures back towards the kitchen. She speaks to him harshly.

REGINA: Yes? What're you doing here, Francis?
FRANCIS: Er…Robert Uncle?
REGINA: What d'you want with him?
FRANCIS: Just looking, Auntie.
REGINA: For a drink, you mean.
FRANCIS (*laughs embarrassedly*): No, no, Auntie…I thought Robert Uncle—I met Uncle just now, afternoon…
REGINA: Go on. Get out. Robert isn't here. We have enough problems as it is, Francis, I'm warning you. You better watch your step.
FRANCIS: I'm gone, Auntie. I'm gone.

(*Francis beats a hasty retreat. Regina pauses for a moment, then switches on the electric light of the Sacred Heart. Then she lights two candles at the altar and says an inaudible prayer. She turns on the light of the porch, just as Georgie enters. He is strangely distraught, pale, hunched, dishevelled. She senses he is in a state of shock, and rushes to soothe him.*)

REGINA: My son!
GEORGIE: Mama! (*It comes out almost like a sob. Like a child, he*

buries his face in her shoulder, embracing her tightly. He appears to be sobbing silently.)

REGINA: What is it? Tell me. (*She consoles, caressing his back and hair.*)

GEORGIE: They're not willing to wait any more.

REGINA: They?

GEORGIE: The builder, my friend. At least I thought he was a friend. Two of his thugs came to see me today. One of them showed me a knife. Look what they did. (*He opens his collar to bare his neck. There is a thin red scratch on his throat.*)

REGINA: My God! (*She tries to put her arms around him once again, but this time he pushes her off.*)

GEORGIE (*gnashing his teeth*): All because of him, that pig, your brother. He's playing games with me. He's playing with my life… They said this was just a warning. That I should keep my part of the deal. Have I not been trying, Mama? Have I not been trying to get him to sign those papers?

REGINA (*consolingly*): He'll sign them. I'll see that he does. I promise you. We just need a little time, son…

GEORGIE: I'll show him. I'll show him now. (*sternly*) From now on I'll do things my way. You don't interfere. I'm going. (*Georgie turns to go.*)

REGINA: Blendina was complaining of some pain. Don't you want to meet her?

GEORGIE: Pain? (*Regina shrugs as if to say, it could be anything.*). I don't have time now. I've got work to do.

REGINA: I'm going out to feed the dogs.

(*The stage is vacant for some moments. A long pause. Then Robert staggers in with Francis, both supporting each other. When they are in, Robert shakes off Francis's arm and gives him a shove.*)

ROBERT: Find Regina and get the can out. No. Better still,

get it yourself. The key will be under the sugar pot.

(*Francis comes in with the jerry-can and two glasses.*)

Pour, pour ... Back to the old country. What you say, Francis? You had the right bloody idea from the start, man. What Scotch-botch? Chchaa! Why make a hotchpotch? That's for the girls. Hop Scotch.

(*He finds his own punning hilarious. Francis joins in the laughter respectfully.*)

Georgie-boy is peeved. No signature, no Scotch. All these fellows, Francis, all after the same thing... (*Francis pours out the drinks, Robert takes a swig.*) I am King of Vasai... What? Robert Miranda, King of Vasai. Nobody dare lay a finger on my property.

FRANCIS (*repeats dutifully*): Nobody dare touch your property, Uncle. Never.

ROBERT: Soon the Prince will be back...

(*Pats the newspapers lying on the sofa.*)

It says so here. Look, read it... What you'll read? Don't know to read also. Anyway, I'm telling you. It says so in the papers. What flight, what time, that all we don't know. But he's coming. Where else he'll go? ...Tell me, where else he'll go?

FRANCIS: He'll come home, Uncle. The prince will come back to his kingdom.

ROBERT: Yes. Back to his kingdom.

(*Pause, during which Robert drinks and Francis dozes off.*)

ROBERT (*whispers*): Remember your mistress, Francis?

FRANCIS (*starts*): Hmmm?

ROBERT: Your mistress. (*Raises his voice, annoyed*) Daisy Aunty!

FRANCIS. How can I forget her, Uncle?

ROBERT: She forgot me. I want to ask her that same question. In such a bloody hurry to go she was... If she was here today, I would have made her so happy, so happy... How much I loved that woman... Pushed off to heaven, halo round her head... Didn't stop to think of me? While I watched my little ones grow up without the love of a mother... Francis, are you asleep?

FRANCIS: What we expect of life—how it all turns out—God knows, there's always a difference...

ROBERT: Why? Why must it always be so? ...If only, if only there was some way...

FRANCIS (*shakes his head*) Umh-hmm.

ROBERT: What?

FRANCIS: Not possible, Uncle. Can't turn the clock back...

ROBERT: I came home so late that night. Slumped here on this sofa and started snoring... In the morning...she had gone... I called the children and told them through tears, Children, your Mama's gone to heaven. She was a saint, and God wanted her close to Him. My Willyboy, he believed me. He cried and hugged me tight... But not Joeboy. Not my prince. He just stared at me in disbelief. In that instant I think I saw the spark of hatred catch fire in his eyes... He just stared...

(A *long silence. Then Georgie enters, carrying a box and a briefcase.*) Georgie, my boy! (*Genuinely pleased to see him.*) Come, join us. A glass, Francis. (*Francis tries to get up but slumps back on the ground.*)

GEORGIE: No, no. Just dropped by for a minute. This is for you. (*Hands over the carton to Robert.*)

ROBERT: What's this?

GEORGIE: All these days I'd been looking. But for some reason, the black market had run dry. Finally, today—found some good whisky.

ROBERT (*opening the box*): Chivas Regal. Ha, ha! Fit for a king.

GEORGIE: I hate to see you drink that rotgut.

ROBERT: Don't you call it that, Georgie-boy. This is pure hooch.

GEORGIE: Oh, I know. From the house of Mirandas. We've been brewing it for the last eighty years. Hundred per cent proof.

ROBERT: Okay, I'll try some of your Chivas. Let see how it compares. Francis, we need your expert opinion.

FRANCIS (*shaking his head vigorously*): No, no, I can't, I can't take anything else.

ROBERT (*tasting it*): Ummm... Tastes a bit funny... But it has a good kick, eh? (*approves*) What about you, Georgie?

GEORGIE: I can't stop. The lawyer's sent some papers for you to sign. He wants them back tonight.

ROBERT: Tonight? What papers? I'm too drunk to sign anything,

GEORGIE: It's a list of all your properties. He wants to submit it in the morning to the Collector's office. We're asking for a resurvey. A revaluation of the land's worth. So, he can ask the High Court to suggest to the government a more reasonable price.

ROBERT: Hmmm...

GEORGIE. I mean, all this will have to be done if you want to go ahead with the appeal. I showed you a shortcut, but you didn't want to take it.

ROBERT: No shortcuts for me, Georgie. Where are the papers? (*Georgie hands them to him*). Can't see anything in this bloody light.

GEORGIE: You don't need to read, just sign. The lawyer's checked the list.

ROBERT: Just sign?

GEORGIE (*offering him a pen*): Here.

ROBERT: Didn't anybody teach you, Georgie? Never sign anything before reading it.

GEORGIE: You did, Uncle. But you're too drunk now to read it. Shall I read it out to you?

ROBERT (*bluntly*): No. I'm not going to sign anything. (*Pauses. Then softly.*) Not unless you first sit down. Sit with me.

(*Georgie hesitates, then sits beside him. Robert puts his hand on Georgie's shoulder.*)

Georgie... I just want to say this once... We're one family. Same flesh and blood... Willy's gone. Now I have only you and Joeboy. Don't think I don't appreciate what-all you've done for me. I'll sign whatever you say. Let's just give it a few more days, eh? In case Joeboy is on his way back?

GEORGIE: Sure. But this has nothing to do with that deal. At least if we've applied for this revaluation, we can ask the court for more time.

ROBERT: Okay, where you want me to sign?

GEORGIE: I'll read it out first.

ROBERT: It's okay, I trust you, Georgie.

GEORGIE: No, no. Just listen please. I'll read: To the Collector, Greater Bombay, etc. Dear Sir, We would like a survey to be done of the following properties belonging to Robert Andrew Miranda listed on the following page (Annexure A), with a view to ascertaining their current market values as per the provisions of Schedule H of the Land Ownership Act of 1933. Kindly provide us... (*Robert nods off for a second.*)

ROBERT: Oh, please stop. I'm falling asleep. Where's the pen?

(*Georgie stands over him and turns the pages as he signs.*) Sign here? (*Slow fade-out begins.*)

GEORGIE: The rest are just copies. Here…here…and here…
(*As the lights fade into a brief blackout, a loud snore from Robert.*)

ACT THREE

SCENE FOUR

The next scene follows without a break. A light comes on in the kitchen. A dim glow spills out from the exit leading to the bedrooms. Georgie emerges from here and goes to the kitchen door.

GEORGIE: It's started, Mama. The pains are getting stronger.

REGINA (*at the kitchen door*): That's good. Why are you so pale?

GEORGIE: I'm alright. Where's Francis?

REGINA: Out on the porch, I think. Hugging the floor.

GEORGIE: Bloody fool! I told him to watch how much he was guzzling. He'd better be awake when we need him. (*Moves towards the porch.*)

REGINA: There's still time. Let him catch some sleep. (*Georgie turns back and heads for the bedroom. Returns.*)

GEORGIE: This is crazy! I mean, there was supposed to be six more weeks to go!

REGINA: It happens sometimes. I told you. She was getting too anxious.

GEORGIE: And the baby…?

REGINA: The baby may be perfectly healthy. There's no need to panic.

GEORGIE: Oh God!

(*Regina goes into the kitchen. The stage remains deserted for some time. The silence is occasionally punctuated by the barking of dogs and other sounds of the night. Then we hear some groaning. Not*

Blendina's voice, but Robert's. We hear him sighing, whining, then retching desperately. Now he stumbles out himself feeling his way in the dark living room.)

ROBERT: Who's here? Help me. I'm sick.

(*Nobody replies. He sees the kitchen light and heads that way, stumbling into chairs and table.*)

Who's here? Regina? Do you hear me? I'm sick. I need a doctor.

REGINA (*offstage*): Go back to bed and sleep it off. You've had too much to drink.

ROBERT: No, no. Not that. Something's gone wrong with my eyes. Can't see. Call Dr Hendricks. Send Francis.

REGINA (*appears*): Francis has done the sensible thing and gone to sleep. Can't send him four miles in the night to disturb Hendricks. He'll probably fall asleep somewhere under a tree. Go back to bed, Robert.

(*Reluctantly, Robert turns back and goes in. More sounds of retching. Georgie peeps out cautiously and crosses the floor to the kitchen.*)

GEORGIE: What's he saying?

REGINA: He's sick. He wants a doctor. The oaf has had too much to drink again.

GEORGIE: Well... That was a very special Scotch, you know.

REGINA (*after a pause, suspiciously*): How special?

GEORGIE (*laughs*) Chivas Regal. Fit for a king.

(*Regina gives him a peculiar stare.*)

GEORGIE: Don't look at me like that, Mama. (*She doesn't answer.*) Mama! You have to stand by me. (*She remains unresponsive.*)

GEORGIE: Mama! I didn't know Blendina would go into labour tonight.

REGINA (*quietly*): Never mind. It's all for the best, son. Have faith in Our Lady.

GEORGIE: Thank you. Mama... But that idiot, Francis! (*He goes out onto the porch to wake him.*)

REGINA (*calls after him*): There's still time, Georgie...

(*Georgie is rough in his attempts to rouse Francis. He shakes him violently, kicks him, pulls him up by the hair, and lets him flop again. The old man is limp as a doll through all this.*)

GEORGIE: Wake up! Wake up, you old fool! Didn't I tell you we have a job to do tonight?

(*Francis makes peculiar cooing and gurgling sounds somewhere from the recesses of his deep sleep. Georgie kicks him again. He cries out and is suddenly bright and awake.*)

FRANCIS: I'm awake, Uncle. At your service twenty-four hours.

(*Like someone in a hypnotic trance, he slowly turns over and flops back into a deep sleep. Georgie kicks and curses, but gives up in the end. Meanwhile, Blendina's gasping has become audible. There is a lot of movement in the dark, going from bedroom to kitchen and back. Georgie has gone back in, but he anxiously keeps coming out to summon his mother. Over all this come occasional and violent sounds of retching and groaning from Robert. He comes out of his room again.*)

ROBERT: What's that noise? Who's screaming?

REGINA: What noise? The only noise I can hear is what you're making. Go back to sleep, Robert.

ROBERT: What are you doing up so late?

REGINA: Go back to sleep.

ROBERT: I can't. I'm very sick. That whisky was bad.

(*Georgie comes out just then. He sees Robert and stops in his tracks, but Robert has already perceived some movement.*)

ROBERT (*alarmed*): Who's there?

GEORGIE: It's me.

ROBERT: Georgie! You here? At this time? Thank God you're here. Georgie get a doctor, quick.

GEORGIE: Who's sick?

ROBERT: I'm very sick, Georgie. Something strange is happening to me. My eyes. I can't see anything.

GEORGIE: You mean you're blind drunk. Sleep it off, uncle.

ROBERT: No, It's not that. It's as if a curtain has fallen over my eyes. A thick net. (*Blendina screams.*) That scream? You heard it. That sounds like Blendina. Can't you hear? Is she sick also? (*Another scream.*) I'll go find out.

GEORGIE (*blocking his way*): Where are you going?

ROBERT: There's some problem. Blendina. I'll go—

GEORGIE: You're not going anywhere. Except straight back to bed.

ROBERT: What's the matter? Why're you talking to me like that, Georgie? Help me. I can't see. Oh, my eyes are on fire ... What're you all doing up so late?

GEORGIE (*takes him roughly by the arm, pushing him along*): This way. Back to bed.

ROBERT: What's going on in this house? What're you all up to? Oh my eyes... Animals! Oh, you brutes! You've poisoned me!

(*Blendina's screams, Robert's retching and groaning and the barking of the dogs mix in a macabre medley, while a slow fade-out culminates in blackout.*)

ACT FOUR

SCENE ONE

(*Morning, two days later. Georgie sits on the sofa, face covered by his hands.*)

GEORGIE: It's all got so messy...

REGINA (*slightly sarcastic*): But you wanted it like this, didn't you?

GEORGIE: Look, Mama, Robert will be alright. I'm sure of that. (*in a stage whisper*) That whisky wasn't meant to kill. Just wanted him out of the way for a while.

REGINA: Well, he's out of the way now. You have your papers. And Blendina has her baby. And Robert doesn't know about either. So what's bothering you?

GEORGIE: Nothing... My baby. I should have taken her straight to a hospital. I just wasn't prepared for all this suddenness... She trusts me, Mama. If she were to find out...

REGINA (*changing the subject*): What did Dr Hendricks say?

GEORGIE: He has written out a note referring Robert to an eye-specialist in Bombay. But that'll be later, once he's strong enough to travel.

REGINA: And?

GEORGIE: Nothing else. Diet should remain the same, he said. Light, boiled food. No tea, coffee. Plus, he's given a list of pills and tonics.

REGINA: Why didn't you call out to me? I was in the

backyard feeding the pigs. I would have heard you.

GEORGIE: Only thing he said we should be very strict about: Robert must never touch alcohol again.

REGINA: Hmm… And how are we supposed to enforce that?

GEORGIE: Keep everything under lock and key. And Francis should be warned not provide him even a sip.

REGINA: His soup must be ready…

(*Regina goes into the kitchen.*)

(*Blendina comes out from the wings. She goes up to Georgie, takes hold of his arms and shakes him.*)

BLENDINA: My baby, Georgie. How is she?

GEORGIE: Shh…Baby's fine. Sleeping, suckling her bottle. Growing up, like babies do. Just forget her for a while, will you?

BLENDINA (*raising her voice a bit*): Why can't I go see her? Why won't you tell me where she is?

GEORGIE: Be quiet. Do we have to go through this every day?

BLENDINA: I can't live without her. I must see her. (*pleading*) Can't I go see her just once? You gave me hardly a few minutes with her, Georgie…

GEORGIE: You have to forget you have a baby. If I were to tell you, you wouldn't be able to stop yourself from going to her. And if the news leaks out—you know gossip spreads like a fire in this village—you won't get even a rupee in alimony. Before you know it, Joeboy will have heard about it in Kuwait… Have to be patient, Blendina. It won't be long before we can all be together again.

BLENDINA: I'll do whatever you say, Georgie. But it's very hard on me…

GEORGIE: I know how you feel. Trust me. We have no choice.

BLENDINA: I trust you.

(*Regina comes out with a feeding cup, muttering.*)

REGINA: As if I didn't have enough to do already...

BLENDINA: I'll feed him.

(*Blendina takes the cup from her hand and goes inside.*)

REGINA (*to Georgie*): Couldn't you have made a clean job of it, you bungler? You had to go and add a special diet and a sick man to my list of duties.

GEORGIE: Hush, mama. What're you saying? It's much better this way. Did you want the police in the house?

REGINA: He's plotting something. From the moment I enter his room, he just glares and glares at me with those ghostly big eyes...

GEORGIE: You're overreacting. He's just trying to focus. He can't see too clearly.

REGINA: Don't tell me what I know already. I can see his eyes dripping with hatred. He knows what happened. If he lives long enough, he'll find some way to hit back.

GEORGIE: What can he do? We just have to wait. And let nature take its course. And if by chance one day he refuses to obey his doctor's orders and is tempted to take one chota peg... We've won, mama. The plot is going to be denotified next month. Construction will start immediately after that. Once it starts, nothing matters. Not whether Robert lives or dies, whether Joeboy comes back or disappears from the face of this earth. Nobody can change any thing after that.

REGINA (*with genuine sadness*): My poor, mule-headed brother...

GEORGIE: This is all his doing, Mama. He brought it on himself.

REGINA: He was always like that. So unreasonable...

GEORGIE: I'll go talk to him again after Blendina finishes. I'll reassure him that it was all an accident. That the police are hot on the trail of the bootlegger. I'll show my anger. And my remorse: that a bottle of spurious Scotch should have made my dear uncle suffer so much…

REGINA (*contemptuously*): He'll never believe you.

(*Blendina comes out with the feeding cup in her hand and announces.*)

BLENDINA: He ate all the soup. But he made me taste it first.

FADE-OUT

ACT FOUR

SCENE TWO

It is evening when the lights come on again. A bulb glows in the dark hall. Georgie is on the sofa, smoking a cigarette, looking relaxed. Regina calls from the kitchen.

REGINA: Have you seen Francis?

GEORGIE: Not since morning.

REGINA (*angrily*): Then where's he gone to? Lying drunk in a ditch somewhere?

(*Pause. Dogs bark. Fr. Rufus enters, gingerly.*)

RUFUS (*in a whisper*): My friends. How is poor Robert?

REGINA: Doctor says he can move about the house now, but he sticks to his room. Just lies in bed and broods and broods… I think he's resting now, Father.

RUFUS: Good. Let him rest. (*Sits*) You know, I always used to stress one thing to him. Moderation, Robert, moderation. But that was one word he never understood. A man of strong passions. Sudden whims. Was it all worth it? Now look at him, poor man, he is not allowed to take even a little drop. How will he manage?

REGINA: He'd better learn to, if he wants to live. Hendricks was very clear about that.

GEORGIE: What about you, Father? Will you take a little something?

RUFUS (*nervously*): No, no…

GEORGIE (*laughs*): Don't worry, won't give you from the same bottle.

RUFUS: No, nothing for me. Definitely. Thank you. But really, it is frightening to consider. One doesn't know what one is drinking, in these days of adulteration. Who do you trust?

GEORGIE: Poor Francis. He's most shaken up. They had been drinking together that night. Fortunately for him, he stayed with his country.

RUFUS: Well, he should worry too. He's older than Robert and drinks much more. I've tried to scold him, but it's like water off a duck's back.

GEORGIE: He went and fetched Dr Hendricks that day, at the crack of dawn. He was in tears, poor fellow. He thought his master was dying.

REGINA: My poor Georgie tried to find Robert the best whisky in town, and this is what had to happen. How much did you pay for the bottle, Georgie?

GEORGIE: Six hundred.

RUFUS: Six hundred! Well, what can you say to these people? Never trust a man who does a black business. Smuggler, counterfeiter, adulterer. What's the difference? One sin leadeth to another. He that loveth silver shall not be satisfied with silver, nor he that loveth abundance with increase.

GEORGIE: You're right, Father. Better to be safe and drink Indian whisky.

(*There is a commotion outside. The dogs begin to bark. Angry raised voices, one of them calling out to Fr. Rufus.*)

MALE VOICES (*offstage*): Father! Father!

RUFUS: Who could that be now? These people don't give me one moment's peace…

FRANCIS (*offstage, in Marathi*): Arre, leave me! Why're you beating me?

(*Rufus makes for the door. But the crowd has already appeared. There are two men, villagers, one of them holding on to Francis' arm. Francis has been roughed up, bruised and bloodied. There is a woman, Louella, who seems to have taken charge of the party. She is middle-aged, dressed in a traditional Koli-style kashti sari. We have not seen any of these people before. Other villagers. All of them appear excited, perhaps even slightly inebriated.*)

REGINA: What's all this? You...

RUFUS (*alarmed*): You, Louella? What're you doing here?

REGINA (*taking charge*): Outside! Outside! What's all this commotion? Don't you know there's a sick man in the house? Go on out! (*She orders the villagers out.*)

VILLAGERS: Father—his fellow came asking—

RUFUS: Please wait outside.

VILLAGERS: ...About the baby, Father...

RUFUS: I don't want to hear anything. Outside!

(*They leave reluctantly sheepishly. But Louella stubbornly stays.*)

LOUELLA: Where is he? Call him out!

RUFUS: But what's all the excitement about, Louella?

REGINA: Speak up, Francis? What's all this nonsense?

(*Francis is whimpering, at least partly because of the beating he's already received.*)

FRANCIS: Georgie-baba...what could I do? As soon as I tried to find out about the infant, she caught hold of me and slapped me. A crowd collected, and they wouldn't stop beating me. They were threatening to hand me over to the police.

LOUELLA: Wait, wait. Where's the landlord? I want him to hear this.

REGINA: You have no shame? To show your face here?

LOUELLA: I have plenty of shame, Auntie. That's why I stayed away for sixteen years. But today I have something to tell him.

RUFUS: Now, now. Let us all be calm first, Louella. Let's talk things over peacefully. I am aware of what all has been happening. No need to disturb a sick man for this.

(*By now, Blendina has emerged, too. We hear Robert's irregular shuffle of footsteps. He comes out.*)

REGINA: Robert...

RUFUS: How are you feeling, Robert? I had thought I would have to go away without meeting you.

(*Robert ignores all of them and approaches Louella. His voice is hoarse, barely audible. He is strangely subdued. He keeps his head bent.*)

ROBERT: Why have you come here?

(*Louella doesn't answer for a moment.*)

LOUELLA: Go on. Not saying more? Why have I come here to set fire to your home? To pollute it with my sinful presence? Sixteen years ago, you forbade me to see your face again. I begged you to take our son under your care. But you said he was the fruit of our sin. You said you wanted to keep your house pure for the sons of your sons...

RUFUS: Louella, I know your Andrew's been having some problems... But I don't understand what Robert can do for him now. And why rake up old stories? Please consider, he's a very sick man.

ROBERT: Speak clearly. Louella what do you want?

LOUELLA: I want nothing from you. I have only come here to open your eyes. To the vileness you've been breeding under your roof. Blind, foolish man.

ROBERT (*softly*): Tell me what you have to say.

LOUELLA: On the night you were taken ill, in the early hours of the morning, a newborn baby was left on the veranda of the orphanage.

RUFUS: Oh yes, I didn't tell you about that, did I? What are we coming to? In this parish? (*incredulous*) Somebody had abandoned a newborn baby under the awning of the orphanage!

LOUELLA: And today this old stooge of yours comes around to snoop, and find out how the baby is! Ask him. (*points to Georgie*) Ask him whose baby it is!

GEORGIE (*brashly*): I don't know what you are talking about.

FRANCIS: But Georgie-baba, I couldn't help it. I had to tell them. I think the ruffians have broken my arm...

BLENDINA (*deeply disturbed*): At the orphanage! You abandoned our child at the orphanage. You promised to take care of her for me!

(*Georgie refuses to meet her eyes.*)

LOUELLA (*to Blendina*): Your child is well, don't worry. Only her little hand, you see. Her little pink palm has got infected. Do you know why? Because as soon as she was born, the baby was branded with a cross.

BLENDINA (*breaking down*): My baby...my poor babe. But why...why... you monster...

(*Rushes towards Georgie, hitting out at him. Hysterical, but ineffectual.*)

GEORGIE (*warding off the blows, protests*): Try and understand, Blendina. I had no choice. It was necessary. For her protection. For her identification later on, when we want her back ...they don't feel pain when they're so small...I had to do it...how else...

(*Robert remains silent through all this.*)

LOUELLA (*to Robert*): We had a little one too, remember? I raised him, single-handed, by the sweat of my brow... I didn't leave him on somebody else's doorstep...

ROBERT (*in a strangulated voice*): A woman became pregnant and had a baby in my own house, and I didn't even know it... I deserved to go blind.

(*Now Robert moves. With some difficulty, he reaches for the gun on the wall and brings it down.*)

REGINA: What are you doing?

(*Robert has difficulty supporting the barrel of the gun with his left arm, but he manages to cock the trigger and takes aim in the general direction of Georgie.*)

ROBERT: I'm going to kill you, Georgie.

GEORGIE: You can't frighten me. That gun is not loaded.

ROBERT: Never used to be. Until I discovered that I live among my enemies.

RUFUS: Control yourself, Robert. Don't do anything rash, I beseech you.

(*Robert fires and misses. Regina easily wrestles the gun out of his hand. He tries to strike her, she ducks. Georgie flies into a hysterical rage that is inspired by fear and shock.*)

GEORGIE: Madman! Murderer! I'll call the police and have you arrested. You tried to kill me. Kill me. I have so many witnesses!

(*Very quietly, another stranger has entered and stands in the doorway, unnoticed. He is dishevelled, unshaven, and carries a small travelling bag slung over his shoulder. When he speaks, his voice has a deep resonance, something pleasant and comforting about it.*)

STRANGER: And now you have one more...

(*Everyone turns and see him. They are transfixed, speechless.*)

REGINA (*in a whisper*): Joeboy...

(Robert slowly drags himself forward towards the stranger, whom he can't see clearly. He brings his face close to his son's, peering into it with trepidation, as if wanting to make sure it's not an apparition that stands before him.)

ROBERT: Joeboy.

(He touches his son's face with both hands. Touches his arms, his torso.)

JOEBOY: It's me, Papa.

(Then Robert takes Joeboy's hands and touches them to his own eyes, his body doubling up with emotion.)

FADE-OUT

ACT FIVE

The stage is in total darkness. Gradually we become aware of a figure framed in the doorway, facing the porch. His arms, slightly raised, rest against the doorframe. His back is to the audience. He is silhouetted by the blue glow of the dying night, which slowly transforms into the first glint of dawn. As it grows brighter, we make out that it is Joeboy standing there, observing this spectacle of the changing light. There is a soft, internal quality to the manner in which he delivers his opening lines, the quality of thought, but there's also a bitter note of suppressed savagery. His first speech can be heard amplified over the P.A., soft, but stylized with a touch of reverb or echo.

JOEBOY'S VOICE (*heard over P.A., softly reverberant*):
Ravaged relics of a forgotten childhood…

Everything same, yet utterly changed.

What did I expect to find? Time frozen, waiting for me to shatter it with the ice-pick of my realizations?

I knew my son was growing up without me. I thought, I was putting together the pieces of my life. It took very long. I came back feeling I had something to share, a revelation to make that would restore kindness and love to this house… What a dreamer I've been. Even as I believed I was being ruthlessly honest.

(*Joeboy turns and—actually—speaks*)

Only a fool could imagine that a change in him will transform the universe.

(*dawn appears*)

I am that fool…

(*He goes onto the porch, and exits. Immediately, the rest of the room lights up. Regina comes out of the kitchen with a pot of tea, goes through her ritual of laying the table. The room is somewhat more disordered than usual. Joeboy's bag is lying on the floor next to the sofa. The gun is missing from the wall. The chairs from around the table have been disarranged; a couple of them have been pulled up closer to the sofa. Enter Georgie, stealthily, on the porch. He surveys the scene before calling out softly to Regina.*)

GEORGIE: Mama…

(*Regina comes out to meet him. He whispers inaudibly, using a gesture to express his question.*)

REGINA: Gone out.

GEORGIE (*coming in*): Where did he sleep?

REGINA: Out here on the sofa. Most of the night they were talking.

GEORGIE: Who?

REGINA: First with Robert. Then Blendina and he.

GEORGIE: Heard anything?

REGINA: Just whispers. Then suddenly a scream, shouting. He must have knocked her about a bit. I heard sobbing as I fell asleep.

GEORGIE: Bastard.

REGINA: I warned you, Georgie. Why do you never listen to me? How could you trust Francis to be discreet?

GEORGIE: It had all been worked out, Mama. I had already given Rufus a bond that we'd take the baby back before she's six months old. And a suitable donation to the orphanage had already been made… He's quite annoyed with Louella for making such a scene yesterday… The next few hours are very important, Mama. Can't let things slip out of our hands now… He's said nothing so far about the papers he signed?

REGINA: I'm sure he remembers very little of that night.

GEORGIE (*agreeing*): Especially not that, since he didn't know what he was signing. But now Joeboy is here, he may want to discuss these things. How's Robert?

REGINA: Sleeping. Woke up before me, full of beans. Started stumbling about the house. Then he wanted to go inspect the back garden and feed the pigs. Tripped on the porch steps and nearly fell. That's what changed his mind. Went back to bed.

GEORGIE: Must be better.

REGINA: He said the fog in his eyes had lifted. But he kept walking into furniture. I held his arm when he stumbled. He was burning with fever.

GEORGIE: Hendricks will be here later on?

REGINA: He's supposed to come.

GEORGIE: Unless, because today's Sunday…

REGINA: What nonsense. He promised he would come.

(*Enter Blendina. She goes to the table and pours herself some tea. She doesn't speak, doesn't look at the other two. They give her quizzical glances. She appears more sombre than usual, grieving. There is an uncomfortable pause. Then Joeboy enters.*)

JOEBOY: Ah, you're all here already.

GEORGIE (*belligerently*): Hi.

JOEBOY: Georgie-boy. Hi. (*uncomfortable pause*)

GEORGIE: I'm sure there are things you want to talk about, Joeboy.

JOEBOY: Later, I'm going to be here now. For a while at least. Where's my father?

REGINA: Asleep inside. Some tea?

BLENDINA: Where's Roscoe? (*to Joeboy*) Have you met him yet?

JOEBOY: I walked up to the old well just now. After a while, I saw Roscoe. He along on his bicycle, to shoot frogs. Introduced myself. Then tried to hug him (*a short, mirthless laugh*); he stuck the barrel of his gun in my ribs and told me to lay off.

BLENDINA: You can't blame him, Joeboy. He doesn't know you. But he'll get to, now.

GEORGIE: Ya. He's never taken easily to strangers.

JOEBOY: Ya?

BLENDINA (*to Georgie*): Stop trying to be hurtful.

(*Georgie and Joeboy stare at each other. The irregular shuffle of Robert's footsteps is heard, as he emerges, no one speaks. They regard him shiftily. His manner of walking and speaking does have a curious edge to it. He seems more energized. The audience, like the other characters, should feel quite unable to decide whether his health has in fact improved, or he is in the grips of a delirium. He completely ignores Georgie through most of the scene, as if he weren't there at all. But even when he speaks to Regina or Blendina, he never looks at them directly, looking elsewhere, into space. Regina breaks the silence.*)

REGINA: How are you feeling, Robert? (*He makes no reply.*) Will you have your porridge now?

ROBERT: To hell with porridge. Slaughter the fat pig. I want a grand lunch. Send word with Francis to Fr. Rufus. And Hendricks. We'll ask him to stay on when he comes for his visit...

(*His tone is gentler when he talks to Joeboy, the only one he seems to address directly.*)

Hendricks never forgot you, son. Not since that time you stole his stethoscope and strung it round the neck of old Nellie, our cow (*a prolonged hearty laugh, in which nobody else joins.*) ... Look, just invite everybody. Invite the villagers.

Invite old Alex as well, and Henry. It's twenty years since Alex set foot in our house. It's time now to let bygones be bygones.

REGINA: Have I twenty hands to dish up a feast for so many mouths? And the cost ...

ROBERT: Well, never mind the villagers, then. Let's keep it a close family affair. But Rufus should be informed immediately. O.K. leave Alex out of it. If lunch is late, he may take a bite out of one of us. (*Laughs again.*) Have I told you that story, Joeboy, of Mad Dog Alex?

JOEBOY: Papa, you're not well. You should rest. There's no reason to celebrate.

GEORGIE (*seizing the moment*): No reason to celebrate? Dammit Joeboy, you've come back after ten years!

JOEBOY: You're delighted, I'm sure... But Papa's sick, can't you see?

GEORGIE: Uncle seems much better to me today.

ROBERT: I'm perfectly okay. And that reminds me. Have to get hold of some good whisky. My Joeboy's not used to our country brew.

JOEBOY: I don't drink any more, Papa.

ROBERT: Don't drink? Why, what's wrong with you?

BLENDINA: Papa, you're forgetting. You're not allowed even a drop. (*to Joeboy*) Doctor said it could be fatal.

ROBERT (*blowing up*): Why do you women keep meddling? Leave me alone. Who said anything about drinking? Can't I raise a bloody toast to my son? (*Nobody says anything. There is a pause.*)

REGINA: Anyway, I'll get on with the cooking. I seem to remember you used to like my vindaloo, Joeboy.

JOEBOY: Make anything. I'm not in the mood for feasting.

(*Regina goes into the kitchen. Robert begins to stride about the room energetically, occasionally bumping into furniture, or reeling, as if intoxicated.*)

ROBERT: I like this. (*rubbing his hands with excitement*) No, no this is a great day... What shall we do? How shall we celebrate? That old girl'll be able to cope with the cooking? Maybe I should send Francis down to the village to hire a couple of helpers, what say? (*shouts*) Francis! (*reconsiders*) No, wait. Francis must first go catch Fr. Rufus, before he goes out gallivanting some place. I can go down to the village myself. And one of you boys, see about the liquor? (*nobody reacts*) I say, get hold of three-four bottles of some good whisky (*He's addressing Georgie*). Willy, what's the matter, you deaf or something?

(*There is a stunned silence, Joeboy slowly approaches Robert and touches his arm.*)

JOEBOY: That's not Willy, that's Georgie.

ROBERT: Where's Willy?

JOEBOY: Willy died some years ago, Papa. You know that.

(*A pained silence. Robert seems suddenly exhausted. He feels his way to a chair and sits down.*)

ROBERT: ...Daisy always told me, I've given you two sons. Two beautiful big boys. What more you want?

JOEBOY (*touches his father's cheek*) Papa, you have a fever. You must lie down.

ROBERT: It's my eyes, they're giving me trouble... You're Joeboy... You've been away..., You're not going anywhere now, are you ...?

JOEBOY: No, Papa. I'm here now.

(*Pause. Once more, Robert is excited. Starts pacing, making plans.*)

ROBERT: We'll go for a shoot tomorrow. Let's start early.

Regina can pack some roast beef for us... And Roscoe, don't forget to take Roscoe, or he'll never forgive you. First class shot. Frogs, pigeons, crows, bugla. And this morning, he shot his first rabbit. That's something, eh? At nine?

BLENDINA: Why don't you have some breakfast, Papa?

(*Robert ignores her.*)

JOEBOY: You should eat something. Then rest.

ROBERT: I'll rest after lunch. (*walking towards the porch*) Now where's that Francis? Has he gone to call Fr. Rufus? (*calls*) Francis! Francis!

(*Dogs bark. A moment later, Rufus enters.*)

RUFUS: Good morning. It's me. The bad penny. Just dropped in to see how everything is.

ROBERT: Why, speak of the devil and he appears. (*Laughs vigorously. Holds Rufus by the shoulders, affectionately.*)

Don't mind my jokes, Rufus.

RUFUS: Why should I mind? Aren't we all devils? Swine of Gadarene? Ha, ha... Hurtling downhill... Ha, ha, ha.

ROBERT: Good thing you came by. I was just about to send Francis to call you. We're having a feast, a grand luncheon in honour of my son.

REGINA (*calling from the kitchen*): How grand it will be I can't promise.

RUFUS: Never mind. However simple, it'll be grand if it's an offering to our Lord. Let us give thanks to Him for our child who has come back safely from the war. Must have had a tough time, Son?

JOEBOY: I've been travelling for almost a month, Father. I had to come by road, sometimes walk for miles. In Pakistan, they took away my car and most of my money. Customs.

RUFUS: Good heavens! What crooks!

ROBERT: Now never mind all that. What's gone is gone. At least you're back.

RUFUS. The horrors of war... We've been reading all about it here. They didn't spare even the women and children, I believe.

GEORGIE: What can you expect in wartime, Father?

RUFUS: It was all foretold in the Book of Revelation. The red dragon is upon us. The day of Apocalypse may be closer than we believe.

JOEBOY: You may be right, Father. Thousands of people stranded in the desert without food or water... I saw some horrible things. At the embassies, at the airports, in the transit lounges, people clamouring and clawing for succour... I saw oil-wells ablaze. The entire sky gorged with mountains of black smoke... But I'll say this, Father. None of it prepared me for the things I found happening here. In peace time. Right here in my own father's home.

ROBERT: Now you're here, Joeboy, everything will be alright. We'll set everything right. I've been waiting for this day... First, where's the booze? Bring it out. I can't drink. Doctor's orders. But what about the others? I want everyone to celebrate. Enjoy!

GEORGIE: I'll get the bottle out. (*He goes in.*)

ROBERT: I really regret selling the jeep. We could have all gone for a drive after lunch.

(*Georgie returns with bottle and glasses on a tray. Puts it on the table.*) Ah, here we are.

GEORGIE: Father...?

RUFUS: No, no, not for me... Well okay, just a drop...

GEORGIE: Joeboy?

JOEBOY: No, thanks.

GEORGIE: Blendina?

BLENDINA: No.

RUFUS: Well, if I'm the only one...

GEORGIE: I'll join you, Father.

ROBERT: Take hold of a glass, Joeboy. I'm going to propose a toast.

JOEBOY: There's no need for all this, Papa.

ROBERT: Where's the glasses... (He *moves to the table and pours out a small drink, shakily.*)

JOEBOY (*sternly*): Say what you have to say. There's no need to drink over it.

RUFUS: Now, now, Robert. We have to be sensible...

ROBERT (*raising his glass, unmindful of protests*): To my son who was lost, but now is found. To my forefathers and their children. May they multiply and see countless generations. And may each generation be happier than the last. (*He raises the glass and brings it to his lips.*)

BLENDINA: Isn't anyone going to stop him?

ROBERT (*lowering his glass*): Shameless whore! What does it matter to you if I live or die? And I had thought I could trust you more than the others. (*Blendina covers her face with her hands and starts sobbing silently. She gets up and goes inside.*)

JOEBOY (*sharply*): Papa! You have no right to speak to her like that. This is between me and her. (*He takes the glass from Robert's hand and places it on the table.*)

ROBERT (*softly*): I had no idea I was harboring a pair of vipers, Son...

JOEBOY: It doesn't matter. Papa. I can't pretend I don't share the blame for what has happened.

GEORGIE: Now that's what I call being fair...

JOEBOY (*in a burst of unanticipated anger*): You keep out of this.

I'm warning you.

ROBERT (*in a hushed voice, conferring with Joeboy*): That man... Who is that man? Is that...is that?

JOEBOY: That's Georgie.

ROBERT (*terribly agitated, in a flurry of quick, uncoordinated movements*): Why is he still in this house? Turn him out! What's that you're drinking? He'll poison us all, Father. He'll poison us all.

GEORGIE (*furious*): I'm leaving anyway. Try to be kind and this is what you get in return. I paid for it, damn you. A bottle of the finest Scotch. That's what it was supposed to be, wasn't it? Is it my fault it turned out to be fake? And he goes on accusing me of trying to poison him.

RUFUS: Stay calm, Son. Don't take it amiss. Robert isn't quite well yet.

GEORGIE: I don't care. He'd better apologize. This is too much. Apologize now, publicly.

JOEBOY: Take it easy, Georgie-boy. We'll take your word for it that you're not a killer. But I know you better than anyone else in this room...

GEORGIE: What does that mean?

JOEBOY: Frankly, it means it would depend on the stakes.

GEORGIE: Hey, watch out, Joeboy. (*closes on him, threateningly*) Watch what you're saying. Who do you think you're insulting?

RUFUS: Children, children, now don't start a fight...

GEORGIE: You come back after ten years. Nice long French leave. And you expect your wife to still be moping for you? You deserted her. You didn't even write to her.

JOEBOY: I sent a lot of money, every two months. Whose fortune was built to that capital? There's nothing left in the account.

GEORGIE: So? She had a right to spend it as she pleased. You think you can buy us with your Gulf money? While you were away who do you think was minding the store? I mean who's been doing all the dirty work?

JOEBOY: You, I'm told. Has it been all that dirty?

ROBERT (*to Joeboy*) What's he saying? What are you two on about? Can't we discuss all this later? I thought we were going to have a party.

JOEBOY: So we are. But there's still time for the party, Papa. You must lie down and rest till lunch is ready.

ROBERT: Okay, I'll lie down. I'll lie down here. (*Rufus gets up to make place for him on the sofa. He stretches out, a cushion under his head.*) I'm feeling a little dizzy—And after lunch, I want you to call my lawyer here. I want to make my will.

(*a pause*)

GEORGIE (*to Rufus*): Let me fix you another.

RUFUS: No, no. I'll wait until lunch.

ROBERT: Why is lunch taking so long? Regina! Regina! What about lunch?

REGINA (*calls, offstage*): The pig is tough. It'll take a while.

ROBERT: Okay, okay, so we'll wait. (*to Rufus*) Must be an obstinate fellow. When he's ready, we'll congratulate him: well done.

(*Rufus giggles. Joeboy goes inside, perhaps to where Blendina is, in her bedroom. Georgie goes into the kitchen. Robert and Rufus are now alone.*)

Tough pig or tender... Now if Daisy were here...you remember, Rufus? She could put together a table full of mouth-watering dishes in a jiffy—

RUFUS: Oh, don't I remember? Daisy used to walk away with all the prizes at our parish cooking contests.

ROBERT: But I never praised her. Not once... A little less salt, something not quite the way I liked it. And I would fly into a rage. (*Jumps up suddenly and sits upright on the sofa.*) Once, I think you were there Rufus, I chewed on a splinter of bone in the kebab. I was so angry, I knocked all the dishes off the table...

RUFUS: All your wedding crockery. I remember.

ROBERT: I was not one to hold back. I'd let her have it. Make a meal of her...

RUFUS (*quoting*): Be not hasty in thy spirit to be angry; for anger resteth in the bosom of fools.

ROBERT: Don't I know it, Father... Was there ever born a greater fool than me?... It's not that I didn't love her. Somewhere down the line, I forgot how it is one loves. Maybe I never knew... I hurt you so much, Daisy... But when you complained, I could not bear that. I wanted to smash you—And all those things you were always reminding me of, by complaining... I could not live with the pain. Aaah... (*he groans.*) ...I think I'll lie down...

(*Joeboy comes out again. Robert calls to him.*)

Willy! Willyboy!... Come squeeze my legs a bit.

My feet and toes as well... That's nice. Ah, how they're aching...

(*Joeboy kneels on the floor beside his father and presses his legs.*)

RUFUS (*aside, to Joeboy*): Poor Robert is missing his Willy a lot today...

JOEBOY: I think he's delirious, Father. What's the matter with Hendricks today? We should send somebody for him.

ROBERT: What? What are you talking about? Is that you, Willy?

JOEBOY: It's me. Joeboy.

ROBERT: Ah, Joeboy... The tramp, the globetrotter. Always

up to some mischief. Knocking down mangoes from Alex's trees, or catching frogs and slitting their bellies with my shaving razor... Then he packs his bags and gets the hell out of Vasai. Doesn't want to know us... Now Willyboy, he's different. Knows what's good for him. Practical, obedient, selfish... Strange, isn't it? Willy, Joeboy?... None of us knew about love. Maybe Daisy was the only one who did. But is that love? All that whining and grovelling and begging? Enough to turn a man's stomach...

JOEBOY: After Mama died, we stopped speaking to one another, Papa. Except in short barks. Like 'Pass the salt'. Or 'Shut your trap'. We froze. I didn't know anything about love. I'd never seen it or felt it breathe between man and woman. Not between my parents, at least.

ROBERT (*in a whisper*): I'm sorry, son... I'm so sorry... (*shaking his head*) I can never forgive myself...

JOEBOY: I'm not blaming you, Papa. And I don't blame Blendina. I failed her too... I failed my son... When I went back to Kuwait after he was born, I started drinking heavily. For months, I stayed pissed day and night. Then, one night, I saw a man die in the streets. He was one of us, a Christian boy. Some things had gone very wrong in his life. He set himself ablaze... I saw him running about in the street, a human torch. He was in agony. But to hear his shrieks, to see his face grinning fiendishly, you would have thought he was in the throes of some exquisitely tortuous pleasure. He fell in the middle of the road, charred, but still twitching... That's when I started thinking about us, our family...and all the fire and hatred that's been raging here for generations... And how, as children, we learned to turn pain into pleasure. It was the only way...

ROBERT: That's why I longed for you to come back, Son. I prayed you should start a family. Make a new beginning...

JOEBOY: I couldn't do it for you. In this, we are each alone. There has to be a real change. Or the cycle continues... And afterwards, Papa, you played the part of the guilty husband. You got sozzled on self-pity. But you never really wanted to find out what went wrong.

RUFUS: Son...

JOEBOY: No, hear me out. I'm not blaming you, Papa. But you blamed her for giving up. You assumed she chose to die.

RUFUS: We don't know the truth, Joeboy. It may well have been an accident.

JOEBOY: It was an accident, Father. But not the kind you mean. I made the same mistakes, Papa. I thought I was making a fresh start when I got married. But the day my wife told me she was pregnant, something horrible happened. I searched my heart for the slightest shred of feeling. There was none. All I could feel surging within me was the loud, clanging horror of that same fury. What had they done to me? My wife, my unborn child? That's when I decided: better to live in a desert, than with the mirage of a make-believe oasis...while all the time the heart is parched with thirst. Of course, there was a high price to pay... My son grew up without the love of a father.

ROBERT. Oh, Daisy... If only we had not been so cruel to each other... If only you could have given me just one more chance...

JOEBOY: I have something to tell you, Papa. Something I had blotted out of my mind all these years... I was only nine...

ROBERT: Are you sure it is wise to talk about all this now, Son?

Joeboy: I may never have another chance, Father. Papa, my

mother didn't want to die. She was only asking for your pity ... The night she died, Mama called me to her bedside and gave me an empty bottle. She told me, 'Give this to your father as soon as he comes back. Tell him Mama said to say goodnight. And goodbye. God bless you, Son. Don't forget.' But Papa, when you came home late that night, I was already fast asleep. And the next morning when you told us that Mama had gone to heaven, my world crashed. I forgot all about that bottle...

Years later, while rummaging about in the godown where our old toys were stacked in boxes, I came across the bottle... Then it all began to piece together, and I remembered... I understood why Mama wanted you to have the empty bottle. It was a desperate message, which didn't get to you in time. I took it with me... And all these years, that bottle of Miltown tablets has been with me in Kuwait. Only when the war began and we had to grab whatever we could and get out, I forgot that bottle once again. I left it there, in Kuwait. I'm sorry, Papa. I had promised Mama I would give you that bottle. But I never did ... All these years I blamed you for her death. The truth is I am as much to blame ... I had blotted out the memory of my own guilt... That's why I never found out about love.

RUFUS: He's fallen asleep. He didn't hear what you said.

JOEBOY: Papa! Papa (*patting his cheeks*) He's passed out. Water, quick!

(*Regina comes out, Blendina come out. Francis rushes in. Georgie brings a glass of water and splashes it on his face. He stirs a little.*)

RUFUS: He's reviving. Give him air.

(*Robert opens his eyes and looks at Rufus.*)

ROBERT (*in a wheezy whisper*): You've come? I want to make

my will…

RUFUS: I'm your priest, not your lawyer, Robert. I can only pray for your dear soul…

REGINA: Move aside. Let him breathe. That Hendricks has really let us down today. Georgie, run down to Henry's place and phone for an ambulance.

(*Georgie rushes out.*)

RUFUS: So sudden… And here we were planning to have a luncheon party.

REGINA: Lift him up. We'll take him inside. He can't breathe on the sofa, slouched like this.

(*Joeboy, Francis, Rufus, and Regina pick him up and try to carry him in, but they stagger under the weight.*)

He's too heavy. Let's put him here on the table.

(*Blendina hurriedly clears the table, and Robert is stretched out on it. Regina puts strips of cloth soaked in water on his forehead. Roscoe comes in.*)

ROSCOE: What's the matter with Grampa? What's he doing on the table?

BLENDINA: Your Grandpa is very sick, Roscoe. Be quiet. (*pause*)

RUFUS: I should send Francis to get the holy oil, first. I think it may be time to administer extreme unction. No sign of Hendricks yet. How irresponsible of him!

(*Regina checks Robert's pulse.*)

ROSCOE: Is my rabbit cooked?

REGINA: Shut up, you fool. This is not the time to talk of rabbits.

ROSCOE (*throwing a tantrum*): What do you mean? I gave it to you this morning.

REGINA: Be quiet.

ROSCOE: I will not. Grampa said he would eat it for lunch. Give him the rabbit to eat, and he'll get well!

BLENDINA: Grandpa's too sick to eat anything, Son.

ROSCOE: It's all your fault. All your fault, and his (*pointing to Joeboy*). He came back and made Grampa sick. I hate him, I hate all of you.

(*Roscoe goes and stands beside Robert peering into his face.*)

You told me we'll go hunting today, Grampa. But you didn't keep your promise. (*He starts snivelling softly.*)

RUFUS: Francis, go, run down to the church. Tell Brother Terence to give you the holy oil. (*Exit Francis.*) Let us pray… (*Rufus prays softly, the others stand around respectfully, their heads bowed.*) O God, whose goodness and mercy are unbounded, the perpetual salvation of them that believe, hear us for thy sick servants, for whom we humbly crave the help of Thy mercy, that their health be restored to them, that they may render thanks to Thee in Thy church. O bountiful Jesus, who upon the cross did shed the last drop of Thy blood for the redemption of mankind, look with compassion on our suffering brother …

(*Georgie rushes in.*)

GEORGIE: The phone at Henry's place is dead. I'll take the cycle and go to the market. I'm afraid the lines may be all down.

REGINA: Francis has taken the cycle to church. To fetch the holy oil… His pulse…I can't feel anything…Oh my God… Robert! Robert! No, wait…I can feel something very faint…

RUFUS: Let us pray. It may be better to let him die in peace in his own home.

(*The family disperses around the room, waiting for the end. Regina and Rufus stand by the table praying silently. Georgie moves aside and has a word with Joeboy.*

GEORGIE: That matter about the will he wanted to make. It's too late now, isn't it? Robert had put all the property in my name, to do as I pleased with it. Anyway, it's all tied up in lawsuits. He wanted me to sort it out. Of course, you'll get your fair share, don't worry, once I disentangle the mess.

JOEBOY: Must we talk about this now?

GEORGIE: No, we can talk later, of course. There's also the other matter of the divorce. Blendina wants a divorce, did she tell you?

JOEBOY (*moving away from room*): There'll be time enough to talk of all that. Clearly, your delight at the turn of events makes you impatient. But let me spoil it for you. If you're hoping to get more money out of me, let me tell you right away—I have nothing left.

GEORGIE: Nonsense. Don't think you can just get away without—

(*Francis arrives with the holy oil, Fr. Rufus anoints Robert on the forehead, on his ears and nostrils, and on the soles of his feet, praying softly. Francis breaks down, whining softly, like a cur bereft of its master.*)

RUFUS (*to Regina*): I think…I'm sorry…Robert is no more…

(*The professional mourners, three or four old village women, arrive on the porch and start a ritual wailing. They sing a traditional Marathi lament for the departed.*)

MOURNERS: O, my beloved, what shadow passed over your forehead that you decided to go away so suddenly…

(*their wailing has an effect on Regina, who breaks down sobbing, loudly calling*):

REGINA: O my brother, my Robert? You've gone? Who shall I make porridge for now every morning? Who will I scold for drinking too much? Oh my brother…my own flesh and blood…

RUFUS: Be brave, my dear, be brave. We all have to go one day. And God takes the ones most dear to Him first…

(*There has to be a certain amount of improvization in this scene, with the characters enacting their grief in spontaneous as well as stylized ways. There is a fair amount of movement and interaction on stage, though of a sombre and subdued nature. The movement of the characters should be approximately plotted out, so that they reveal themselves in little vignettes occurring in different parts of the stage. A shifting pattern of lighting can highlight some of these vignettes as they come together. The village women stream in to pay their last respects to the dead landlord. Roscoe is crying inconsolably. Blendina soothes him, but is herself much affected. Georgie is busy. He keeps moving in and out of the room, presumably making arrangements for the funeral, now and then stopping to have a word with his mother or Fr. Rufus. Joeboy's grief is not manifest, except in the dignity of his bearing, in his concern for Roscoe and Blendina. The first exchange that is highlighted is between Georgie and Blendina.*)

GEORGIE (*finding themselves alone for a moment on the porch away from the mourners*): What a stroke of luck that our Joeboy should have turned so holy-holy. And a teetotaler to boot. He's quite resigned. Even blames himself for everything.

(*Blendina turns her face away from him.*)

We have to plan now. We can get our baby back quite soon.

BLENDINA: I've nothing to say to you, Georgie. My baby won't remain at the orphanage for even one more day.

GEORGIE: Sure, we can arrange that.

BLENDINA: I have my own plans.

GEORGIE: Oh come on, don't be angry, darling…

(*She doesn't reply.*)

You're just stressed out. All of us are. We'll talk about this later. (*Some villagers arrive. The next vignette focuses on Joeboy and Blendina.*)

BLENDINA: Joeboy... What will you do now?

JOEBOY: Don't worry about me. I can start again... All along, on the way back, one thought sustained me. That I was going home... That at last, after all these years, I had been able to resolve something within myself. Find and pluck out that thorn of hatred that had been lodged in my soul... At last, I thought, I will be able to make peace with my father, offer him some peace, perhaps. Build a home based on care and sharing, I came too late, I see...

BLENDINA: Is there no second chance for us?

JOEBOY: I'm sure there is. That's what you're trying, isn't it? A second chance with Georgie. I wish you luck.

BLENDINA: That man has grown despicable in my eyes. I want a second chance for us. Can't we start all over again?

JOEBOY: You're joking...

BLENDINA: If only you had come back earlier...if only you had stayed in touch, only written once in a while...none of this would have happened.

JOEBOY: Who knows, Blendina? There is no formula for happiness. Is there? I could have been right here with you, and the very same things could have happened ... They happen all the time. Women are adulterous, children are born out of wedlock.

BLENDINA: O, forgive me, Joeboy...please, forgive me.

JOEBOY: You have a baby with Georgie. He can't be all bad.

BLENDINA: I want nothing to do with him... Do you think you'll be able to accept her, Joeboy? Please accept her. A little sister for our Roscoe? (*sobbing quietly*) If you can't, then what you said this morning…it doesn't make sense. If you can't forgive me, the cycle will continue… I know it…

(*Joeboy doesn't answer. He looks down. In another part of the stage*):

REGINA: Who called these mourners?

GEORGIE: I don't know. Maybe Francis spread the word?

REGINA: What business did he have to do that? They'll have to be paid.

GEORGIE: Never mind, Mama…

REGINA: You'll make all the arrangements, Son?

GEORGIE: I'll do it.

REGINA: Don't forget to tell the butcher to keep four kilos of tender beef for us tomorrow. There'll be lots of people over for lunch after the funeral.

GEORGIE: I will, Mama. I'll do everything. Don't worry.

(*The lights begin to go down, very slowly. Joeboy is standing at the side of his father, who is lying on the table like a sacrificial offering. Clearly, Joeboy's thoughts are far away from the melee of ritual mourning he is surrounded by, which has already begun to take on the air of a celebration. Outside, the dogs are howling.*)

A FLOWERING OF DISORDER

CHARACTERS

DOLLY (Dorab, affectionately abbreviated):	Short, muscular, hirsute, quintessentially a low-brow vulgarian.
COOMI:	His wife, fully guarded in speech and manner, precious in her ways: yet, alarmingly close to a veneer of sophistication, lurks the real possibility of hysterics.
RUKHSANA or ROOKY:	Their daughter, who has suffered a genuine nervous breakdown. Befuddled and resentful, unable to grasp what overwhelmed her so soon after marriage.
RATAN:	Rukhsana's husband, newly-appointed branch manager of a bank in Bangalore, whose voice we hear perhaps only once on the phone to his in-laws.
NOSH or NOSHIR:	Rooky's younger brother who believes he has wisely opted out of 'the family madhouse', although still living under its roof: grudgingly allotted a fair share of familial respect on account of alleged 'maturity', and an equally notional ambition of becoming a philosopher/writer.

SOHRABJI:	Elderly widower. An average mediocrity it would seem, yet full of surprises, and unsuspected inner perspicacity.
PIROJA:	A neighbour.
RUZWA KARANJIA:	A faith healer, in his seventies.

THE SET

Living room of a blandly middle-class Parsi dwelling in Andheri East, Mumbai. The rhythmic clamour of passing suburban trains and prolonged hooting of long distance ones afford a persistent, yet sparingly used, sound backdrop for the unfolding drama.

Upstage left, a front door, with two low concrete steps leading to the threshold. Upstage right, a section of screened passageway presumably leading to (offstage) family bedrooms. Centre-stage, at an angle, is an easy chair facing a TV set perched on a moveable wall bracket. A square table draped with a checked tablecloth and four wooden chairs around it. Carelessly abandoned beside the steps at the front door (at least during the opening scene) are a large suitcase and a smaller overnight bag.

Dolly, a short, squarely built man in striped pyjamas and sudrah paces about, muttering. Occasionally, he peers into the passageway, hackles raised it would seem, by the sound of persistent sobbing: his resolve to stay aloof from this doleful fracas seems to falter occasionally, but is at once reinforced: he strides firmly, hesitates, shuffles across the living room and back again, clearly on edge.

The action of the play takes place in the early years of the new millennium, i.e. about twenty years ago.

ACT ONE

SCENE ONE

(*Momentary hush.*)

COOMI (*offstage*): Drink this...drink this, dear...

RUKHSHANA (*offstage*): (*sobbing, through cries of sorrow*): Why did you have to bring me here...? I want to die! I just want to *die*—

(*Dolly can't take it any more. Charges towards the passage—*)

DOLLY: I'll straighten her out. Bloody bitch, two tight slaps across the face—

COOMI (*appears from the passage and blocks his way*): You stay out of this...!

DOLLY: Screaming and shouting like a drunken whore—!

COOMI (*in a stage whisper*): Why don't you understand? She's not herself, Dolly. Can't you see? She's lost control...

DOLLY: I'll teach her control...!

(*Tries to shove her aside, but* COOMI *prevents him access to their daughter.*)

COOMI: She needs to be soothed...Stop it, Dolly! Control yourself! Try at least, please!

(*Dolly glares suspiciously at her, unsure if there isn't a slight sputtering somewhere in her admonition.*)

DOLLY (*yells, as she disappears offstage*): Then handle her with your caresses. Afterwards don't come to me for help; when the case is out of hand!

(COOMI *disappears into the passageway, and Dolly resumes his pacing. A pregnant silence. After a while,* COOMI *re-emerges, heaving great sighs of relief.*): O dear mother, dear God…

DOLLY: What the hell is the girl doing now?

COOMI: Shh…sleeping…

DOLLY: Did she take her drops?

COOMI: In her favourite rose sherbet. Drank it all without stopping. My poor babe was thirsty. Then she lay down, mumbling some nonsense, and went out like a light.

DOLLY: Your poor babe…? (*Waves his arms in exasperation.*) Shrieking and wailing like a tom on heat! Does she have no sense? Maderchod, all eight tenants popped their heads out to listen: delightful diversion for our 'B' block bhadwas.

COOMI: Shut up, Dolly! How can you talk filth at a time like this? She's ill (*tearfully*)…Our little one has completely lost her grip on her senses…I can't believe this is happening to my Baby…

DOLLY: Well, I don't either, let me tell you: not one word. Sounds more like melodrama to me… High opera! (*Produces two dramatic cries, in mock-operatic style.*)

COOMI: Don't mock her pain, Dolly.

DOLLY: Sheer idiocy, if you ask me. Pure fucking self-indulgence…. And don't we know who's responsible?

Coomi (*not understanding*): What?

DOLLY: I mean, who's been feeding the flames?

COOMI: What flames? What do you mean, Dolly? (*shocked, yet somehow still unable to grasp what he's insinuating*)…For fifteen days she was chewing my brains: every single day! Half an hour, forty-five minutes? Sometimes two or three times a day.

DOLLY (*muttering to himself*): I'll straighten out her maderchod madness, you see…

COOMI: Do you have any notion what kind of bill you're

running up, I said? What will Ratan think?

DOLLY: Then itself I told you, didn't I? Make her snap out of it! Don't indulge her nonsense...But no, you ignored me. Relished...chewed on every juicy piece of gossip.

COOMI (*shocked*): This is too much, Dolly! You call this gossip? (*Even now she disregards his growing meanness, the swear words he continues to mutter under his breath.*) Rooky's reply was always the same: bill doesn't matter; company will pay... But company, company—even company has some limit, no?

DOLLY: 'She's worried, she's lonely, she's this, she's that...' Dollops of simpering you fed her, day after day, day after day! Now see where it's got you? Which gherchodiya husband will tolerate such behaviour from his wife?

COOMI: Dolly...?

DOLLY: Or for that matter, from his mother-in-law?

COOMI: I still can't understand a word you're saying, Dolly. Ratan never listened in to any of our conversations. Rooky always spoke to me after he left for work...

(*pause*)

But I'll admit one thing—haven't been able to figure it out myself—we just don't know what happened to our poor baby. Even after going all the way to Bangalore to fetch her I still don't know what could have brought this on...

(*Pause;* DOLLY *only shakes his head as if lamenting a lost cause.*)

Same things day after day...over and over again... First, on the phone, then on the plane...I begged her, stop it, Rukhshana! Stop obsessing on your marriage problems, everyone goes through difficulties in marriage; let's talk of other things, but no... Stubbornly she refused to listen... And now they're so horribly stuck in her head: the same delusions spinning round and round, crackling like an old gramophone record....Only...

DOLLY: Only what?

COOMI: Now my Baby feels the pain...

DOLLY: Just what are these damn delusions, can you tell me?

COOMI: For one thing, she didn't want to come home... This is my home, my palace, screaming her head off... At the airport, in the taxi, appealing to rank strangers for help! Where are you taking me? Help! Help! I'm being kidnapped!

I felt so ashamed. I had to keep gesturing... (*demonstrates by tapping a finger at her temple*) discreetly. A few showed concern...but most looked away... And I tell you one thing, Dolly, many...so many were amused... The swine!

DOLLY: What do you want me to say? And what is her bloody pain all about? Two tight slaps across the face would bring her back to her senses.

COOMI: She needs our help, Dolly. When will you understand? She's not pretending... Ratan's doctor—the bank's official physician—wrote out a prescription for her. And a note to a specialist here, in Mumbai. Phone him tonight, why don't you? Maybe this fellow can pay us a visit in the morning?

DOLLY: One more quack? And what's he going to do, may I ask? Feed her more pills and potions?

COOMI: A trained psychiatrist will know what to do. Maybe he'll just talk to her, advise us... Oh, I'm scared, Dolly. What if he tells us she has to take shocks...? Please God, don't let it come to that...please, God...

DOLLY: Let him do whatever's best for her. So long as he gets results.

(*pause*)

COOMI: All the way back on the flight, I tried... Baby, don't do this, don't give up. Talk to me, tell me what's upset you so...But I could see in her eyes she wasn't hearing a word I said...She's lost in her own private world... Some terrible fear has gripped her: dug its claws deep in her soul...

DOLLY (*dreamily, as though he hasn't heard a word of what his wife has been saying*): We found her a nice boy, well-stashed... She's living in a picture-book bungla. Servants, cook, car, a chauffeur on call... What is she scared of? To go walk out on her husband—and fall, plop, back into the lap of her ageing parents?

COOMI: She didn't want to come, believe me, Dolly... Oh no. In fact, she accused me of conspiring...

DOLLY: Conspiring?

COOMI: To clear the path for her husband's lechery.

DOLLY: What the hell is she talking about? Where does the girl get all these ideas...at last we'll have some peace I had thought, some leisure time. But no, she's back. As if this place is some—charitable hostelry!

COOMI (*quietly*): It's her home, Dolly. If we don't help her, who will?

DOLLY: Yes, it's her home alright. And with the kind of 'training' she's got from you, maybe it'll be her home for life. Maybe she'll never be able to leave it.

COOMI: What on earth are you talking about? Stick to facts. A girl should know how to cook, keep her home clean, how to market, how to economize. Sure, I taught her all those things. No one can say I didn't. It was my duty.

DOLLY: Oh yes, we know all that (*with a hint of sarcasm*), you never fail in your duties.

COOMI: And she'd learnt it all pretty well too, believe me.

DOLLY: Then what happened?

COOMI: Ask yourself. Ask yourself that question! Ever since she was a child what did you do to her? Not healthy, I warned you even then. So much petting-cuddling? Even after she was a fully grown girl?

That child has never heard a 'no' from your lips. Doctor's sets, papier-mache dolls, rasgullla tins, whatnot? At the drop of a hat?

DOLLY: Is it a crime then to show love to one's child?

COOMI: But even there, when were you ever consistent? One minute you are the kindest, best father in the world. Next minute, you're consumed by terrible wrath...

DOLLY: Soo ghelu gandu bakech? Terrible wrath?

COOMI: Even now, if I think of how savagely you would yell at them, it makes me shiver...

DOLLY: And when was the last time I yelled? At you, or at your children? Are you saying I have scarred them for life? Let's ask them then—what they feel about Papa's bhayankar gusso? Let's ask them.

COOMI (*shakes her head*): What are you saying? For years as kids they were terrified of you... I know. I pleaded with you, I prayed to God to cool down your rages...for the sake of my children... Please...let's drop this?

DOLLY: You don't understand, Coomi. Children have to be trained. Ek-be phatka pare (*raises his hand and gestures as if slapping someone*) only then will they learn... Have I raised my hand on them after they grew up? No. I didn't need to. Because they learned their lessons well, and learned them early...

COOMI: I can still see the terror in their eyes, when you would get angry... They were only kids then. You think they have forgotten that fear? In today's world beating children is not at all acceptable.

DOLLY: Not acceptable? Says who? They are my children. And I can't give them a good whacking? To teach them what's good for them and what's not?

COOMI: Let's just drop this, Dolly, please…Fear remains…it never goes away… But do you remember, Dolly, the walkie-talkie doll you gave her? On her twelfth birthday? Turn her to one side and she broke into peals of laughter…turn her the other way and she started a doleful boo-hoo-hoo? Do you remember?

DOLLY: Oh yes, I remember. But where's it gone? Haven't seen that doll in…a long, long while!

COOMI: It's gone; God knows where. Or when. But please listen to what I'm saying carefully, Dolly—your 'baby doll', too, is no more. We won't hear any gushing or giggling from her… Groans and cries of pain is all we can expect from our Rooky… (*restraining involuntary sobs*) But we have to accept what she has become, Dolly. Don't reject her, I beg you…
(*slight pause*)

DOLLY: I hear you Coomi, loud and clear. But don't pretend that beneath those fine sentiments, you're not saying something quite different.

COOMI (*shocked*): What? What are you hearing, Dolly?

DOLLY: That my showing love to our child is the root of her problems? Isn't that what you're trying to say?
(*A long silence.* COOMI, *now dry-eyed, stares at the floor.*)
When everything's said and done, there can only be one villain in the piece: your husband! Speak clearly!
(*More silence.* COOMI *shakes her head in contradiction.*)

COOMI (*remorsefully*): If we don't help her, Dolly, who will?

DOLLY: Did I say we won't? Of course we'll help her... She's our child. But to create such a rumpus? Past midnight? Ran up the stairs to Goolmai's while you were paying off the taxi! Luckily, I scrambled after her and dragged her back before she could ring their doorbell. Bachao, bachao, Goolmai...! Screaming her head off! As if some psycho was about to slice her to pieces!

(*pause*)

COOMI (*softer*): For a while she was quiet. But by the time our flight landed, the pills Ratan made her swallow...their effect must have worn off...

DOLLY: Don't mention that man's name here. Solicitous pig... And did he say why he had to call you all the way to Bangalore to fetch her? Does he feel no responsibility in this matter at all?

COOMI: He's just been made branch manager, I told you...at least he insisted on paying my fare—both ways.

DOLLY: Oh thank you, thank you so much. Your airfare? And what about doctors' bills?

COOMI: Put them in an envelope and post them to me, that's what he said. He'll cover everything.

DOLLY: O thank you, dear, thank you again. So he can charge it to his company's expense account? But how will he compensate us for the tension and grey hair? The churning of our guts...? We raised our girl, taught her everything she needed to know. She was fine when he married her. Now he returns her to us a broken woman, babbling like a moron? A little peace in our old age...I thought we were entitled to that at least?

COOMI (*bitterly*): So back to harping on your favourite theme, Dolly? Sitting in your easy chair you may not have noticed how grey I've become... With all the peace you gave me for so many years? Maybe you don't remember... next week will be our thirtieth.

DOLLY: What?

COOMI: Anniversary!

DOLLY: Oh yes, I do remember. Most things I do.... How much I made you suffer... What a selfish bastard I've been... but understand, Coomi. All I wanted was to enjoy life. Just a little bit, if you don't mind.

COOMI: Ha! Don't try to fool me, Mister Dolly! Enjoy life? Why, even today! Even after our children have grown up, not a single woman crosses your path without your making a compulsive bid to charm her. Do you think I'm blind? Don't you realize how old you've become...? Yet, like a frisky puppy, you still want to lick everyone's smelly—toes?

DOLLY: Ah, so now you're calling me a great womanizer, eh? An old fogey obsessed with cunt?

COOMI: Chhi!

DOLLY: Say it. Say it aloud. Why, then I must be the raunchiest Parsi alive since Casanova... But maybe it's you who needs a new pair of lenses. It's you who never learned to be happy? Always worrying and fretting, fussing and muttering, fearing the worst, the most God-awful.... That's been the story of your life. And mine, too.

COOMI: Don't give us your big talk! Just because I put my finger on what you've always hankered after.

DOLLY: Perhaps you haven't noticed how you conspire with fate. Dwelling always on the most dreadful...mulling over it so deeply, non-stop!

Oh, that would be alright too...if it affected only you. But we all live in the shadow of your gloom. On a permanent footing…And now your daughter has picked up your ways too, don't you see? In line with your training, your crackpot fears and superstitions?

COOMI: Crackpot fears? Superstitions? Then tell me… What's this thing that's happened to our Rooky? Suddenly our daughter's brain goes into a tailspin? Who could have contrived it? What jealous black heart wished for it?

DOLLY: There you go again: imagining the worst!

COOMI: A simple girl from a simple family. Suddenly she finds a boy who transforms her entire life. Do you think people are not going to be envious? I don't say this for a fact… But I won't rule it out: someone's done this thing to her.

DOLLY (*raising his voice*): Let's not go round in circles, please. Get this clear once and for all. There's nothing wrong with Rooky. All she needs is a good hiding!

COOMI: Hiding! So you would thrash a sick person?

(COOMI *is shocked. He climbs down.*)

DOLLY: Well, what I mean is…a good shaking down. That's all she needs. Wallowing in all this drama-baaji!? Maybe she was just feeling lonely in Bangalore. Maybe she just wanted— some attention…?

COOMI (*distractedly, softly, as if speaking only to herself*): Bengaluru…they call it Bengaluru now…

DOLLY (*implodes*): Arrey rahva de ni…maderchod. Bengaluru…

COOMI: They insist… Everyone calls it Bengaluru… I know. I've just come from there.

(*pause*)

A bit lonely, you say? A little attention? (*Joins her hands in mock supplication.*) Oh yes, dear God, help me face this new calamity. I'm all alone, I know. Can't expect any help from this—

DOLLY: Say it, say it aloud. From this hardened, unfeeling monster of a husband?

COOMI: What else should I call you?... But those are not my words. You used them...

DOLLY: Call me anything you like. Carve out my liver and scramble it in red chilli. Make a nice aleti-paleti of my entire life. What have I ever done for any of you? Office and back, office and back... All the way to Vikhroli!—and back! You think it was a joke? Just to earn a pittance?

(*brief pause*)

COOMI: Please, please, Dolly. This is no time to think of ourselves. You see, there's something else I haven't told you. Something Rooky said to me, on the plane... It terrified me.

DOLLY: What?

COOMI: A steno at Ratan's office...she thinks he is infatuated with her!

(*No response, long silence.*)

DOLLY (*casually*): Arrey? There was a bottle of Benadryl here. Where's it gone?

COOMI: Are you listening to me at all, Dolly?

DOLLY: There was a full bottle here yesterday. Where's it gone?! Won't be able to sleep without a swig or two...

COOMI: Dolly. We have to do something for our baby, please. She's given up...

DOLLY: Well, let the doctor decide. We can't break your heads over it... All I'm asking is: why pack her off to Mumbai? Are there no psychiatrists in Bangalore?... Oh sorry, Bengaluru.

COOMI (*exasperatedly*): But I explained to you! He has to be at his bank. Every morning at ten... He was afraid to leave her on her own... She had one narrow escape as it is...

DOLLY: Narrow escape?

COOMI: Yes…only last week. She locked herself in the kitchen and turned on the gas… Luckily, one of the windows wasn't latched properly. The cook climbed in and saved her… That's when he decided to call us for help…

DOLLY (*after a stunned silence*): And we thought we had found her a lucky catch… The bastard. He must have been beating her, or something. A girl doesn't just wake up one fine morning and try to kill herself?

COOMI: Oh, but I thought you were convinced it was only delusion, self-indulgence on her part?

DOLLY: It better be. Or that little punk is going to eat my shit.

COOMI (*shakes her head*): No…he swears he's done nothing… Weeks ago she became convinced he was fooling around with his steno… She would follow him quietly when he left home, make surprise visits to the bank, create scenes in front of the staff… Not just that. She was confiding to neighbours at their housing colony. Ratan says he's become the laughing stock of their enclave…

(*brief pause*)

And our Rooky? How furious she became when she realized I was there to bring her home?!

(*embarrassed silence*)

First, she accuses me of trying to assist Ratan's lecherous intent. Then she accuses me of trying to seduce him myself, can you imagine?

(*brief pause*)

DOLLY (*chuckling*): Well, don't think I haven't noticed… You always did have a soft spot for the boy.

COOMI (*screams*): Have you no shame to talk like that?!

DOLLY: Nothing so awful about it, dear Coomi. Everyone has

their needs. Even at our age.

COOMI: Sinful creature! That's what you've always craved, don't I know it? And to lament about it now!

DOLLY: But what's so terrible, darling? About a little jig-jig? Just now and then? I know I have never been able to satisfy you.

COOMI: I don't care to be. We've given birth to two children, that's enough for me... But you're trying to provoke me, aren't you?

(DOLLY *bursts into prolonged, disparaging laughter.*) How could you? At a time like this? O God, help me! One mad daughter, one perverted father. Little surprise we have come to this pass.

DOLLY (*chuckling*): Okay, okay, call me pervert, if you like. But what's life without a little fun and mischief?

COOMI: Selfish man! You can sit there and chuckle as much as you want. But do you know what I've been through in one day?

DOLLY: One day?

COOMI (*yells*): Today! I mean Today! The shame, the humiliation! Holding on to that girl's wrist tightly with one hand, managing her suitcase with the other. And she: calling out to rank strangers to rescue her. I had to keep doing this (*tapping her temple with a curved index finger*). Then I bundled her into a cab at Santa Cruz airport. And the bloody cabbie tries to blackmail me.

DOLLY: How so?

COOMI: When we reached here, he demanded five hundred rupees. Police ka lafda ho sakta hai. I'll have to report the matter, he says.

DOLLY: So?

COOMI: So what, for heaven's sake? I gave it to him. He could have created such a nuisance for us. Bringing police into our lives...at a time like this?

DOLLY: Are you crazy? Five hundred rupees! Why didn't you yell out to me? I would have squeezed his balls for him. Maaderchod, suvvar ni aulad, you shouldn't have let the bastard get away so easily!

COOMI: If you had so much concern, why didn't you meet us at the airport?

DOLLY: And get my spine jigged all over Mumbai's potholes? You know very well...(*puts his hand on his lower back*)...my slip-disc, dear, don't forget...you have no idea what pain I go through every evening.

COOMI: And what about me? Low blood pressure, vertigo, insomnia...! But still, I do what I have to, without fussing or complaining?

(*Key turns in the latch, and the front door opens.* NOSHIR *enters.*)

NOSH: What's this? Mum? Inventory hour? Or are you compiling an encyclopaedia of family illnesses?

DOLLY: Get inside and shut the door. (NOSH *does that.*) Here comes another inmate of our charitable hostelry for derelicts...At midnight.

NOSH: Sorry, dad. By the way, it's only just past eleven.

COOMI: Where were you? Is this the time to come home?

NOSH: I had to attend a function. At a friend's place.

DOLLY: Function? Friend? Don't bullshit us, you rascal. Why don't you just say you were with your black beauty?

NOSH: Well, I'm not denying it. I was at her brother's engagement dinner... You're not wrong, Papa, to call my friend Amelia dark. But she's also very beautiful. I never dared tell you this before…but I like her very much…if all goes well…

DOLLY: Nothing so amazing about all that. We know you like brown arse, boy. Don't announce it with so much fanfare… Or should I say fanny-fare?

NOSH (*mumbles*): At least, I'm thinking, our kids will be spared the insanity of consanguineous coupling with some pale Parsi bitch.

DOLLY (*fulminating*): Look at him, mouthing big-big words at me. Behnchod, he's grown too big for his boots. Ek bae phatka parsey ne, maderchod, then you'll understand everything. Punk!

COOMI: He's drunk. He's been to some party and got drunk. Now you don't get overexcited, Dolly, please.

DOLLY: So what are you saying? That you and your sister are mad because your mother and I are second cousins?

COOMI: Stop it. Stop it at once, both of you!

DOLLY (*angrily*): This home-fucker's got one big jig-jig on his mind. Let's hope he doesn't get stuck to his bitch while mating!

COOMI (*screams*): I won't tolerate such language in my house. Have you no shame? (To NOSH) And even on a day like this you were not here to help us. Your poor sister's having such a bad time (*breathlessly*) your mother had to go to Bangalore—

DOLLY: Bengaluru…

COOMI: —all alone to fetch her…

NOSH: Where's Rooky?

COOMI: Asleep. In your bed.

NOSH: Poor girl. I guessed as much.

COOMI: How would you?

NOSH: From all that Ratan has been saying.

COOMI: To you?

NOSH: Oh, no. I mean all the things he had been saying to you. On the phone.... Agitation... Temporary mental disturbance... Poor sis. Marriage can be a difficult business, I guess.

DOLLY: Difficult business, hunh? What philosophers we've been breeding under our roof!

NOSH: But how would my presence have helped, Mum? You know very well how Rooky feels about me. One look at my face—first thing on arrival—and she might have gone into a fresh attack...! Maybe?

COOMI: You pull out the dholki—quietly—and sleep in the passage. Don't want to hear another word from you.

DOLLY: I'm going to watch *Santa Barbara* before sleeping. At least I'll try to. (To NOSH) Tell me, Nosh. Have you been glugging down my Benadryl?

NOSH: Benadryl? Come on, Dad. Not my kind of poison.

(DOLLY *glares at his son.*)

COOMI (*approaching closer to* NOSH): Now listen, I want you to be kind to your sister when you see her in the morning. None of your silly pranks or nasty wisecracks. Do you understand? She needs our love. To make her well again... Let's all sleep while we can...

DOLLY: Your Mama's right. We'll just pretend everything's normal, that Rooky's come home for a routine visit. Okay?

COOMI: But honestly, Dolly, I'm dreading this. How will she behave when she wakes up...? You didn't phone the doctor when I asked you to. And now it's too late to call anyone...

NOSH: Tell me, Mum, is she—? I mean...has she—lost it completely?

DOLLY (*reacts intemperately*): Chupp! Salo badmaash! Naguno!
COOMI (*she decides to ignore his imprecations, but her voice cracks under the weight of emotion as she whispers*): Yes…Completely! Now get to bed! Both of you!
DOLLY: But I just told you, I won't get sleep unless I can watch a little TV first—
COOMI: Oh, you watch your *Santa Barbara* if you must. Please keep the volume down.
NOSH (to himself, aloud:) I wonder sometimes… What are we? A family of loonies? Whose turn will it be next?
(*Lights begin to dim, as the signature tune of Star TV cross-fades into the hooting of a long distance train.*)

BLACKOUT

ACT ONE

SCENE TWO

Next morning. An elderly, dhoti-clad bhaiyya from UP sits on the floor of the Shroff living room beside a heap of crumpled clothes; examines, sorts, and counts. COOMI, *seated in a chair near him, tidily records totals in a notebook.*

DHOBHI: Ek, do, teen... Chaar lehenga... Chhe sudrah... Do ganji... Do kameez... Teen chaddar... Ek double chaddar...

COOMI: Total kitna?

(DHOBHI *counts again.*)

DHOBHI: Kul mila ke athra kapda hai, Mummy... Ek pyjamas pe yeh dekho—bada daag laga hai. (*shows*) Poori koshish karonga, saaf hoga to kar doonga...

COOMI: Aur bhoolna mat dhobhiji, last time ka ek pant bhi baaki hai...

DHOBHI: Woh aa jayega, Mummyji. Agley guruwaar ko...

(*A pause, while* DHOBHI *wraps unwashed clothes in a bedsheet, knots the bundle, and prepares to leave. Just then,* RUKHSANA *emerges from the passage, dopey, distracted, and moving slowly as though in a trance. She sees* DHOBHI *and joins her hands in a respectful pranam.*)

DHOBHI (*seeing her, reciprocates*): Arrey Baby...! Aap kab aiee? Kaisi hain...?

(*She doesn't answer, but continues to gaze at him demurely, hands folded—as though he were a living god she must pay profound obeisance to.*)

COOMI: Rukhsana, dear...? Did you sleep well? ...Baby ka tabyet theek nahi hai... Kal raatko hi aiee...

DHOBHI (*hitches the bundle on his shoulder*): Apna khyal rakho, Baby... Aur Mummy ka bhi. Achcha to, mummy, main chalta hoon... Baby, Namaste... (DHOBHI *exits.*)

COOMI: Rooky! I'm so glad you remembered our dhobhi... He's aged a lot, of course. With so little water left to the city, it's a wonder he still gets clothes to look well, somewhat clean.... But I don't understand, Rukhsana...tell me. Why did you greet him like that? With so much—reverence? As though he were a holy man? ...No harm in that, of course, it's very good of you, my dear. But he's just our old dhobhi, you do remember him, don't you?

(*Just then* NOSH *emerges in the passageway, dishevelled, bare-chested, wearing crumpled pyjamas and yawning loudly.*)

ROOKY (*aggressively*): He's a good dhobhi let me tell you that... I know him better than you...And now I know what it is to suffer, I'll never disrespect any living creature again...

(*Long pause.* COOMI *looks baffled.* NOSH *listens admiringly.*)

NOSH: Wow...! Last night they told me Sis is bonkers...she's lost it completely. And this morning she wakes up teeming with wisdom. A sage, almost... You might even say a fully fledged guru...!

COOMI: Noshir! Stop that at once...! Didn't I tell you something last night? Barely out of bed and already you're poking fun at your sister! Have you no shame?

NOSH: I'm not, Mum, I'm not...poking anything at her. But booking, yes. Booking a berth, if I may, for her next public discourse... Azad maidan, Rooky. Or Cross? So I too can imbibe those pearls of wisdom as they drop...

COOMI: Stop being ridiculous, you clown!

(*a pause*)

ROOKY (*suddenly immersed in deathly gloom*): I have nothing to say…to any of you…(*yells at the top of her voice*) JUST LEAVE ME ALONE!

COOMI: Arrey, but why're you yelling like that? You want to inform all our neighbours, too? (*to* NOSH) She's not feeling so good, Nosh. Please don't trouble her.

ROOKY (snaps angrily): Who says? Who says I am not feeling good? Stop putting words in my mouth! (*gloomy, depressed again*) But you may be right. I'm not…I'm not feeling so good at all… In fact, I'm finished. Done with. There's nothing left to me now…I've become a beggar…for life…

COOMI (*almost in tears*): No, no, my baby, don't take it so hard. You still have everything. Your whole life before you. Your Mama, your Papa—

NOSH: Your bro.

COOMI: We'll find a solution to every problem you may face. Don't worry, Baby…

ROOKY: No problem.

COOMI (*not understanding*): I'm sorry?

ROOKY: I said, there's no problem! Get this clear in your head! I have no problem at all… (*softly, wondering to herself*) Of course, now that you mention it…and why do you keep reminding me? There is that one problem: my marriage, would you say that it's—?

COOMI: What?

ROOKY: Over? …Over. Over. Fucking over!… My marriage is over. Why did you bring me here? Back to this hellhole? I was so happy in Bengaluru… In my bungalow. You saw it, didn't you? I took you on a walking tour of the whole place... Mon Repos...that's what it's called. Now suddenly I'm back here where I began. Back in Katpitia Baag, 'B' block! Why would you do such a thing to me, Mama? Are you crazy? Now I'll never, never be able to go back home... (*she begins to weep softly*)

COOMI: No, no...my baby...

ROOKY (looks up): Don't baby me. It sounds disgusting.

(DOLLY *emerges from the bedroom.*)

DOLLY: Tea. Tea... Please... My kingdom for a cup of tea...

COOMI: Your kingdom will have to wait, bawa... Please wait.

(DOLLY *resignedly sinks into his easy-chair. But presently,* COOMI *does fetch him a cup of tea from inside.*)

DOLLY: Thank you, my dear... Aaah...

(*He savours his first hit of caffeine, just as the doorbell rings: ding-dong.*)

Arrey, ai kaun? Savaarna porma?

(COOMI *goes to the front door. Looks through the peephole and opens the door. It is* SOHRABJI, *their elderly neighbour from upstairs.*)

COOMI: Kem? Soli Uncle?

SOHRABJI: Maaf karjo mai, early morning I am disturbing you...?

COOMI (*agitated by the very sight of him*): Pun thayu su? Bolo ni?

SOHRABJI: What can I say, mai? I have nothing to say in my defence. Yesterday I am going to Andheri, main market. Full shopping doing. And all the way, a voice is telling me: SUGAR, SUGAR...

COOMI: Hunh...Bawa, I don't have all morning to listen to your long stories. What do you need?

SOHRABJI: In my head. Must remember to buy SUGAR!

Believe it or not—everything else I am buying. Somehow sugar only forgetting…

DOLLY: Arrey, arrey, Soli, come on in. What's the big deal? Come on in. (*calls out*) Nosh…

COOMI: (*hands the cup to* NOSH): Go on son, fill him some sugar from our kitchen barni, please.

SOHRABJI: Tomorrow… First thing tomorrow I'll return… I don't mean myself: sugar, I will return… First thing in the morning. Thank you so much, my kind neighbours, my good friends.

COOMI: Yes, yes, thank you… No problem, Sohrabji.

DOLLY: Arrey, Soli-ba. Little sugar between neighbours? Why make such a big fuss?

SOHRABJI (*apologetically*): No, no, I mean it. Definitely… Promise! Tomorrow! Without fail! God bless you all (*exits*).

DOLLY (*in a soft voice*): Tomorrow morning, eh? Or tomorrow evening? Or maybe not at all?

COOMI: Oh, we know very well why. His tomorrows never come…that's why. (*Repeats, with emphasis.*) That's why!

(*All through* SOHRABJI's *entry and exit, Rooky has been seated quietly in a low-lit area of the stage.* SOHRABJI *didn't notice or address her at all. Now she speaks up.*)

ROOKY (*with anger and venom*): See? Just how nasty you can be? About an old man who borrows a small cup of sugar…? Don't want to live in this place. Not for even one minute… Why did you bring me here? What will you say about me after I'm gone?

(*Both parents speak simultaneously, rapidly, alternating lines.*)

Arrey? What's wrong with you, child…?

…Just now you were sitting peacefully…

…Woke up happily, too, I noticed. I was so sure you were

feeling better...much much better...isn't that true?

...I've absolutely no doubt about that even now... But she is, isn't she looking better?... So much brighter today, our Rooky.

...You don't know Soli Uncle, my dear. He's always borrowing things from us, never returning... It's an old habit...

...And always, he'll say 'tomorrow'... That's why I said his tomorrows never come! Ever! Don't judge us, Baby, not on his account.

ROOKY: Tomorrow I'm leaving.

DOLLY: Oh no, you're not!! Sit down quietly.

ROOKY: I am! I'm taking the next flight back to Bangalore.

COOMI: You mean Bengaluru...

ROOKY: Yes! Bengaluru! Today if I can get one.

DOLLY: See? The more kindness you show the more they will sit on your head.

ROOKY: Nonsense. I am a married woman, I can go wherever I like.

DOLLY (*peremptory, threatening*): STOP IT! Stop it I say. You can't travel alone. Ask your husband to come and fetch you if you want to go anywhere!

COOMI: Baby, please don't do this. Don't fight with us, please. We want to help you...I'm going to phone your doctor right now...

ROOKY: I don't need a doctor. I need a travel agent...

DOLLY: Behave yourself, Rukhsana. I'm warning you. From now on, you're not dealing with your sweetly pliant Mummy. You're dealing with me. Your Papa!

ROOKY: So what will you do? Beat me up? Tie me with a rope and thrash me? I won't stay in your pokey flat for another minute.

DOLLY (*yells*): Just sit here quietly for one minute and don't talk back. SIT! Pokey flat, eh? It's where you grew up... Madam has grown accustomed to aleshaan bunglas! In Bengaluru, if you please!
(*She sits down in a chair quietly for a moment lost in thought. No one says anything.*)

ROOKY: Okay, then. I'll ask Sohrabji. He won't mind if I move in with him.

COOMI: Sohrabji! Don't be so silly, child. You can't do that. Even if you know him since you were so little... Word will spread in a flash. Soon whole colony will start gossiping.

ROOKY: I don't care... Give me one good reason why I shouldn't? It's just one flight upstairs ...And Sohrabji lives alone. He'll be happy for some company. I'll go ask him first.

DOLLY: Look at her stubbornness?

NOSH (*who has been silent all this while*): What about me, Rooky? I need your company, too. I missed you so much when you got married and went away...

ROOKY: Ha! Ha! Tell me another, bro.

NOSH: We've not had time to catch up on anything. I miss those heart-to-heart powwows we used to have as kids.

ROOKY: I'm not flying to another city, please. Just one flight upstairs. Any of you can come and see me whenever you want... If you miss me too much just yell, and I'll come down myself... I'm going up now to ask Sohrabji if I can move in for a few days.

COOMI (*whispering to* DOLLY): I'm thinking maybe it's not such a bad idea, Dolly... It may help her relax. (*to* ROOKY) But when we go to see the doctor you have to come along... Do you promise?

ROOKY: I'll come; I'll come whenever you want... Promise.

Now I'm going up to find out if I can stay there. See you later... (*Goes out the front door, leaving it open.*)

DOLLY (*angrily*): Let her go stay with Sohrabji if she wants. What do we care?

COOMI: You don't understand, Dolly? Within hours the word will spread like wildfire.

DOLLY: Whose word? What for heaven's sake?

COOMI: Not only did she walk out on her husband, even her parents' flat she abandoned to shack up with—

DOLLY: Sohrab? Ha, ha... That old goose? Don't be funny, Coomi. Nobody's going to think like that.

COOMI: Won't be funny once the word gets around. No joke—except on our family name!

DOLLY: Who, tell me, which idiot will see her sharing the flat with Sohrabji in that peculiar twisted way you have? ...He's an old man. For heaven's sake!

COOMI: (*backs down*) Old man, yes. But all alone? With a young, deserted bride?... We'll see who's right, who's wrong...

DOLLY: We'll see.

COOMI: Already this morning, when I was taking in the milk, Piroja came down the stairs... Pretending it was just by chance.

DOLLY: Piroja? (*points upwards*) You mean—

COOMI: The very same.

DOLLY: But—

COOMI: She's no friend of mine, it's true. Never speak to her if I can help it. But listen—temerity of the woman (*imitates nasal tone*), 'But doesn't her husband mind? How will the poor man manage all by himself?' Bitch!

DOLLY: We'll see, we'll see... Let her say what she wants...

But don't forget. It's her husband who sent Rooky home. She's not a young bride visiting us on holiday.

COOMI (*shocked*): What're you saying, Dolly? That's what she'll always be for me... Always. Ovaaryu, ovaaryu! (*snaps her fingers*).

NOSH (*after a long and shocked silence*): Stop it, Mama-Papa! Stop bickering like kids... In the end does it matter what people say? Let them talk, who cares?

DOLLY (*approvingly*): Spoken like a true philosopher. I agree entirely with Nosh, by the way. You're taking the whole thing much too seriously, Coomi. Give your daughter some time, some breathing space... Everything will soon be as it was again...(*Drains his cup of tea, and puts it down with a clink.*)

(FADE-OUT)

ACT ONE

SCENE THREE

It is evening. RUKHSANA *and* SOHRABJI *are seated beside each other on a sofa in what could possibly be misconstrued as romantic closeness. They are whispering to each other softly. Their interactions have the muted quality of mime.* RUKHSANA *has been crying,* SOHRABJI *consoling, whispering.*

RUKHSANA: If only he had told me…confessed there was someone else… I'm sure by now it would all be over…

SOHRABJI (*shakes his head*): No, no. What you're saying is silly, frankly…That's impossible!

RUKHSANA: But why?

SOHRABJI (*thinks before answering*): Well, the truth is, people can't bear the stench of their own guilt. So they deny it, create self-justification. They have to, there's no other way… They pretend, make-believe, retaliate—sometimes viciously…

RUKHSANA: But I'm sure it would never have developed into more than just a fling…

SOHRABJI: So you say. But had he told you, you think you would be able to accept it…?

RUKHSANA (*considers for a moment before speaking*): No…I suppose not…I would have killed him first. Or myself.

SOHRABJI: There, you see…

(*He gets up and switches on a light.*)

RUKHSANA: It was as if only by excluding me—blocking

every trace or smell of me from his very consciousness he could enjoy his new partner. Didn't have it in him to partake of illicit pleasure, and yet be civil to me... So he turned me into the bitch—the jealous, neurotic other.... And the sad thing is I played the part willingly—to the hilt.

(*Long pause before Sohrab attempts to reply*)

SOHRABJI: I keep trying to explain... That's the way we are made. When the brain is ... split in two by duplicity, none can bear to live with such falsehood. One flees from it. By turning the world upside down and inside out.

RUKHSANA: But why should that make me so insecure about myself?

SOHRABJI: But naturally, my dear...you felt excluded, disbarred from his magic circle...that you believed he had created for himself with someone else... Am I right? ...The problem was that you let it affect you so much... Mustn't take it so hard.... There's no point, really, Rooky.

RUKHSANA: But how do you know so much about this? I mean, you, a bachelor? You are one, aren't you, Sohrabji?

SOHRABJI: Call me Sohrab, please. No, I was married once... When my wife died she was only twenty-seven...

RUKHSANA: I'm so sorry, I didn't know...

SOHRABJI: Cancer... The doctor—in those days—had termed it 'galloping' cancer. Galloped away with my wife... my life.

RUKHSANA: I'm so sorry, Sohrab. Thank you for confiding in me... You've helped me so much by talking to me today...I was wondering....

SOHRABJI: What?

RUKHSANA: Could I stay up here with you for just a few days...?

SOHRABJI: Here…? You mean in this flat? Well there *is* a spare bedroom…But your parents? Your mother, your father? What will they think? Have you asked them?

RUKHSANA: I've told them. They don't have much choice in the matter.

SOHRABJI (*alarmed, very doubtful*): Arrey, pun… Don't hurt them, child… They are in shock themselves. They're trying to help you… (*Long* pause.) But before we consider all that, there's one thing I want to know. You must decide first.

RUKHSANA: What, Sohrab?

SOHRABJI: Do you want him back? I mean, your husband… If it were possible, would you want to have him back?

RUKHSANA (*overwhelmed by emotion, she cannot find words at first, but nods emphatically*): Yes…I want him back…I do.

(FADE-OUT)

ACT TWO

SCENE ONE

Well-appointed living room of a large flat at Marine Drive, where COOMI *and* ROOKY *are in queue for a meeting with* RUZWA KARANJIA, *clairvoyant and soothsayer. Three or four other supplicants are also seated and waiting, as at a doctor's waiting room.*

To one side of the room, at an angle, is a sort of altar cluttered with indistinct ceremonial objects; above these, a large garlanded portrait of KARANJIA's *own hoary guru.*

COOMI (*softly, to* ROOKY): Be patient, my dear. In a few moments he will emerge… Ruzwa Baba. Most amazing, wonderful man. He'll put you totally at ease, within minutes…and we'll know exactly where the trouble lies—I mean, between you and Ratan. He has a penetrating, infallible third eye: a healer par excellence…And besides, Ruzwa Baba is also a clairvoyant and philanthropist: a man who sees the future clearly!

DEVOTEE 1 (*who has been listening in*): And also—the past, mai! Don't forget.

RUKHSANA (*confused*): But Ratan? How does this Karanjia know Ratan? Is he related to him? Does this flat belong perhaps to Ratan's parents?

COOMI: No, no. Nothing of the sort, my dear… Be patient. In just a few minutes—with the blessings of Baba—we'll know everything… Many souls he has rescued from physical agony, unthinkable afflictions! After we go home, I will tell you some amazing stories of his wondrous deeds.

DEVOTEE 2: Who can forget that case of Berjis Fafra? 'F' block, Rustom Baag? Yaad chhe, mai?

COOMI: Of course, I remember. Rooky, you should hear this. Bergis Fafra was virtually paralysed—lay in bed all day unmoving, like a block of wood...

DEVOTEE 2: Until Baba pinched a nerve in his leg...Oh yes, he knew exactly where to pinch him.

DEVOTEE 1: So hard, so hard, that Bergis screamed in agony! But immediately after, he climbed out of bed and started walking!

DEVOTEE 2: Every evening now, two, three kilometres at least, he must go...walking!

DEVOTEE 1: At 6 p.m. sharp, if you stand at the Byculla Bridge corner you'll see Bergis Fafra. Striding stiff and upright like a British soldier. Come rain or shine—

COOMI: But you know, Rooky, these are almost legendary tales from long ago. Berjis Fafra must be at least ninety now! But there's another story I have, my favourite. That too took place quite a long time ago. The case of Aimai Acharwalla.

(*Devotees nod and murmur.*)

DEVOTEES 1 and 2: Hanh vari, hanh vari...That was sheer chamatkaar, who can forget?!

COOMI: You see, Aimai, was a very good woman who made only one big mistake in her life. Of allowing unscrupulous paying guests to move in with her... A man and his wife. Such scoundrels! Day in, day out, they harassed her, creating every possible problem for her so that life became a living hell for poor Aimai. They would dump their garbage in her portico, pour mugs of slushy water in their shared passage, turn on the radio full blast in the middle of the night! Until things came to such a pass that Aimai herself was willing to move out and surrender possession of her flat to those rascals.

DEVOTEE 1: That's exactly what they were after, believe you me!

COOMI: At last, this lady—poor Aimai—took her problem to Ruzwa Baba. Baba gave her a very simple solution: a piece of bitter gourd—you know, karela?—a piece of raw vegetable? Said some prayers over it, and asked her to drop it discreetly on their side of the flat. Within a week, you won't believe it, the tenants gave Aimai notice to vacate.

'These lodgings are just too hot—oh-ho-ho so fiery hot, like a furnace!' the husband began to complain. 'Can't stay here one more day!' And the wife? She started to lament, 'Everything I cook in this kitchen turns bitter—bitter and rancid, smelling like fermented hooch! Can't eat a morsel in this flat!...Ughh...' She too wanted out. Rooky, don't ever underestimate this man's amazing powers...

(*Just then, KARANJIA emerges from the wings: in his seventies, skinny, with a slightly comical handlebar moustache, smartly dressed, almost dapper. With kohl around his eyes, a large black smear of it on his forehead, he has a slight limp, and uses a walking stick. Looking around at the audience first, he turns his attention now to those waiting in queue.*)

KARANJIA: Arrey, Coomi-mai! When did you come in? I had no idea ...Never mind, tell me, how can I be of service to you? (*He looks at RUKHSANA, seated beside the older woman.*)

COOMI: Yes, Baba, we need your help. This is Rukhsana, my daughter...Her husband has sent her home. From

Bangalore...They were having—some marriage problem...
KARANJIA: Emm? Arre, arre... H'mm...
(He takes her hand in his, feels her pulse and gazes into her eyes. Someone provides a chair for him. A shift in lighting creates a subtle ambience which isolates KARANJIA, Coomi and Rukhsana.)
COOMI: But not just that... My poor child is in some state of shock...Her mind ...is quite disturbed, I'm afraid...!
KARANJIA: Well...What to say? These days people are up to such kinds of nastiness... I'm not referring to her husband, no, people in general...But this young man, Ratan, I have to tell you... he does have some lafru going on,
RUKHSANA: How do you know his name, Uncle? And how do you know about his—?
KARANJIA: I don't. But *you* know...you're telling me... That's how I can read it. In the drumming of your blood... in the sadness of your soul...Never mind, dikra, we'll find a way around this one, too.
COOMI: But how?
KARANJIA: H'mm...Let me think...(*after a few moments of listening to her pulse again*) You were right. It's not a simple matter of affections distracted, or love gone astray... There is mischief brewing here.
COOMI (*reacts*): Mischief! I knew it!
KARANJIA: But please do stay calm... I need to focus my energies...
COOMI: Yes, of course...
KARANJIA (*calls out*): Dahya!
(*His Gujarati butler responds in a bit.*)
DAHYA: Saheb?
KARANJIA: Gloves, please...From my bedside drawer...

(*Butler exits. Returns in a moment with a pair of latex gloves, enclosed in plastic wrapping, on a small tray. As* KARANJIA *rips open the plastic and wears a glove on his right hand, lights dim further, his voice, amplified by echo and reverb takes on a hypnotic, measured cadence, as soft music enhances the suspenseful moment.*) Let us be silent now in this deeply important moment. (*praying aloud*) Help us Great Universal Mind, help us to help this child. We know you will…without fail. As pointedly we focus our hearts…on plucking out this young lady's grief from its very root…

RUKHSANA (*alarmed*): What are you going to do, Mr Karanjia? Are you a dentist?

KARANJIA: No, no… This won't hurt at all, my dear Rukhsana. No pain, no anaesthesia… Just relax. Open your mouth, please…let me look inside…(*Bends over her; for a few moments, the lights dim further, and in the increasing gloom on stage, we hear* RUKHSANA *gagging, protesting loudly.*)

Bas, bas… Thay gayu. It's done… Thanks Universal Master, for giving this child a new lease of life. May the evil designs of those who wish ill upon her…be forever thwarted… Here! See what I found. Lodged deep in her throat!

(*lights go up again*)

(*He holds up something so tiny in his gloved hand that* COOMI *has to rise from her chair and draw closer to him to examine it. When he doesn't let her touch it,* RUKHSANA *becomes curious too; although she remains seated, looking dazed and disturbed.*)

COOMI: What is it?

KARANJIA: No! Don't touch it…!

COOMI: Looks like an elaichi to me!

KARANJIA: Yes…Something of the sort. But endowed, undoubtedly, with evil intent… Never mind now, it's out…

Tonight, in a brazier of sacred fire, I will destroy it.

RUKHSANA: No, no, wait… Let me see it first…

KARANJIA: From afar please…don't touch…. (*He shows it to her.*)

(*she reacts loudly*) YAACK! (*and starts retching*)

(*Fade-out begins*)

KARANJIA: We have extracted—the unholy root of evil implanted in your life. From this moment on everything will be normal again…between you, your husband, your mother, your father… You are going to be well again, my child…

(*As lights begin to dim—the stage is almost in darkness now—* RUKHSANA *jumps up as if in a trance and laughs, chillingly, like one possessed.*)

RUKHSANA: So Mr Healer…! You say I am healed?… But how the fuck can you know that?

COOMI: Rooky!

(*But* ROOKY *ignores her Mum and glares at the audience: in her unabashed use of the expletive and the savagery of her grimace, she appears to be deliberately cocking a snook at the healer's rosy prognosis.*)

BLACKOUT

ACT TWO

SCENE TWO

Back at home, COOMI *is apprising* DOLLY *of the morning's events.*

DOLLY: Hmm. All terribly mysterious, I'll say… How much more bizarre is this drama going to become?

COOMI: Well, he actually did pull something out—from deep in her throat. He showed it to us. I saw it—and Rukhsana too! Odd thing is: …after he had pulled it out, she began to behave even more—irresponsibly!

DOLLY: Irresponsibly?

COOMI: Yes. I'm beginning to wonder. This whole visit to Karanjia may have been a mistake after all. It seems to have driven her deeper—into her weirdness.

DOLLY: Frankly, I never did trust that Karanjia bloke of yours. Not one bit.

COOMI: Sorry, Dolly, What you think makes no difference at all. He has proved his powers innumerable times. I could tell you some—

DOLLY: No, no. Spare us, please…. I've heard all those stories many times before… But in this instance—it's common sense—the crazy coot was using sleight of hand, don't you see? To convince you and Rukhsana. That with his amazing powers he had plucked out her troubles by their very root! Like a louse from her scalp! Or a worm from a child's bum! Smacks of melodrama to me! Don't you see?

COOMI: Can't ever hope to win an argument with you.

DOLLY: Well, the kindest thing one can say about it is that his intentions were good. But naturally, our girl—why, anyone—would react perversely to confidence tricks of this sort. Not surprisingly, it left her feeling madder—and angrier—than before.

COOMI: Luckily, by the time we got back home, she was so tired and hungry, she forgot entirely about wanting to move in with Sohrabji.

DOLLY: Thank your lucky stars for that, Coomi dear... But boy, was she hungry? Did you notice how much she tucked in at lunch? Ate non-stop—like a pig!

COOMI: Touch wood, touch wood. Let her eat well, sleep well, become healthy again... Only after she wakes up, we'll know whether she's really better or not.

DOLLY (*obligingly touches a wooden teapoy next to him*): Of course...that's our only hope. But I still can't get over the way she cornered the choicest pieces of meat! In one fell swoop. Myself I got only one small chichra and a bare bone...

COOMI: Never mind...my poor babe was famished. Don't grudge her her appetite at least, Dolly...

DOLLY: Please, I'm not such a glutton as you make me out to be.

(*Picks up a newspaper and starts reading, while* COOMI *tidies the room; for a while neither of them speak.*)

COOMI: Tried ringing up that Dr Bharucha this morning...

DOLLY: Uh-hmm...? Where was I?

COOMI: You were still asleep...

DOLLY: And?

COOMI: His secretary said doctor is on holiday. At his

Panchgani bungalow. Anyway, she said, there's heavy demand for Dr Bharucha (*imitates stylish accent*) so the earliest appointment I can give you is for next month…!

DOLLY: Next month! Well? I hope you took it?

COOMI: Of course. But we have to reconfirm before going anyway.

DOLLY: Didn't know so many lunatics were wandering loose in our city… But frankly, I am not at all impressed by these hotshot physicians. Bomanji Bharucha may be much in demand but he'll probably turn out to be a churlish old fool…

COOMI: You don't know him. Nor do I… But I often wonder, who or what does impress you, Dolly…

DOLLY: See for yourself. He'll keep us waiting two hours, then meet us for twenty minutes, and make us cough up— three thousand! Rupees!

COOMI: What to do? That's how much these specialists charge nowadays.

DOLLY: I could bring my daughter back to her senses for far less.

COOMI: Ha! Don't be so brash, Dolly. Something terrible has happened in our lives…how can we even think of scrounging on expense at a time like this?

DOLLY: Am I saying we should scrounge? No. I'm asking another question—is what happened really so terrible?

COOMI: How can you even talk like that? I'll tell you what has happened…! I'll tell you. On our way home from Karanjia's—

DOLLY: You mean your faith healer?

COOMI: Which other Karanjia do we know? On the way back, outside the gates of the Hindu colony Rooky saw some chalk patterns on the footpath, and a discarded garland... Right there she froze! Frightened out of her wits, Black magic, she stutters, pointing to the pavement. No, no, that's only on account of Ekadashi, I explained to her, the Hindu festival that just passed... Rangoli and flowers are leftovers of that day! But no. Stubbornly, she insisted on crossing the road and walking on the opposite pavement... She wasn't pretending, believe me. She was terrified!

O Khodaiji! There we stood, balancing on a divider in the middle of the road—cars and buses grazing past us—my tears started to flow, and wouldn't stop... Our poor girl has completely lost grip of her senses...

DOLLY: We mustn't panic, Coomi dear. Please. We just have to be careful that she's not reminded too often of her failed marriage. Therein lies the real cause of her anguish.

COOMI: At the moment, little chance of that, I should think...

Although I do feel, that as Rooky's father—and man of the house—you should call up Ratan and speak to him.

DOLLY: Man of the house? What do you want me to say to him?

COOMI: Speak to him a little sternly. Don't you have any questions to put to him? Why did you send our daughter back to Mumbai...? Are there no psychiatrists in Bangalore? What are your plans for her? These are all the things you should ask him—man to man.

DOLLY: Ah! So there are some virtues to masculinity, then? I was beginning to see myself as our colony's 'luchcha-lafanga' blackguard! Mavaali with a capital M!

COOMI: Stop playing the fool, for heaven's sake! You're no better than Noshir!

(*Just then the phone rings.*)

Can you take that, please? Dolly? I've got something on the gas.

DOLLY (*gets up, rather reluctantly and speaks into the receiver*): Yes, Dolly speaking… Hello? …Kaun? …Ratan…? Arrey, what a surprise… Rukhsana is okay…she's resting now… I'll tell her, I'll tell her… Definitely… But just hold on. One minute. (COOMI *is gesticulating frantically to get his attention.*) Aunty wants to say something to you (*hands the receiver to* COOMI)

COOMI: Hello, Ratan… No, no, no. That's out of the question. I can't disturb her while she's fast asleep. But earlier today—why, ever since we came back to Mumbai—she's been very upset… Please call and speak with her. This is not right—what has happened is not right at all.… Next time you call we have to work something out, we have to find a solution… She's upset, naturally she's upset… You say she was like that even with you in Bangalore? Well, frankly, all that we don't know. But please understand, Ratan, there's no smoke without fire…You must call again. You must call again and speak to Rooky. I have to go now. Goodbye! (*disconnects*)

DOLLY: Wasn't expecting to hear that bugger's voice on the line, by god… Took me completely off guard. Coomi… but how superbly you handled him. Put him in his place, I should say.

COOMI: Thank you. I really do believe he shouldn't be let off scot-free. He has to be made to feel more accountable for what's happened.

DOLLY: The way you handled him—I'm impressed—that will give him something to think about… Maaderchod!

COOMI (*hisses irritably*): Shh! Dolly, please… Is that all you can think of saying? Control your tongue!

(*Quick* FADE-OUT)

ACT TWO

SCENE THREE

COOMI *and* ROOKY *are seated at the dining table.* ROOKY *is silent through most of the scene. Both mother and daughter seem too disheartened to make conversation; yet intermittently, the mother does say a few revealing things; occasionally, the daughter does too.*

COOMI: At times, things do happen, my dear…
(*She waits a moment before continuing, partly to ascertain if* ROOKY *is taking anything in.*)
…which seem frightfully beyond one's control.
ROOKY: Hmm…
COOMI: But at such moments, especially…it's crucial not to give up…to hold on tightly…
ROOKY: Hmm…
COOMI: Hold on to your belief in yourself… In who you really are…Yes, you should…
ROOKY (*blankly*): But who am I, Mama?
COOMI: That's just what I mean! You know very well who you are! You are Rukhsana Shroff, my lovely first-born… now Rooky Kavarana. Once head-girl at Girton High… A playful child in her younger years, but later an excellent scholar, a topper, an all-rounder! Darling of so many teachers, good at sports, too…and so creative… Who, in her final year wrote and directed a skit that brought the house down with unstoppable laughter—don't you remember? On Parents' Day, the entire school hall was filled with

guffawing parents... You lampooned every teacher you ever studied under.... But with such tenderness that the teachers themselves applauded loudest, with tears in their eyes...

I kept all your prizes, your cups... But when you got married, and I asked you to take them with you to Bangalore, you said no, that might 'diminish my husband's self-assurance!' ...Just imagine, Rukhsana... How kind and thoughtful of you to say such a thing... And look at you now. What's become of your own self-assurance? Don't allow this to happen to you, Baby... We love you so much, Rooky...

...Your Papa, too, feels no different... I'm certain he loves you very much...Whatever happened in the past, we have to forget. When he was younger, he was a rough, violent man, that's true... He could be quite beastly, in fact. I tell you. He firmly believed that children should be 'trained'—by means of corporal punishment... Oh, you won't remember much about this...and I'm glad for it, too. Often I'd say to him: but you lack the very discipline you want to instil in your children...How is that fair?!

ROOKY (*shakes her head*): Can't remember anything... My head feels hollow...like an empty coconut shell...

COOMI: Older now and less frisky, the truth is he does care. That's why he's caught the train to Vikhroli this morning... To meet an old friend who prepares these good luck charms—a family secret taught to his father by some sadhu decades ago—and known to soothe mental distress. He's getting one for you today.

ROOKY: I'm telling you right away. I'm not taking anything.

COOMI: No, no, it's nothing to eat. All we have to do is store it in the house...and it will work its magic quietly... In the cupboard, perhaps, under the bedsheets... Out of sight of prying eyes. Your Papa believes in very little, as you know... But he swears by the efficacy of this lucky charm...I'm afraid, though, he won't be back in time for lunch...

ROOKY: What's for lunch?

COOMI: Are you hungry already...? That's a good sign... I've made your favorite meal: dhandaar ne machchi no sauce!

ROOKY: Yumm!

COOMI: I'm so happy for you, Rukshsana. Macchiwallah brought pomfrets early in the morning. So fresh and glistening, they looked almost alive! ...And do you know what day is today? Mehr roj! Your birthday roj!

ROOKY: Nonsense! My birthday is in August. August 17.

COOMI: Yes. And thanks, dear God, that my girl still remembers the day she entered this world.

ROOKY: What do you mean? Of course I remember my birthday !

COOMI: But that's according to the Roman calendar. I'm talking about Roj, the day of the month you were born on, according to our Parsi calendar. That's today. Mehr Roj! Isn't that great? That's why we are eating dhandaar-sauce!

ROOKY: What are we waiting for? Let's start!

COOMI: Sure. In fact, dal and rice and fish are all still piping hot. Help me set the table...

(A swift scene transition occurs: minor changes in lighting and some movement to and fro the kitchen: in moments they are seated at the table eating.)

ROOKY: We can save some...

COOMI: When he was younger he had such a nasty mouth, a foul temper... What's that?

ROOKY: Save some for Papa. To eat at night...

COOMI: Oh you mean dhandaar-sauce? There'll be leftovers, I'm sure. But he probably won't want to eat it at night—it's an afternoon meal really... Never mind, we'll see... But what I want to say is, he's become so much less selfish in his ways now... I can hardly believe it myself.

ROOKY: I don't remember very much about those days... Only how annoyed you would get when he brought home gifts for me.

COOMI: After a day at his office that's all he could think of... Rarely came home empty-handed... Dresses for you, big-big dolls, sutarfeni, barfi, mavaa na khaaja.... He'd spoil you so. But we had only his salary to live on, Rooky. And of course, I was worrying about rising expenses. Your school fees and Nosh's, and all the extras they would keep demanding from time to time...

ROOKY: One dress I still remember. He bought it for my ninth birthday. Ninth? Or was it tenth...? Lacework down the front, bows and flounces all over. I hated it, to be honest. It made me feel like an old woman! And with five days still to go for my birthday, I had set my mind on another I'd seen at Banaji's boutique—that little shop under the Andheri fly-over...?

COOMI: Oh, that shop's gone now...long ago.

ROOKY: I wanted that dress, the one in Banaji's... It was so cute and sleek. But then something happened... Can't remember what...

COOMI: Just as well, Baby. And it was your eleventh birthday actually. But is there any reason to try and remember everything? The past is over and buried.

ROOKY: But that dress? How could it have just disappeared? I don't think I ever saw it again! The one Daddy bought for me? It just vanished... Oh my God, that's fantastic!

COOMI: Ah, Baby... What use is it to recall past unhappiness? Do memories soothe present-day afflictions? Oh dear, I'm not sure. But yes, I'll be truthful with you...I do remember it very well...your dress... In fact, it was I who destroyed it... Burned it in the colony courtyard late one evening, by the garbage dump...

ROOKY (*shocked*): But why? Why would you do a thing like that?

COOMI: Frankly, out of sheer disgust, my baby! ...In less than a year you had shot up so much, it would never have fitted you again. Forget that dress, dear. I don't wish to—I can't talk of it—

ROOKY (*yells*): But why?! Tell me why!

COOMI (*yells back*): I can't...! ...I told you. I'm too ashamed.

ROOKY: Please, please, tell me. Please tell me! Why did you burn that fancy outfit Daddy brought for my ninth—or eleventh?—birthday?

(*No reply. Hesitantly,* ROOKY *repeats.*)

Later, I might have tried it on again! I would have worn it, I'm sure...

(*pause*)

COOMI (*more quietly*): Even at the time, I felt too broken, too humiliated.... No, nothing to do with you, or the dress... But your Papa... There, you see. You've made me say it.... When he felt rejected, he could turn into quite a monster really...

He couldn't take it...that you should actually prefer another dress to the expensive one he had bought for you outraged him. He got into such a fit of anger...that to spite you—or maybe to spite me—

ROOKY: What?

COOMI: He pissed all over your dress...

ROOKY: (*astonished*) My God! Pissed?

COOMI: Well, no. I can't bring myself to say it. Something worse.

ROOKY: Tell me? Please. I beg of you.

COOMI: Well, you're old enough to know, I suppose.... He shagged all over your dress...

ROOKY: Shagged? You mean—oh my God, he masturbated on my dress?!

(COOMI *nods*.)

COOMI: In the end, it was such a crumpled, sticky, foul-smelling mess... I poured kerosene on it, and set it on fire... Burning with shame for him, for all of us... And now to have to recount this bizarre story to you...? God help me... Yes, there were times like that with Dolly, when a beastly, primitive side of him took over. Then he became a mad man... I'm so sorry, sweetheart. I shouldn't have told you... Please forgive him...Rooky? Everything's changed now. Everything's better now...

ROOKY: Oh my God...! I can't believe this. He really did that?

COOMI: Well, I'm sure he feels awful about it, too. As he must about so many of the things he did in those days... Once, do you remember? He locked you and Nosh in the toilet from morning to evening. Took the key with him to work, so I couldn't let you out... For a while both of you children cried piteously. My heart was breaking. But I could only talk to you from outside the locked door. Didn't have the courage—or the strength—to break the lock...

Perhaps, that's why he's gone to Vikhroli today... To make

up for all the things he did to us in his crazy moods. Perhaps he feels just a little responsible. For things that have gone wrong in our lives. This good luck charm, he believes, will restore your mental...stability. And maybe it will, too... Don't doubt it.

ROOKY: By the way, there's nothing mentally unstable about me... Let me make that clear right away. I'm feeling fine... Besides, I don't remember anything at all about being locked in the toilet all day.

COOMI: Well. God bless you, Rooky, that's wonderful... I'm so glad you don't... You must have been only five. And Nosh was just three... A very cruel thing it was on your father's part.

ROOKY: But that doesn't mean I don't want some time on my own...

COOMI: What are you saying?

ROOKY: No, I don't mean locked up in a toilet or anything like that. But upstairs...I mean at Sohrabji's.

COOMI (*sighs*): Oh no! Please don't start on that again! But why Sohrabji's?!

ROOKY: Why not Sohrabji's? You tell me? If I'm to stay confined here with you and Papa, what chance do I have of getting better? Don't you see?

(FADE-OUT)

ACT THREE

SCENE ONE

In one corner of the stage a bed and pedestal lamp. RUKHSANA *is reclining on pillows against the bedstead. Behind her, a window overlooking a street, from which emanate traffic and street sounds.*

ROOKY: Alone, at last… (*she sighs; when she speaks again, her voice sounds uncannily like her mother's*):

How do you feel today, Baby…?

(*after a pause, she replies, once more sounding like herself.*)

ROOKY (*in her child-like voice*): Loss….great loss….My life, my world…None of it built on solid rock…Everything strewn, everything scattered…

On the other hand, weren't you always a whix at cracking jigsaw puzzles?… Don't remember?… Can't solve this one? Put the pieces together again! Every scrap, every shard of your splintered life…

And what if fragments have washed away… so far I don't even know they're missing…Some crucial bit might have drifted downstream in the filthy effluence of my life… leaving a gaping hole at the very centre of my being…?

Last night….oh yes…

Vast fun-fair throbbing with life… Loud music, lights… merry-go-round, two giant wheels, roller coaster, candy floss and dabeli roti stalls… Hundreds of revelers, laughing, dancing, making merry… Mama, Papa, Granny, Grandpa, my whole family. Generations—even those I've never seen except in faded black-and-white photographs... We were all there.

The weird thing was...we were moving on roller skates. Performing complicated twirls, pirouettes, zigzagging expertly through crowds of other skaters on a congested skating rink...

Oh, but in a flash—it was all gone. Poof! No people, no rides, no music: everything had turned silent. Only me, alone on a vast barren field of ice; I could feel the chill entering my bones. Immense walls of ice were closing in on me...It was only a matter of moments, I knew, before I froze to death...

(*Enter* SOHRABJI. *He ambles across the stage, and speaks.*)

SOHRABJI: Rooky, dear? Will you take some hot porridge? In the morning, I mean?

ROOKY: I'm sorry?

SOHRABJI: Some Quaker oats? What time should I wake you for breakfast?

ROOKY: Don't worry about me, Sohrab. I'll make something, when I get up.

SOHRABJI: But I could keep it ready. Some porridge? I have some myself every morning.

ROOKY: Please don't. Just pretend I'm not here...

SOHRABJI (*laughs*): How could I? You are my ward now. I am responsible for you.

(ROOKY *stays silent, and perhaps* SOHRAB *doesn't expect a reply. Presently, he exits. and* ROOKY *resumes talking to herself.*)

A child, lost in a vast gathering of people...how does she find her way home again?

Sits down somewhere, sobbing helplessly...until a kind stranger notices, and takes her home... Ah, but then I do still believe in fairy godmothers?..... I was a Girl Guide once.

Our troop's instructress would teach us: if you get lost, don't panic. Just walk back along the path you came by, and you might pick up the trail once more... All those treks we went on...I still remember them... Deolali... Khandala... Alibaug... Wonderful days...Learning to tie knots, erect tents, light bonfires...cooking large meals in the open for twenty-five girls, and two chaperones.

(*Doorbell rings faintly, in the distance.*)

SOHRABJI (*calls, offstage*): Rooky dear, a visitor to see you...

ROOKY (*puzzled, alarmed*): Visitor? Dear God!

COOMI (*calls, offstage*): It's only me, Rooky. Your Mama, darling!

ROOKY (*in a sharp undertone*): Can't leave me alone, can she?

(*A quick fade-out, fade-in—and* DOLLY *appears on stage—instead of* COOMI.)

ROOKY: Now you? But Mama just came up to see me a minute ago!

DOLLY: That's all very well. Am I not your Papa, too? I love you just as much and more.

ROOKY: I'm not saying don't come up to see me. Please do, anytime, I'm sure Sohrab won't mind, he's a good man.

DOLLY: And how are you today, Baby? Top of the world, I'm sure?

(*slight pause, as though* ROOKY *is making an effort to remember*)

ROOKY: But wait. Early this morning...I had another visitor.

DOLLY: Really? Who was it? Before Mama came up?

ROOKY: Oh, very early, even before the sun was up. Sohrab wasn't even awake.

DOLLY: That's bullshit. What are you saying? *Who the hell* would come so early in the morning to see you?

ROOKY: But what's to get so agitated about, Papa? Do you mind? It was my husband, Ratan.

DOLLY: What're you saying, baby? How is that even possible? Ratan is in Bangalore.

ROOKY: So? He took the first flight out at 4 a.m. Truth is… he was dying to have sex with me. He was… Tossed and turned all night in throes of desire, then caught the early morning flight out. And when he came to my room, we had a fucking great time. Such a great, fucking time!

DOLLY: Ah! What's happening, Rukhsana dear? Have you started imagining things again?

ROOKY: If you don't believe me, ask Sohrab… Although he may not know—he slept through the racket we were making… The nuts and bolts on this cot need tightening. It's terribly squeaky.

DOLLY: You're talking nonsense now, Rooky. Please try to talk sensibly… I've never heard you use such vulgar language before… And I see you're on first name terms with Sohrab Uncle?

ROOKY: We're all fucking grown-ups here, aren't we? I could do it myself, you know, if Sohrab has a spanner. Just a few twists and turns would render it firm and erect again. So one can fuck in peace…

DOLLY: Mind your language, dear! Doesn't do credit to a lady to talk so loosely.

ROOKY (*laughs*): But I'm not a lady, Papa. No way. And you're no gentleman either. Sometimes you spatter your seed all over the place. Like a gardener with an engorged hose.… Or maybe even a bloody Flora Fountain.

DOLLY (*angry, but also dumbstruck*): What on earth are you talking about? I can't understand a word you're saying… Tell me. So you say you had a good time with Ratan? Then where is he now? Where is your Ratan now?

ROOKY: Oh, he had to get back to work. Couldn't leave his subordinates to run the bank—for more than just a few hours. Asked me to give you and Mama his warmest.

DOLLY: By God, Rukhsana! What's going on? I don't believe a word you're saying. Did you tell your Mama all this?

ROOKY: No, no, of course not. Can't discuss the pleasures of sex with Mama. With you it's different; you are more broad-minded, I've noticed.

DOLLY (*yells, panicky*): Sohrab! Are you there? Just see what my girl is saying. I think her case has gotten worse. And all because she came up to live here with you! I was against the idea from the very start!

(*Standing to one side of the stage,* DOLLY *and* SOHRAB *confer urgently in inaudible whispers.* SOHRAB *is reassuring an agitated* DOLLY, *while* ROOKY *stands at the window behind her bed, gazing out. Sounds of car and bus horns float up, some yelling in the streets. She seems oblivious of the two men talking at the other end of the room, as they of her. When she speaks, her lines have the distracted, disengaged quality of soliloquy.*)

ROOKY: Traffic, traffic everywhere... Ah, but see there: an impatient fool tries to squeeze between a heavy lorry and a posh sedan—he's done it, I knew he would!—left a deep gash on the side of the sedan!... Drivers at each others' throats. One finds a rock in the ditch on the side of the road and hurls it at the other's windshield! Cracks appear out of nowhere like a map of the globe. Now this guy's enraged... Steps out of his vehicle with a knife—or is it a long screwdriver? He engraves deep gashes on the bonnet of the offending car... Amusing, all this would be...if it weren't also so deadly.

DOLLY (*going to the window, and standing beside* ROOKY):

Welcome to the real world, Rooky…That's what they call road rage! It's routine, my dear…happens all the time. Don't let it bother you.

ROOKY: But look: now he's attacking the other guy with his screwdriver—man's bleeding profusely! What frenzy, my God…? A traffic policeman arrives at last and begins to gesticulate… Cars inch forward slowly…

DOLLY: Ah, Rooky… Here a car, there a car, what do you expect? Fights are bound to happen… Don't think about it, Baby, it's nothing to do with us… You please try to relax. (*Hugs her and plants a kiss on her cheek.*) I'm going down now. (DOLLY *exits.*)

ROOKY (*alone now, shakes her head*): I can't. How to relax…? Late last night, I was woken up from deep sleep by terrible shrieking… What's going on? Is it a riot, some communal clash I wondered?… But no, only pavement dwellers fighting, with ferocious intent. A woman had woken up in the night to find her husband molesting their child. …Maybe it wasn't her husband… Or maybe the little girl wasn't even their own kid. But the woman totally freaked out! I might have done the same thing I suppose—if it were my husband. Or my child!… Ratan…so keen on having a child when we got married… Then he lost interest completely…

(*slight pause*)

…Last night, after I was woken up, I got out of bed and stood at the window. Streetlights were out, sky black as pitch. Not a star in sight… And I realized in that moment, this is a picture of my life: yes, enveloped in utter darkness…without a glimmer of hope. …God knows where Ratan is, what he's doing, what he's thinking? I have no clue. Will I ever know? (*Enter* SOHRAB. *He overhears her last words.*)

SOHRABJI: No one knows anything, my dear. No one can know anything for sure... We have to learn to live with not-knowing.

ROOKY: At least, no child is suffering on our account. ...Because finally, it does seem that in time everything disintegrates... I realize this now. Perhaps it's in the nature of our universe... Sooner or later everything collapses... That's called the law of entropy, isn't it?

SOHRABJI: I don't know. Maybe it is.

ROOKY: But then, if everything disintegrates, what law—or force holds it together?

SOHRABJI: No idea... Gravity? Maybe? Or God?

ROOKY: Who knows? Maybe our lives were just intended to crumble, turn to fine dust and disperse in vast open spaces of nothingness...

SOHRABJI: Maybe, maybe... But do remember, dear... There's also great reason that binds everything together. Keeps it ticking, in impeccable synchrony. Like a perfect clockwork machine. There is order everywhere. In the way our lives are played out—or in the way they unravel. No randomness there at all.

ROOKY: Ha, ha, you amuse me, Sohrab. How profound you make that sound.

SOHRABJI: But it is so, it is...

ROOKY: Well, look at it slightly differently and what you're saying becomes totally meaningless. If anything, it's randomness that claims the lion's share in this clockwork universe of ours.

(*For a moment there is silence as* SOHRAB *considers this.*)

SOHRABJI: Okay. You may be right, I'll admit. But let me rephrase: what I really meant to say is: choices we ourselves make determine the course of our lives. And these choices, inevitably, have very far-reaching consequences.

ROOKY (*to herself*): Then tell me, Sohrab, if everything's so crystal clear to you: what was it I did that made my husband stop caring for me? So irrevocably? Tell me, please, if you know?

(ROOKY *can't suppress an involuntary sob.*)

SOHRABJI: No, no. Please don't cry. Try not to feel so pessimistic…

ROOKY: That's easy for you to say…

SOHRABJI: Always remember, dear Rooky: there's only one thing in life that's irrevocable.

ROOKY: And that is?

SOHRABJI: But you know the answer, yourself we all do. From the moment we're born—the only thing in life that's permanent, unchangeable…is death. When my wife passed, I would have given anything to bring her back. My right hand, my liver, anything at all… But it just wasn't possible…

(ROOKY *stays silent.*)

ROOKY: I think I sense what you are saying, Sohrab. Sorry it took me so long to grasp. Value life for what it offers, even if the final result never quite squares up to what one had hoped for. Isn't that what you're saying?

SOHRABJI: Yes, something like that… But certainly, I'm not saying to give up dreaming… No, not at all, Rooky… Someday our dreams could come true…

(FADE-OUT)

ACT THREE

SCENE TWO

DOLLY *and* COOMI *are seated at a bare dining table, fidgety with expectation.*

DOLLY: No sign of her yet?

COOMI (standing up): What do you want me to say? I have no control over her, or anyone else, Dolly…

DOLLY: She'll come, she'll come.… It's only just ten.

(*Long, restless pause, during which both husband and wife seem on edge. The front door has been left ajar for* ROOKY *whom they are expecting to enter any minute. She does, presently, empty-handed.*)

COOMI: Arrey? Your valise?

(ROOKY *stares, uncomprehendingly.*)

I mean all your things? You've come back empty-handed?

DOLLY: Okay, it's okay. She'll bring her things down later on. What's the great hurry…? But I hope you've had enough of being on your own, my dear? With Sohrab Uncle?

COOMI: Exactly a week. She's been with Sohrab a whole week!

ROOKY (*combatively*): Any problem with that?

COOMI (*sarcastic*): Problem? No problem? So long as you don't mind making a laughing stock of your parents? Shaming them in full public gaze…?

ROOKY: My God, Mama! Didn't know you had such talent for high melodrama…

DOLLY: Melodrama, nahi dikra. Understand: what you are putting your parents through would drive the most stoical of philosophers to hysterics.

ROOKY: So both of you have decided to gang up against me now? In fact, Sohrab offered I could stay longer, if I wanted...I should have.

(*Her parents' faces express surprise, and a hint of disapproval.*)

COOMI: But wisely, you decided to come home, right? Back to your parents?

ROOKY: Well, for the time being, at least.

COOMI: And what else? What else did Sohrabji advise you?

ROOKY: He told me I shouldn't stop dreaming.

COOMI: Ah...!

DOLLY: Dreaming?

ROOKY: About all the things I desire. In life.

COOMI: He would certainly be the right person to advise you on that, I'm sure... (*contemptuously*) First-rate dreamer that he is...

DOLLY: Who, Sohrab? But why do you say that, Coomi?

COOMI: Don't we know him? Every few days Sohrabji rings our doorbell. (*imitates*) Mai, forgive me. Went all the way to market, but just imagine—completely forgot. Forgot what? Tea powder, sugar, milk, everything and anything he forgets... But, of course, he can always pick up supplies from his local bhandaar, free of cost.

ROOKY: When will the two of you stop this backbiting? Don't you find it shameful? Please learn to be a little more generous with your neighbours!

COOMI: I like that! See how she defends her new-found friend.

DOLLY: But that's a good sign, isn't it, dear Coomi? A very good sign indeed I would say. She's learning to appreciate others, learning kindness.

Although…(*doubtfully*) what she needs most urgently, I'd say…is to learn to be kind towards herself.

ROOKY: What? Then you think I'm cruel? To myself?

DOLLY: I just mean it's time to forget. Get over whatever went wrong in your marriage.

ROOKY: Nothing went wrong. My husband just got the hots for another chick.

DOLLY: Well, try to overlook his mistakes, Rooky. It happens. See it as—human folly.

COOMI: Mistakes! Human folly! Ha!

DOLLY: The sky hasn't fallen on our heads. Don't let domestic discord overwhelm you so… To make you lose your wits, your very presence of mind?

(*A moment of quietness. All three are silent. Then*)

COOMI (*sarcastically, and softly to* DOLLY): Such sound advice from a papa to his daughter, isn't that marvellous?

ROOKY: Oh, I know, I made a mistake…

COOMI: What mistake?

ROOKY: We should have had a baby right away, while Ratan was keen on one.

COOMI: Yes! Of course. That would have brought you two much closer. If you ask me, never presume to meddle with God's plans.

ROOKY: But how did I? It's not as though I got preggers or something, and had an abortion…. That would be meddling, surely. What're you trying to say, Mama?

COOMI: Just that we can never know what's good for us. He has a time for everything, a plan for everyone.

ROOKY: You mean if I decide I don't want to be changing nappies and giving suck to a little imp every two hours—while I'm still only twenty—I have no say in the matter?

COOMI: How you talk?! It was you who wanted to get married at that young age, we didn't force you...

ROOKY: I was in love.

COOMI: And with a boy of your own choosing.

ROOKY: At least I believed I was.

COOMI: Did you not consider then everything that marriage involves?

DOLLY: No reason to start doubting that, my dear. You were in love, and you wanted to marry Ratan. At any cost, and only him.

COOMI: Of course! That's how it was.

DOLLY: In fact, I remember Mama suggesting you should meet other boys. Before jumping into marriage with your first, bright-eyed beau.

ROOKY: Yes, I do remember that, too...

DOLLY (*proudly*): But you know our girl, Coomi. When she makes up her mind about something, even wild horses couldn't drag her away—

ROOKY (*giving vent to unprovoked anger*): What are you going on about, Papa? ...I am responsible, of course I accept that. I wanted to marry Ratan. And we were very happy, too. Until that bitch got in the way...

DOLLY: Yes, my dear... But don't you know? The world is full of bitches.

(COOMI *and* ROOKY *both glare at him.*)

Present company excepted...

ROOKY: But then...tell me what should I do now?

DOLLY: Do?

(ROOKY *nods.*)

Now?

(ROOKY *nods again. There is a moment of awkward silence.*)

Well…get your act together, my dear. As you youngsters are fond of saying nowadays…

COOMI (*softly*): Again. What edifying moral instruction! From a father to an abandoned daughter…

ROOKY: (*sits up*) Abandoned? Am I abandoned, then?

DOLLY: Nonsense! There you have your answer—to what you were just asking me: what should you do now? I'd say, build your life again… Do all those things you always wanted to but couldn't, because you got married so young… Not abandoned, my dear. The proper term is unattached. That's what you are! Not tied down by marriage or domesticity. Free again, to reconstruct…using the building blocks of your own past, the vast panorama of your own life.

COOMI (*in a more positive tone*): Now for once there's some good advice from a father to his daughter. Why, you can start reading novels again. Maybe, join your school's theatre group, even write another skit or two… Contact old school friends again…What a lot you can do, Baby. So long as you don't give up…

DOLLY: And do you know what else? I have a great idea. Yesterday, my friend, Adil Bhesania, phoned to ask if I was interested in a Dalmatian pup. His dogs have littered again. He has eleven pups to sell, or give away. He was almost pleading with me to take one off his hands. Would you like that, Rooky? A little puppy to take for walks, to play with all day?

COOMI: Oh please. Don't create more headaches for me, Dolly…Puppies need a lot of looking after. Besides which, he or she will chew up our sofa cushions, and all our slippers too while teething….(*The others remain silent; then* COOMI *reconsiders*) But, on the other hand, if you promise to be responsible and look after him, Rooky, maybe it's not such a bad idea…

ROOKY (*reproachfully*): Even as kid, you never let me keep a dog.

DOLLY: Yes, Coomi, that's true. I remember you raising the same objections twenty years ago…! So, that's settled, then, okay? I'll phone Adil today itself, and we'll go pick a pup. Maybe tomorrow? You can choose one for yourself, Rooky.

ROOKY: Can't we go today itself? If it's okay with your friend?

(FADE-OUT)

ACT THREE

SCENE THREE

The final scene unravels at dizzying pace. Chaotic entries/exits heighten the sense of anarchy, bedlam; the annoyingly persistent yapping of a puppy dog (offstage) contributes in no small measure... Repeated rings of the doorbell, loud hammering on the front door.

COOMI (*rushing to the door in panic*): Good God! Who can that be?

(*She opens. It is* SOHRABJI): What happened, Sohrabji?!

SOHRABJI: Maaf karjo...maaf karjo, mai...Nathi khamaati...

(*He rushes past* COOMI, *holding his crotch. Perplexed, she watches as he disappears into the interior of her flat; a minute later, he re-emerges, sighing with relief.*)

Sorry mai, very sorry mai, prostate trouble... Please excuse.... If I had tried to walk up to my own toilet by now my pants would be soaking wet.... But, of course, I must tell you, all the way through marketing somehow I managed. Able to control. Only one minute ago, while passing in front of your door, I knew I wouldn't be able to... Just had to go... Please forgive me, mai.

COOMI: It's okay, it's okay, Sohrabji... Never mind.

SOHRABJI: Oh, one more thing, Coomimai, if you won't mind... Can you spare a few drops of milk, please...? I'm thinking I'll go up and make myself a nice hot cup of tea...

COOMI: But tea is the main culprit, don't you see? That's why you can't control su-su.

SOHRABJI: Oh, is it really? But I only have two cups. Ek savarna, ek baporna...

COOMI: And just now? Weren't you on your way up to have one more? Keep proper count, Sohrabji... Anyway, to tell you the truth, I'm out of milk. Very sorry, bawa.

SOHRABJI: O never mind, never mind, dear Coomi. You always help in so many ways, I won't have that extra cup today. You're right, you're right... Maybe you're right...

COOMI (*after* SOHRAB *shuts front door*): First time in my life I've spoken a white lie—about milk! But it's for his own good: too much caffeine, not prostate trouble is the problem! (*Offstage commotion erupts as soon as* SOHRABJI *shuts the front door behind him.* ROOKY *and* NOSH *are yelling at each other.*)

ROOKY (*offstage*) You better behave yourself! Or I'll slap you so hard, arsehole! Behave yourself!

NOSH: Who the hell are you to slap me? I'll spit in your face if you dare to touch me!

ROOKY (*emerging*): Tell him, Mama, tell him! Tell this mad brother of mine!

COOMI: What's happened? What's he doing?

ROOKY: He's torturing Rustom! Throwing him up in the air and catching him before he lands. Pretending he's a ball!

NOSH (*emerging to make his case*): But Rustom loves it. That's why he keeps yapping for more!

COOMI (*scolding*): What's the matter with you, Nosh? You're supposed to be a philosopher, aren't you? Can't behave sensibly with your sister?

ROOKY: Or with a baby pup?

NOSH: But I didn't do nothing, Mama. She won't let me play with Rustom. He's my dog too.

ROOKY: Bullshit! He's my baby (*screams*). And I won't let you torment him, you sadist!

(*Now a sleepy-eyed* DOLLY *emerges.*)

DOLLY: And you won't let your old man catch forty winks either? So much screaming and shouting since early morning—enough to wake the dead.

COOMI: About time you woke up too. It's ten-thirty!

DOLLY: But I only just fell asleep! Believe me. Someone had finished off my bottle of Benadryl! I was up all night, tossing and turning!

COOMI: That someone can only be you, Dolly. You're getting so forgetful, really! Anything you need, please write it down. Noshir will pick it up for you on his way home from college.

ROOKY: I could pick it up too. I like going out, especially if there's errands to run.

DOLLY: Then don't forget: One big B. One full bottle of Benadryl! Without fail! I want it by this evening...

ROOKY: Are you addicted to it, Papa?

DOLLY: Addicted to Benadryl? Oh no, it just gives me good sleep. (*pause*)

ROOKY (*speaking to herself, thoughtfully*): Am I, then? Addicted to my husband? Ratan gives me such a good sleep... Well, most nights. At least when I am with him. Question is: will I be able to live like this? Without him? Forever and ever?

(*pause*)

How do I start to build my life again... Without my partner? The time has come...the walrus said to talk of many things... Of shoes and ships and sealing wax... Of cabbages and kings... And why the sea is boiling hot—and whether pigs have wings...

No, no, but please...Tell me. Where do I start...? How do

I start...Someone please tell me?
...Thick and fast they came at last,
And more and more and more—
All hopping through the frothy waves,
And scrambling to the shore...

DOLLY (*alarmed, whispers to* COOMI): What's she babbling on about? Good God, has her brain gone for a toss again...?!

COOMI (*whispering to* DOLLY, *excitedly*): No, no, listen. Don't you remember? That's the poem she recited on stage, in her school hall. For which she got first prize! In the sixth standard.... It's all coming back to her... Touch wood, touch wood.

ROOKY: I weep for you, the Walrus said:
I deeply sympathize.
With sobs and tears he sorted out
Those of the largest size,
Holding his pocket-handkerchief
Before his streaming eyes.

(COOMI *and* DOLLY *listen to their daughter's recital, mesmerized.*)

DOLLY (*whispering to* COOMI): That means... She's getting better, you're saying?

ROOKY: O Oysters, said the Carpenter,
You've had a pleasant run!
Shall we be trotting home again?
But answer came there none—
And this was scarcely odd, because
They'd eaten every one.

(COOMI *starts applauding,* DOLLY *is silent.* ROOKY *ignores both.*)

My question is: how do I start? Where do I begin...?

COOMI: But you have already! You've started already, don't you see? That entire poem you recited from memory! Something you learned maybe eighteen or twenty years ago! Isn't that marvellous…

DOLLY: Yes, your mother's right… You must believe in yourself. There's nothing wrong with you, Rooky. That's what I've been saying from the start.

ROOKY: Then tell me, Papa.

DOLLY: What?

ROOKY: It still bothers me no end. But I really want to know the answer. Why did you soil my dress?

DOLLY: I'm sorry?… (ROOKY *stays silent*) What're you talking about?

ROOKY: My birthday dress. Why did you stain it? …So Mama had to take it to the garbage heap, and set it on fire?
(DOLLY *looks genuinely baffled*.)

DOLLY: What dress? How did I soil it? I haven't a clue what you're talking about.

COOMI: Past is finished and gone, Rooky. No sense in raking it up again… Your Papa has changed completely. He doesn't remember any more…those fleeting moments of madness. Nor should we. Some things are best forgotten.

DOLLY: Can't remember a thing about any dress I stained… Now listen, dear Rooky…We aren't getting any younger, your Mama and I. Ten years from now, we may not be here to support you.

COOMI: (*softly, snapping fingers*) Ovaaryu, ovaaryu…

DOLLY: With our love or advice… Before that happens, we would like to see you settled and happy…

ROOKY: (*distracted, to herself*): I would too… My question is: where do I start? How do I start…? Maybe I should talk to

Ratan. Let him see I'm okay now…

(*A moment later, the phone rings.* ROOKY *answers. Initially, dumbfounded by the voice she hears at the other end, she cannot speak. Then she stutters*)

Yes, yes. I can hear you quite clearly, Ratan. I'm feeling much better now… How are you?… Okay…I am okay too… No, no, of course not. No question of it. My parents will never object. They'll be delighted…

(*Before Ratan's call can come to an end, it is interrupted by another loud banging on the door, and the shrill and persistent ringing of the doorbell*)

COOMI (*disbelieving*): Now what? Sohrabji ne paachhi pisaab laagi?

(*She hurries to the door and throws it open. But it is* PIROJA *standing there, their neighbour from the flat adjacent to* SOHRABJI*'s.*)

PIROJA: Thank God you're at home! Come quickly, please! Come quickly!

COOMI: But what's happened?

PIROJA: Aapra Sohrabji! What a ruckaas! Good thing I was at home and heard his cries for help. Good thing too he leaves his front door open in the morning… Otherwise we would still be looking for a locksmith…

COOMI: But what has happened, Piroja—?

PIROJA: Slipped in the bathroom and fell, while taking his bath! I'm sure he's broken something… He's in terrible pain. Whole body twisted, wet and shivering. We have to dry him first, then we'll phone Dr Damri!

COOMI: Bichara aapra Sohrabji…?! O Parvar Daegaar! Why do you concoct new disasters for us every day?

PIROJA: Come quickly, please…I have no idea how to help

him. And there's nobody else with me.... Shirinbai and Nusli have both already left for their offices.

(*Slow fade-out, fade-in, signifying passage of time.* DOLLY *and* COOMI *are seated at their dining table.* ROOKY *is on the phone to Ratan.*)

ROOKY: I'm sorry, Ratan, I had thought I'd take the first flight out. But I can't. Not right away.... Our neighbour, Sohrabji—do you remember him at all? He's had a fall and broken his thigh bone. At least that's what our family doctor believes. He's had him admitted to the Parsi General where they're taking X-rays to be sure... Tomorrow morning a surgeon will examine him and decide when to operate. Sohrab is in terrible pain.

No, no, Ratan, it's nothing like that, please... Don't be silly. You do remember meeting him once? ...Yes, you did.

He's a sweet old man, who's helped me a lot in these past few days while I've been away. Mum has spoken to a nephew of his in Navsari, and this guy's agreed to stay with him at hospital. But he can't get away for another three days, he says. No, I can't leave Sohrab alone. Until I'm sure he's getting the care he needs... I am very fond of him, Ratan. Now don't be jealous... An old man, over eighty. And a widower... You have no idea how much he's helped me—to understand...about life...our marriage—helped us, I should say—I'll tell you all about it when we meet... Won't be long now... Ratan, I love you... Great. I'm waiting to get back as soon as I am able to. Love you, too. (*disconnects*)

(*pause*)

COOMI: Dada Hormuzd, taro gano gano upkaar...
DOLLY: So he wants you to come back, Rooky?
ROOKY: Yes, Papa. He wants me back... Very much.

DOLLY: And what about that other girl, Rooky? The one he was feeling turned on by?

ROOKY: At his office? No. There's no one else, he swears. It's possible I got it wrong...

NOSH (*coming out*): So you're going back, then? That's great news!

ROOKY (*nods*): But not just yet.

(*Lights dim very gradually to a blackout.*)

ACT THREE

SCENE FOUR

Hospital ward. SOHRAB *shares a room with another male patient.* SOHRAB's *leg is in plaster and suspended in traction. A thick curtain divides the two patients. We never see the other occupant of the room, only occasionally hear his gruff, unhappy cussing in a heavily accented Irani voice, conversing with* SOHRAB, *or with a ward boy or nurse—or simply groaning in pain.* ROOKY *enters, and greets* SOHRAB *effusively.*

ROOKY: Sahebji Sohrab! Hope you are feeling much better now?

SOHRAB: Rooky! Hi, Rooky! So good of you to drop by.

ROOKY: Not at all, Sohrab. It's the least I can do. Mummy says she'll come to see you this evening, during visiting hours.

SOHRAB: No need. Tell her no need. I think Dr Hadvaid has done a pretty good job of stapling my broken femur—with a pin. There's much less pain now.... But they keep me sedated a lot...I may well be asleep when she comes.

ROOKY: I'll tell her to wait another two or three days then before she visits.

SOHRABJI: Yes, that would be better. Please explain.

(*From behind the curtain come sounds of a raucous argument between a nasty ward boy and the old Irani gentleman.*)

WARD BOY: Again pisaab? There should be some limit. Just a few minutes ago I emptied the whole bottle!

IRANI: Pun paachhi laagee to su karun, mara Shezaada? ... Aastey, aastey! Remember, last time in your ghai-ghai how you wetted my whole mattress?! And nurses had to change all the bedsheets...?

WARD BOY: All that you remember very well, kaka. What a good memory you have! Only my baksheesh you always forget. Ask doctor to fix a permament tube for you. I don't have time to give you your bottle every few minutes.

IRANI (*exasperated*): But he tried to put in a tube, you know that. And I got an infection. That's why he removed it.

WARD BOY: I tell you, I have lots of other patients also. ... Whole ward gives me five rupees per pisaab! I'm taking only two rupees from you. Even that you grumble about.

IRANI: Before I leave this place...you'll make me a pauper. I'm telling you I need to piss every half hour!

WARD BOY: Nonsense. Learn to control. Every half hour pisaab? Whoever heard of such a thing?!

(*brief pause*)

ROOKY: Sounds like a real tyrant, doesn't he?

SOHRAB: What to do? We are at their mercy... And for no. 2, they won't accept anything less than ten rupees.

ROOKY: Gosh! How trapped you must feel here, Sohrab. And helpless... No news of your nephew from Navsari?

SOHRAB: No. I'm still waiting...

ROOKY: Maybe I could stay here with you, if I can be of some help, Sohrab?

SOHRAB (*laughs*): Even if I agreed, the hospital would never permit it. This is a male ward. Tell Mama no need to visit me in a hurry. Maybe after a few days, when I'm feeling better...

As for Irani saheb, poor man, ward boys are the least of

his troubles. Lying there all day he's developed bed sores, you see...

Around midnight, two nurses arrive to haul him physically and turn him over—to air his back, apply lotion, whatever—even as his leg is still in plaster. You should hear him, his cries of horror, especially if they rouse him from deep sleep...'They've come again to turn me. Take me, Khodaiji, take me, please. Can't bear this agony any more...' As if it were the Prince of Darkness himself on his rounds at night.

ROOKY: But why wake him up so late?

SOHRAB: Bed sores can't be neglected. And I suppose it's the only time nurses find, after they're free of other routine duties. As hospitals go, I suppose this is quite a decent one. And charitable too...But in any situation where so many patients have to be attended to, mistakes are bound to happen... Yesterday we heard of an outrageous incident. A man was anaesthetized and taken into the theatre, but he was operated on the wrong limb ...right, instead of left, before the error was discovered. Can't confirm if it's true or just a tall tale...

IRANI: I can hear every word you're saying, Sohrabji. Won't you take pity on me and let me meet your niece? You know I never have any visitors...

SOHRAB: She's my neighbour, Irani saheb, from Katpitia Baag. Sure you can meet her, if you want to...

IRANI: Nomo khodo, nomo khodo...

SOHRABJI: Let me ask her. Rooky...?

ROOKY: Of course.

(*As she crosses the barrier of the dividing curtain, we hear her voice introducing herself.*)

ROOKY's voice: Hello, uncle. I am Rukhsana, or Rooky...

IRANI's voice: Hello Rukhsana... What a sweet girl you are... Nomo khodo, nomo khodo... Myself, Yezdiar Irani... Thank you for meeting me, dear Rukhsana...
ROOKY: My pleasure entirely...
IRANI: God bless you, dear Rooky...
ROOKY: Please get well soon, uncle...
IRANI: I'll try, I'll try...

(*Slow fade-out, fade-in. When the lights come on again, the hospital scene has been transformed (swiftly, by a stroke of set-designer wizardry) into an angular view of* ROOKY *speaking on the phone in her living room at home. The hospital bed and other paraphernalia could perhaps be pushed out of sight behind the curtain.*)

ROOKY: No, no, Ratan. There's absolutely no reason for you to come. I can travel alone... Yes, I'm sure... And besides, Sohrabji's nephew—my Mum spoke to him again—will be arriving this afternoon from Navsari, so Sohrabji will have his helper at the hospital. And I'll leave for Bangalore soon after he gets here. Isn't that great?

(*She disconnects, and* NOSH *barges in*)

NOSH: Yay boy, Rooky! That is great news... But one thing I want to make clear. Rustom stays here with me.
COOMI: Oh come on, Nosh, don't be so selfish. Let her keep her mind busy playing with her pup.
NOSH: Nonsense. Her mind is okay. I could have told you that right at the start. She's fine. Papa's been saying it all along. Besides, she can have her own baby now. A real one. Not a toothy canine one. That's the great advantage she has over me, don't you see!
ROOKY: In fact, that's precisely what Ratan said he would like...He just told me that. You can keep Rustom, brother.

Only, don't pitch him so high in the air. And if you do, be sure to field him before he lands, I beg you. You're no Kapil Dev. One day you could drop the catch.

NOSH: I'll never. I swear, Rooky, I'll never. Don't worry… He loves it. Well, that's settled, then (*whoops again with joy*). YAAAY!

ROOKY (*speaks aloud to herself, ponderously*): And what if… Ratan fumbles and drops my catch? Wouldn't that make an awful blotch of my life? But he says he loves me, he swears it… But what if he finds—I'm still not …all there?

COOMI: (*embraces* ROOKY) Nonsense, Rooky. Every bit of you is right where it should be, every nut, every bolt in its precise slot.

ROOKY: At the moment, I feel that way myself: every piece in its proper place. Yet, what fresh jolt or tremor could send my lofty edifice toppling again? Honestly, I'm happy now. But also…a little scared…? No, that's not completely true. I can feel my strength coming back. No matter what happens, I know I'll face it… Without terror or dislocation.

NOSH: Yaay…! But in parting, let me offer you the same advice you were giving me a minute ago. No matter how fast the ball is coming at you, DON'T drop the catch… Got it?

ROOKY: Yes, bro. Got it. Holding on for dear life.

NOSH: Yaay…! That's the way to do it, sis…

DOLLY: Oh yes, after all we are a nation of cricket lovers, aren't we?

(*Offstage, Rustom responds hysterically to* NOSH's *every excited yell; he doesn't stop yapping until after lights fade and the stage darkens.*)

NOTES

DOONGAJI HOUSE

Doongaji House was first produced by *Stage Two* and presented at the Alliance Francaise auditorium in Bombay on 6 July 1990, with the following cast:

HORMUSJI	Nosherwan Jehangir
PIROJA	Meher Jehangir
AVAN	Sherezad Rastomjee
FALI	Torak Pavri
CAWAS	Denzil Smith
DARABSHAA	Soli Marker
PERIN	Kashmira Patel
YOUNG HORMUZ	Rustom Warden
PURVEYOR	Liyakat Fruitwala

Director: Toni Patel
Lights: Michael Nazareth
Music: Avaan Patel
Production in-charge: Vijay Shetty
Backstage assistance: Anuradha Sethi
Sound recording: Luke Paul, Indo Studio

Doongaji House was first published by Xal-Praxis in 1991. A second edition was published by Sahitya Akademi in 2006.

THE LEGACY OF RAGE

The first performance of *The Legacy of Rage* took place on 20 November 2005 outside 'Bubbles', the residential bungalow of the Miranda family, opposite St. Anne's Church, Mumbai. An Attic Salt Theatre production (in association with Rachel Productions), it was presented by the Celebrate Bandra Trust and featured the following players:

ROBERT	Shivkumar Subramaniam
REGINA	Nilufer Fernandes
GEORGIE	Alekh Sangal
BLENDINA	Dilnaz Irani
FRANCIS	Remy Fernandes
JOEBOY	Saurabh Agarwal
FR. RUFUS	Mukul Chadda
LOUELLA	Merlyn D'leema
ROSCOE	Jeremy D'Souza

Director: Joy Fernandes
Lights: Sailesh Hejmadi
Sound: Dhaval Shah
Backstage and production: Gautami Vegiraju, Yogesh Rao
Make-up: Arvind Shilpkar
Costume: Shakeel

The Legacy of Rage was first published by Sahitya Akademi in 2005.

A FLOWERING OF DISORDER

A Flowering of Disorder has been first published by Aleph Book Company in this edition. It hasn't been staged to date.